Duet in September

The Calendar Girls Series
Book I

by

Gina Ardito

The following is a work of fiction. Any resemblance to real persons, living or dead, is purely coincidental and not intended by the author.

Cover Art by Elaina Lee of For the Muse Designs

Copyright © 2013 by Victoria Ardito
All Rights Reserved

No part of this book may be reproduced or stored in a retrieval system or transmitted in any form, whether by electronic, mechanical, photocopying, recording or otherwise without express written permission of the publisher.

Dedication

For all my Long Island friends, who know the unique beauty of sunrise over the Atlantic and sunset over the Sound. Yes, we have traffic. But that's only because everyone wants to live here!

Chapter 1

Nia

"It's one lousy month, Nia. Come on! It'll be fun."

Seated inside our favorite local coffee shop, I stared in amazement at my twin sister, Paige. Staring at Paige isn't exactly like looking in a mirror, by the way. She's a candy box blonde, and I'm a redhead. She's petite; I'm five-foot-ten—in flats. Her eyes are a really cool blue, mine are boring hazel. Yet, despite the disparities in our appearance, we're generally more alike than not.

Generally.

This new scheme she'd divulged over our morning caffeine get-together would probably widen the gap between us. More than that, I had to consider the possibility she'd finally lost her mind. It was bound to happen, particularly after what had become known as the Kevin Event. I sighed. Time to dazzle my other half with flawless logic.

"Not all guys ask for the waitress's phone number during a dinner date, you know. In fact, the good guys actually pay attention to *you*. The whole time. Sometimes, they even call again." Not that I knew by personal experience. My love life wasn't any more successful than my sister's these days.

Paige's lips twisted like a strawberry Twizzler. "This has nothing to do with Kevin the Cretin."

I quirked a brow until she visibly squirmed in the comfy wingback chair.

"Okay, it has *a little* to do with Kevin the Cretin," she conceded. "But not entirely. I mean, let's face it. You and I are both in a rut. Coffee, work, home, weeknight television, Friday night chick flicks. Day after day, week after week, nothing ever changes. I saw this psychologist on *Dara* the other day…"

Tilting my tall coffee toward my mouth, I stared at the ceiling to keep Paige from seeing my eyes roll. Not Dara Fitzsimmons, that talk show host, again. *God, give me strength.*

Years ago, Dara's daddy bought a local cable station and found himself with an empty hour of airtime, which he offered to his daughter. Within one season, she'd become a syndicated voice for those ladies still maneuvering the shark-infested waters of fishing for careers and Mr. Right simultaneously. Paige, as one of Dara's Disciples, not only watched the show every weekday, she firmly believed Dara Fitzsimmons held all the answers to the hunt for love and happiness. I, on the other hand, thought Dara was a prissy, sanctimonious, spoiled little rich girl who knew nothing about the Real World.

Just another checkmark in the Different column for us.

"Think about it." Paige picked at the edges of the cardboard ring wrapped around the cup that held her mocha latte. "Every day for thirty days, you change one thing in your life. *One thing.* Easy, right? You take a different route to work one day, you go out for lunch instead of choking down a sandwich behind the counter." Her index finger popped up near my nose. "One simple thing."

Simple. Right. Over our childhood and teenage years, I'd learned to avoid anything Paige deemed "simple."

In elementary school, Paige said sneaking our cat into school would be "simple." In hindsight, smuggling Fluffy into the class had been easy. Keeping her hidden in my backpack for six hours? Not so much. Before we finished the Pledge of Allegiance, Fluffy had ripped her way out and dashed around the classroom like a whirling dervish, hissing, spitting, and scratching. Thirty manic minutes later, the janitor had cornered our poor calico and stuffed her into a drawstring bag while I sat in the principal's office waiting for Dad to come to school. I lost television privileges and my allowance for two weeks over that little escapade.

At fifteen, Paige insisted we'd have no problem climbing out our bedroom window to meet our friends for a midnight rendezvous at the schoolyard without our dad ever knowing we were gone. And of course, *she* had no problem at all. I slipped on a patch of wet leaves, caught my foot in the rain gutter, and fell off the roof. Three manic hours later, I left the emergency room with my left arm in a cast and my father's disappointment weighing down my shoulders. I lost my allowance for two months.

"Come on, Nia." My sister's urgent whine broke through my memories of those...*ahem*...good times. "It'll be fun. And maybe it'll break us both out of our funks."

I was going to regret this. I knew someday soon, I'd be sitting somewhere—an alley, a police station—ruing the day I agreed to my sister's *Thirty Days to Break Out of Our Funks* plan. Which made my quick surrender that much more pitiful.

At least no one could take away my allowance this time.

"All right, all right," I relented on a heavy sigh. "I'll do it. When do you wanna start?"

"Today. Right now. It's September 1, the perfect time. From now until the thirtieth, you and I will both do one thing differently every day." Her eyes took on an electric glint. "Me? I'm going to walk to work today. What about you?"

I took a sip of coffee to buy time—a stay of execution.

"Nia! Answer me." Paige pushed a hand into my shoulder.

Coffee sloshed up to my nostrils, but thankfully, didn't spill over the top and onto my spotless white blouse. As a precaution against further possible damage, I set the cup down on the table and grabbed a napkin to blot my upper lip. "I don't know yet. I haven't exactly had time to map this all out the way you obviously did."

"Don't you dare welch on me on the first day," she warned in low tones, her lashes fluttering like a bat's wings at me. "Don't welch at all."

"I won't. I'll come up with something. I promise." I glanced at my watch. Twenty minutes to nine. "But right now, I gotta dash to get the store open."

Before she could protest, I grabbed my purse from the seat next to me and sprinted out the door. As I settled into my car in the parking lot, I sighed again. Paige would only continue to nag me until I played along. Might as well give in right from the start. Leaving the gear in park, engine idling, I dug out my cell and dialed her number.

"Yeeeeeessss...?" she answered after the first ring.

"Just so you know, I'm going to take First Avenue to work today, okay?" Since my gift and souvenir shop, Nature's Bounty, sat in the middle of Snug Harbor's Main Street, this new route would make me late. But only by about five minutes, and it would get Paige off my back until tomorrow. Well worth the time sacrifice.

"Purr-fect." Her satisfied smile bounced off satellites in space and zinged through my earpiece.

While fine hairs danced on the back of my neck, I gripped my cell phone tight enough to crush it. "I hope you get caught in a sudden thunderstorm on your walk to work," I grumbled.

Paige only laughed. "Have a nice day, Nia. If anything exciting happens today, call me back. I'll do the same."

I hung up, shifted the car into drive, and took step one of this dumb thirty day challenge. Two blocks after I turned onto First Avenue, I remembered why I never drove this route to work. On the Thursday before Labor Day weekend, tourists poured into our tiny oceanside village by ferry, car, and—for the rich ones—private plane. All entrances into Snug Harbor used First Avenue as the main artery to beach homes, inns, and motels. At 8:50 a.m., the visiting throngs forced traffic to a dead halt.

Penned in between an RV larger than my house and a Manhattan-to-East End luxury bus, I rubbed my fingers at the pain piercing my head just above my eyebrows. This was going to be the longest September of my life. The traffic light changed from red to green, and I managed to squeak past the bus on my right. Naturally, at the next block, the traffic light jumped from green to yellow, and the car in front of me stopped before entering the intersection.

Kathump! My head snapped forward as the whole car jerked, and the crunch of metal resounded in my ears. Or was that the sound of my neck cracking? *No, no, no.* As dread crept over me, I slowly turned to look into my rearview mirror—in time to see a Jeep full of teenagers jump the curb on my right and speed away in the road's shoulder.

Perfect. Just perfect. As soon as the light changed to green, I eased out of the traffic and toward the curb.

Picturing Paige in my head, I stared at the graying sky and amended my wish from earlier. "I hope we get a tropical storm this morning."

Once I managed to pull into an empty restaurant parking lot, I stepped out of the car to survey the damage. Smears of blue paint and black impact marks framed the crater-shaped dent in my rear fender. A crack ran through my right taillight like San Andreas Fault: no damage yet, but one good bump away from total destruction.

Yet again, I pulled out my cell phone—this time to call the local police. The female dispatcher answered before the first ring completed its chime.

"I need to report a car accident," I said.

"What's your name?" the woman asked.

"Nia Wainwright."

"Nia? It's Emily. Emily Handler."

Emily Handler had grown up as Emily Forletti, three houses away from Paige and me. Shortly before beginning her senior year in high school, she'd married Roy Handler and promptly given birth to their first daughter a scant seven months later.

"Is anyone hurt?" Emily asked. "Do you need an ambulance?"

"No. A bunch of kids in a Jeep hit my car and then took off. I just want to file a report."

Emily expelled exasperated breath into my earpiece. "Tourists. Think they have the right to wreak havoc and drive away without owning up to their responsibilities. You sure you're okay, Nia?"

I rubbed a hand over my neck as I assured her, "Yes. Annoyed, shaken up, late for work. But physically, I'm all right."

"Where are you? In a safe place?"

"I'm on the corner of First Avenue and Maple Street." I glanced at the sign perched on the gray-weathered clapboard building behind me. "In the parking lot of The Gull and Oar."

Emily remained quiet for a moment, but computer keys clicked in the background. "Sam Dillon is pretty close to that area, I think," she said at last. "I'll send him over. Are you on your cell?" She rattled off my phone number to me.

"Yes."

"You got enough juice in it to send and receive calls?"

"Yes, it's fully charged." Thank God I hadn't changed *that* routine.

"Okay, sit tight. Any problems, call me back. I'll have Sam there in a jiff."

I looked at the gridlock on the road. Not in this traffic. "Tell him to come up Maple. First Avenue's a nightmare right now."

Emily laughed. "Well, *duh*. I don't know why you didn't go down Main Street. You've lived here long enough to know to avoid First Avenue in the summer."

I gritted my teeth just as the first fat raindrop splashed my nose.

~~~~

Paige

So Nia thought I was nuts. What else was new? But we really did need to shake up our lives. Especially Nia. This town, crammed with the same people we'd known since we were born, had sucked all the excitement out of her. While I welcomed this thirty day challenge for myself, I also hoped to see the return of the animated, fun, passionate soul Nia used to be.

As I left the coffee shop to start my stroll to work, I studied the storm clouds gathering over the rooftops of the stores. The atmosphere felt heavy with moisture. Not the kiss of ocean spray that normally swirled in the air, thanks to the town's location directly on the Atlantic. This much pressure could only herald a thunderstorm—a big one. My sister's revenge in full-blown three dimension. Nia had an uncanny knack for wishing misfortune on me and getting her wish. If she'd ever channeled her energy toward good rather than evil, I probably would have won the lottery a dozen times by now.

The black clouds rolling in required a quick detour before work. I ducked into the drug store at the end of the strip mall in search of an umbrella. Nothing would stop me from completing this thirty day plan. The guests on Dara's show all swore only good things had come from their participation: new and better jobs, new romances, new outlooks on life. All from changing one little thing every day for thirty days. Nia's black magic would have to be more ominous if she thought to sabotage me. A thunderstorm on Day One wouldn't put a dent in my hope shield.

I strode through the automatic doors, and past the shoplifting sensor gates. Mrs. Justine, the cashier who'd been a fixture in this store for at least my lifetime, peered at me over her blue-framed cat glasses. I offered a quick nod in greeting.

"Keep those hands where I can see them, Paige," she shouted in her two-pack-a-day smoker's rasp.

Oh, for crying out loud. When I was four years old, Mrs. Justine caught me shoving a package of M&Ms in my pocket. Thirty years later, she still couldn't forgive that one toddler crime spree? I flashed her a brilliant smile. "Not to worry, Mrs. J. I'm a reformed felon these days. Just got out of the Big House, you know." Well, sort of. If Albany and the state comptroller's office could be considered the Big House. I'd only moved back to Snug Harbor six months ago when Dad got sick.

As I rounded the corner toward the seasonal aisle, where back to school supplies and scarecrows fought for attention with sunscreen and sand pails, I stopped short. Naturally, a cluster of tourists blocked the end of the aisle. Shocked expressions on the adults' faces let me know they'd heard my remark about my so-called prison record.

The dad, big-bellied and eye-catching in vivid orange surf shorts with splashy brown flowers and a tan t-shirt that proclaimed him the World's Greatest Golfer, narrowed his eyes to slits. Puh-leez. Like that outfit wasn't a serious crime against fashion.

Mom, in her wide-brimmed straw hat and white tank dress meant to show off her bronzed skin to perfection, had better taste, but no more sense than her husband. With her candy-apple-red manicured fingers poised over the postcard rack, she craned her neck to a nearly forty-five degree angle. "Kids, come over here, please."

Two dark-haired boys, both under the age of ten, poked fingers into the cage of colorfully painted hermit crabs. "We're right here, Mom," the bigger one whined.

"Well, stay where I can see you," the woman replied.

I rolled my eyes so far back, I saw my brain blink. I never should have come back to Snug Harbor. I belonged in Albany, where I'd gone to school. Where I was just another face in the crowd. Where people only knew what I told them about my past. Where I was never compared to Nia. Where one day didn't meld into another. Unlike Snug Harbor, where the only things that changed were the faces of the steady stream of sun-worshipping strangers coming and going.

Somehow I managed to weave around the disapproving faces with my dignity intact. On a sigh of relief, I spotted the end cap where rain gear dangled from hooks. I rifled through the various sizes, shapes, and hues of umbrellas until I found a purse-sized automatic in Barbie pink. Just the bright spot this miserable day needed.

As I played with the button to open and close my new toy, a familiar baritone voice drawled, "Paige! That *is* you. I thought so."

I cringed. I didn't have to turn around to identify the speaker, but I whirled anyway. Sam Dillon. Of all people to run into, why did I have to run into Sam Dillon? In full police uniform regalia, of course. Because my wisecrack about being a felon still lingered in the air like a bad odor.

Apparently, Nia's voodoo was stronger than ever today.

As Sam strolled toward me, floppy-hatted mom made a quick grab for her kids and pulled them into her protective embrace. Annoyance trickled down my spine like an ice cube on a hot day. Did I look dangerous? Really? I'm a CPA, about as far from a thrill-seeker as a sloth. Maybe if I wore a pencil behind my ear and nerd glasses, I'd appear less menacing.

Not that I cared what a bunch of tourists thought. Most of them would evaporate by Tuesday. But the locals were a different story. Nia and I would forever be known as "the Wainwright twins" to every person who lived in this teeny, nosy town. I could find the cure for cancer, and Mrs. Justine would still insist I keep my hands where she could see them every time I walked into this store. Which brought me back to Sam Dillon.

"Well, well," I said with forced exuberance. "If it isn't Marshall Dillon."

True to form, he glowered at me. Sam always glowered at me, whether or not I used the goofy nickname I'd given him the day I learned he'd become chief of Snug Harbor's village police force. Small recompense for all the harassment he'd dished out at me when he was the varsity quarterback and I was the nerdy math major. I could only be happier if this former high school heartthrob had become paunchy and bald while I'd blossomed into a swan. Fate, however, has a quirky sense of humor. I blossomed into a nerdy accountant with few swan qualities except for my long neck and my habit of looking calm while paddling manically below the surface.

The adult Sam Dillon had kept his thick dark hair that begged to be tousled, broad shoulders that tapered to six-pack abs, and the sexy swagger of a man sure that he could have any woman in town. Except me.

His ursine gaze raked over my pink sundress, then down to my cotton ankle socks and beat-up sneakers. "Interesting workout attire."

I quirked my lips. "For your information, I'm on my way to work."

"In that outfit?"

"Makes for a quick getaway after I swipe a candy bar from here." The retort zinged out before I could stop it.

Sam snorted and slowly shook his head. "That smart mouth of yours is going to get you into big trouble one day, Paige."

Yes, Daddy. I managed to clamp my lips around that

riposte so it stayed inside my smart mouth.

Jerking his fingers at me, pistol-like, he asked, "Seriously. What's with the dress and sneakers getup? Is there a marathon for urban professionals I don't know about?"

I patted the computer case slung over my shoulder. "I decided to walk to the office and didn't want to ruin my work shoes." No way I intended to tell him about the Thirty Days to a New You plan from Dara's show. Sam already suspected I was an idiot. Too much conversation on my part would only *confirm* I was an idiot.

"Walking, huh? What happened? Your car break down?"

"No, it's such a nice day, I just…felt like walking."

He cocked a dark, feathery eyebrow. "In this weather? You know there's a storm blowing in, don't you?"

Ha! He thought he'd clinched my idiot title. Not quite, pal. I gestured to my umbrella. "Hell-o? Why do you think I stopped here?"

"Uh-huh." His gaze scanned the shelf of pain relievers and cold remedies in the opposite aisle. "You need a ride?"

"With you?"

His glower snapped back to me, darker now, and his honey brown eyes turned hard as topaz. "That's right, I forgot. The perfect Princess Paige can't be seen fraternizing with the local yokels. Someone might start to think you were one of us."

I couldn't speak. Could barely breathe beneath the man's outrage. I'd been joking. But Sam obviously didn't see the humor. Questions whipped through my brain with the force of a tornado. Was that really what he thought about me? That I considered myself better than the people I'd grown up with? Better than my own sister?

The sudden static squall of his radio cut the tension with the subtlety of a chainsaw at a funeral.

"Sam," the dispatcher squawked. "Check in, please?"

Turning away from me, he unclipped the mike from his hip. "Yeah, Em. What's up?" He never looked back, just strode away, leaving me to ponder his accusations.

Long after he'd left the store, I stood at the end of the aisle, the dopey umbrella dangling from my hand.

Chapter 2

Nia

Sam must have been around the corner when Emily contacted him. I'd barely managed to duck into the car, turn on the engine, and flip the wipers a few times when he appeared from the back of the restaurant.

He pulled up alongside and signaled me to roll down the window. When I complied, he leaned sideways toward me. "Hey, Nia," he shouted over the heavily falling rain. "You okay?"

"Yeah." I sighed. "I can't believe, today of all days..." I let the statement go unfinished. What could I possibly say? It wasn't like any day was a good day for a hit and run.

"As long as you're okay. The car's just metal and leather. Remember that. Nothing there that can't be fixed. You, on the other hand, are irreplaceable."

For the first time all day, I smiled. Who would have thought the guy who tormented Paige all through junior high and high school could grow up to be so sweet? And hunky. "Thanks, Sam."

Waving off my gratitude, he jerked his head at the hood of my car. "Is she drivable?"

I assured him she was.

"Drive around to the overhang near the main entrance," he directed. "Colin won't open the restaurant for another two hours. And at least we'll be out of the rain while we handle the paperwork."

"Got it." I shifted into drive and followed Sam under the blue-and-white-striped awning attached to the front of The Gull and Oar.

With both cars lined up beneath the shelter, we stepped

outside to survey the damage together. Sam and I had very different reactions.

He blew out one long exhale through pursed lips. "Well, this isn't too bad."

I winced and sucked in a sharp breath. No? My poor Passat would definitely need major cosmetic surgery. Aside from the dent in my bumper and cracked taillight, on closer inspection, I also noticed the trunk no longer aligned perfectly with the back end of the car.

A pad and pen in hand, Sam fired off questions at me. Where exactly was I when this happened? Was the light red? Did anybody stop to help or leave contact information as a witness? What did I remember about the Jeep? Color? Model? How many passengers were in it? Did I get a plate number? Even a partial?

Once we'd completed the paperwork, he told me to stop by the station later for a copy of the accident report. Then I could contact my insurance company and start the ball rolling on repairs. "Don't worry, Nia. Brice will take good care of you," Sam said, referring to our local auto body pro. "Drive safe now." With that, he climbed into his patrol car.

Now a full forty-five minutes late for work, I figured I'd more than fulfilled the requirements of Paige's thirty day challenge for today, and opted to head back onto Main Street to get to Nature's Bounty as quickly as possible.

At last, I pulled into my parking space behind the row of stores that sandwiched my gift shop. High-tailing it out of the car, I snagged the strap of my purse on the seatbelt clip. The hiss of stitches tearing on the soft leather handle only added sharp bitterness to my anxiety, like acetone on a ripped cuticle. I smothered an unpleasant wish aimed at Paige and wrangled my purse out of the seatbelt's greedy clutches.

Dodging sheets of rain, I jogged to the back door with the store's keys in my outstretched hand.

Once I stepped inside, I gasped. The air conditioning, set on a timer to turn on every morning at eight a.m., sliced cold air into my damp skin. I hugged myself against the shivers as I headed for the front door. While warmth slowly seeped into my body, I unlocked the main entrance, flipped the sign from "Closed" to "Open," and turned on the lights. A rainbow of colors greeted me. Although Nature's Bounty sold the usual souvenirs prevalent in a beachside town—seashells, sand dollars, towels, key chains and bottle openers—what made my little shop different from the others in Snug Harbor was my hand-blown glass. Shelves with artfully displayed Christmas ornaments, jewelry, wine goblets, hurricane lamps, photo frames—all created in my workshop at home—lined the walls to dazzle the eyes of prospective buyers.

I barely stowed my purse under the counter and tied my sales apron around my waist when the bells tinkled as the front door opened. Without looking up from the counter, I greeted the first customer of the day. "Welcome to Nature's Bounty. May I help you with something?"

"I hope so."

A smooth baritone voice wrapped around me like a velvet cape on a snowy afternoon. I glanced up. Thank God I was empty-handed, with a stool behind me to support my weakening knees. Because the man who spoke had just stepped out of every dream and fantasy I'd entertained since I was thirteen years old. Glossy, tight curls—the color of a latte—swept off an angular face with a high forehead and slightly stubbled chin. Shoulders wide as the ocean fairly burst from a baby blue button-down shirt, open at the neck with the long sleeves rolled up to the elbows. Dark eyes flashed beneath raven brows.

He was the pepper to my salt shaker, the spice that my bland life lacked. He topped me by a few inches—a nice contrast since I normally wound up around men who stood at eye level or, worse, looked me straight in the bust. As I locked eyes with Mr. Tall, Dark, and Delicious, my palms grew sweaty and my hands shook. One surreptitious glance downward on my part confirmed no wedding ring on that significant third finger of the left hand. I stifled the urge to pump my fist. Yes! Maybe Paige was on to something. Today could be the start of something wonderful after all.

"Oh, thank God you're finally open! I've been sitting in my car for over an hour." A nubile blonde in a lime green zip-up hoodie and vivid floral sarong skirt entered my store, along with a blustery wind that whistled around the sales floor. Only in a beach town could someone wear that outfit and not look stupid. She pushed the hood off her flawless face, allowing thick waves of honey blond hair to tumble to her shoulders.

My welcoming smile widened to encompass both customers, but the full wattage flashed on the one with testosterone. "I'll be with you in just a minute," I told the newcomer. *Or more, if Cupid gets involved here.*

"You're Nia, the glassblower, right?" the woman asked.

Nia, the glassblower? Growing up, I was "Nia, the redheaded twin." When Paige left for college, I became, "Nia, the one who stayed behind." After I opened Nature's Bounty and Paige returned home to take over Dad's accounting business, I earned the title, "Nia, the artsy one." Paige, on the other hand, gained "the smart one" as her surname in second grade and kept it to this day. "Nia, the glassblower," however, was a totally new moniker and almost a separate identity from my twin. I'd take it. Happily.

"I guess that's me, but as I said—"

"We're looking for wedding favors," the woman said. "Something totally unique. Paul Ivers at Snug Harbor Liquors recommended you."

We. Wedding favors. *Thud!* My heart crash landed back on Earth, and my smile faded to black. Of course, this gorgeous guy was already taken. Did I really expect my love life to take a one-eighty because of Paige's silly challenge? I swallowed my disappointment and pasted on a professional mien. "I'll have to thank Paul for thinking so highly of my work. What did you have in mind?"

The woman sashayed over to my counter in a cloud of sex appeal and expensive perfume. "You tell me. I was thinking, perhaps, heart-shaped wine stoppers. But then I realized that's too cliché. I want something totally unique. Not the same mass-produced trinkets everyone else gets." Removing her rhinestone-studded pink sunglasses, she looked up at my fantasy guy, batting neon blue eyes framed in lush black lashes. "Right, Aidan?"

"Whatever you say, Camille," he replied and picked up a cluster of glass grapes from the nearest shelf. His long, slender fingers danced over the delicate orbs the way they might caress a woman's curves: slowly, gently, tentatively, but with a look of desire that stole my breath. His dark eyes, the hue of Kahlua, gleamed beneath the high intensity lighting. "This is amazing."

"Thank you," I murmured and fought the urge to fan my face. Despite the dampness still clinging to my skin, heat emanated from me in waves. Beneath my canvas apron bib, my heartbeat kicked up tempo.

Down, girl, I told myself. *He's taken.*

He hefted the sculpture a little higher, pointed to the tiny dent in the bottom where my pontil had held the red-hot piece during the final construction phase. "You made this?"

This time, I could only nod. My mouth had dried to dust.

The clusters, available in both green and dark purple glass, were wired with miniature lights in the center so each plump grape appeared to glisten with dew.

"Electric lights shaped like grapes? That's not a wedding favor," the woman named Camille insisted. "I told you—"

"This isn't for the wedding, Camille. I thought I'd like to get something like this for the business."

Camille's face mottled an ugly reddish purple. "How about we focus on what we came for right now? You can come back on your own time and shop for those seagulls, or whatever they are."

"Piping plovers," he replied blandly.

I stood, stunned. Sure, love was blind sometimes. But this guy must have been deaf and dumb, as well. Why else would he do nothing when she spoke to him in such a nasty way? I surreptitiously glanced around them, looking for television cameras from that *Bridezillas* show. At least her rudeness had one benefit. My attraction to Mr. Delish had shriveled shorter than his backbone.

I should have realized that we were incompatible from the minute he walked into my shop. He was, after all, a *tourist*—a necessary evil in Snug Harbor, with the emphasis on "evil." Twenty-five years ago, my mother left her husband and twin daughters for a rich tourist. Since then, the Wainwrights tolerated the presence of interlopers in our town, but *not* in our family.

"Whatever." Camille's caustic tone obliterated my ugly memories. "Today is about me, not you."

A boyish smile lit up her companion's face, as if Camille's attitude was simply an amusing diversion. My knees wobbled. Okay, maybe my attraction to him hadn't completely shriveled up.

"Trust me, Camille." His gaze intensified on me. "I'll *definitely* be back."

Was he flirting with me? While my pulse indulged in an invisible happy dance, my conscience burned with moral outrage. Clearly this marriage wouldn't last a year. That didn't mean, however, that I wanted to be a featured player in their divorce proceedings.

I stepped out from behind the counter and took the

sculpted lamp from him. His hands clasped mine, squeezed lightly. Oh, my God. He *was* flirting with me.

Little jolts of electricity zinged through me. A problem with the wiring in the grapes? Had to be. Which meant I couldn't put the piece back on the shelf until I'd had a chance to fix whatever was wrong.

Smoothly removing my hand and the sculpture from the man's grip, I offered an apologetic smile. "Obviously, this one's not for sale."

He quirked a brow. "Obviously?"

"Well, yes, there seems to be a short in the wires."

"Is there?"

What kind of game was he playing? "You didn't feel that buzz?" Up close, his charming smile melted my kneecaps.

"No."

Of course he did. He must have. The tingles shot through my nerve endings so strongly, I still experienced aftershocks. I frowned. "Oh, well, maybe it's because I'm still a little damp from getting caught in the storm outside. Either way, I can't sell this piece as it is. If the wrong person touches it with wet hands, *zap!*"

My fingers grasped at the white power cord and my imagination went into overdrive. Sweaty palms, damp clothes, and an electrical short could add up to a life-altering event for me. And not in a good way. *Zap.* How exactly was I supposed to unplug this thing from a live outlet and not risk electrocution?

My hesitancy must have been obvious.

"Here." The man's fingers cupped mine over the cord. "I'll unplug it."

He stepped closer, and I quickly withdrew my hand and backed away until my butt hit the edge of the counter behind me.

"Thank you."

"You're welcome. But I really don't think there's

anything wrong with this piece."

He ran his fingers over the globes again, and I nearly sank to the floor in a puddle of goo. What I wouldn't give to have those fingers touch my bare skin with such tenderness, such total adoration.

"In fact," he said, "I'd like to order a hundred or so."

That snapped me to attention. "A hundred?!"

"Umm…excuse me." Camille's breathy demand sliced through the bubble I'd created with this delicious man. "Can we get back to my wedding favors, please?"

God, where was my head?

"Of course, I'm so sorry," I stammered as heat rushed into my cheeks. To avoid scrutiny from these two, I skittered behind the counter again and perched on the stool, the grapes sculpture on the shelf beside me. "If you want wine stoppers, that's certainly an option. The uniqueness could come in their shape and the fact that each is hand-blown and not mass-produced." I pulled out an order form and pen from the drawer beneath the counter. "About how many do you think you'll need?"

"Five hundred."

The pen slipped from my fingers as I gripped the counter edge to remain standing. "Five hun…" I couldn't finish the thought, couldn't move. When Aidan picked up the pen and replaced it on the counter, I could barely eke out the words, "Thank you."

"Well, we're having five hundred guests," Camille amended. "Many of those will be couples. So maybe three hundred? Or three-fifty? How long will they take to make?"

I fumbled for the pen, attempted to write something on the pad, wound up with illegible curlicues. "It would depend on the intricacy of the design, of course. When do you need them for?"

"Valentine's Day."

February. Less than six months from now. Barely five

months from now. I paused, calculating all the hours I'd face with my hands painstakingly swirling around two thousand degree heat. There went my social life. And the grapes? "Would this project run concurrently with the grape lamps?"

"No," Aidan replied at the same time Camille said, "Yes, of course."

Camille whirled on him, hands on hips. "Aidan!"

"What?" he retorted. "I need the lamps sooner. And I only need a hundred. I want these lamps, Camille."

"And I want the wine stoppers. The wedding comes first."

"The wedding's not for six months."

Wow. The more time I spent with these two, the more I knew their relationship was doomed. Couldn't any of their friends or family members see how incompatible they were? Like a lit match and gasoline?

Whatever. I didn't want to get involved. On any level. Working with normal tourists was hard enough for me. Working with this pair would probably kill me—or drive me to insanity. My back tightened, a sharp reminder that only a tourist would rear-end me and take off. Because only tourists would assume we locals didn't matter except to serve their needs.

"Look, I'm sorry," I said to the couple. "But I couldn't possibly deliver what you both need." Like a few years in therapy. "Honestly. Thanks for thinking of me, but I don't have the resources—"

"I'll pay you double your normal fee," Camille interjected. "Forget about the lamps. The wine stoppers are a really big deal. My wedding could put your little shop on the map. There'll be reporters and photographers from New York in attendance."

I shifted and backed away from the counter. Why did every privileged snob think he or she could buy us poor schlubs? Regardless of the untold riches and publicity I might garner, I didn't relish dealing with these two. "No, really. I can't. The time involved to make that many pieces..." I shook my head. "It's much too big a project for me."

Camille slapped a hand on my counter. "Do you have any idea who my fiancé is?"

Ooh, the trump card. Frankly, I didn't care if her fiancé was the U.S. President. I swerved my attention to Aidan, who dipped his head and covered his brow with a cupped hand. "Camille, don't."

"Shut up, Aidan. You've done enough damage. I should have known better than to bring you here with me."

Okay, I'd had enough. Hands fisted, I strode around the two combatants and opened my front door. "Thanks for coming in."

As a wet breeze whistled inside, tinkling my glass wind chimes, Camille turned and slid her sunglasses into place. "You've made a very big mistake, Nia."

Maybe. But somehow, I'd find a way to live with the consequences. Besides, if these two went through with this marriage, they were making a much bigger mistake than I ever could. Still, their story was none of my business. Thank God.

Flipping her hood over her expensive salon hair, Camille blew past me with more ferocity than the storm whipping outside. I watched her retreating back as she climbed into a cute red sports car at the curb and breathed a sigh of relief. The minute she disappeared down the road, the atmosphere inside my shop lightened considerably. Until I spotted the groom—Aidan—still standing near my counter, a bemused smile on his face.

"Well done, Nia the glassblower," he murmured. "Not many people come up against Camille and survive unscathed."

I was so done with this man's games. To prove it, I opened the door a little wider. "I'd like you to leave as well, please."

"Ouch." He winced and sucked in a breath. "Ordinarily, I'd bow out gracefully, but, you see, I still want those lights."

"They're not for sale," I said firmly. "I suggest you and your fiancée shop elsewhere for what you want."

"My...?" His eyes widened, and a second later, he burst out laughing.

Every chuckle had me burning a little hotter.

"You mean Camille?" When the laughter died, a smirk lingered on his face. "She's not my fiancée. She's marrying my father."

Oh, good golly, Miss Molly. I swallowed my stupidity with a very large gulp. "Your father?"

His laughter ebbed away. "My father," he repeated. "Ogden Coffield."

Ogden Coffield. My heart fell to my feet. Ogden Coffield, owner of one of the most popular wineries and half the real estate in the area. Now I understood Camille's threat. Had I agreed to create her three hundred fifty wine stoppers, I might have been able to gain a place at Coffield's Bluff Vineyards for *all* my glassware.

I'd screwed up. Big time. I'd insulted the most powerful family in the county.

"You've got guts," he said. "And talent. Your ambition, however, just took a serious nosedive."

I resisted the urge to plant my palm on my forehead. "How about if I just throw myself on a red-hot pontil as penance?"

He shook his head. "I don't know what that is, but it sounds painful."

"It is," I admitted, thinking about the glowing end of the wand used for melting and cooling glass.

"So would you consider having dinner with me instead?"

"Dinner?" Disbelief stole my sanity. I stared at him,

Duet in September

eyes narrowed in confusion. "You want to take me out to dinner? Why?"

"Yes, I want to take you out to dinner, preferably to a steakhouse. As to why, because I think you need the red meat after coming to blows with my soon-to-be stepmother. You're lucky she didn't drink your blood." He leaned a hip against my counter, those elegant fingers once again caressing the grapes still perched there. "And because, I told you, I still want these lamps."

My world had tipped upside-down once too often today. I gripped the doorknob tight enough to crush the brass handle to dust. "And you always get what you want, don't you?"

"Always." His grin was cocky, self-assured, and downright annoying.

I swept my arms to the open door. "Not this time. Have a nice day, Mr. Coffield."

Chapter 3

Paige

By the time I got to the office of Wainwright Financial Services, I was soaked. My pretty pink umbrella had turned inside out on the first gust of wind. Ten bucks destroyed in sixty seconds. Cabs, not exactly plentiful in our town to begin with, tended to become rarer than money falling from the sky on rainy days. Today was no exception to that rule.

Luckily, I kept a spare set of clothes at the office for emergencies. Yeah, I'm *that* girl. Miss Ready-for-Anything. I actually kept two sets of clothing at my office: one professional business outfit for days when I got caught in a sudden weather catastrophe. And another dressier ensemble in case Prince Charming showed up to have his taxes prepared and swept me off my feet on the spot. So far, His Royal Highness had yet to make an appearance. But a single gal doesn't ever lose hope. Thus, the pretty blue dress that brought out the color of my eyes sat waiting. Just like me.

At exactly 9:15, I was dry with makeup refreshed, my ruined hair now tied into a quick braid. Seated at my neat desk—no Post-It notes or folders out of place, I retrieved the office's voicemails. No surprise that the only message on the machine came from Lou Rugerman, who had called to make sure his quarterly taxes would be paid on time. In the fifteen years he'd been a client of Wainwright Financial—originally as my dad's responsibility—his finances had never been close to unstable. But the man still sweated over every penny and every detail.

I'd need another caffeine jolt before I could deal with him. My office has a mini-kitchen and when I first came to work here, I'd splurged on one of those single-serve coffeemakers. Not only that, I'd added a shelf filled with flavored syrups, cinnamon, and chocolate shavings. When I'd told Dad about the new addition, he'd remarked that a new coffee bistro would snap up the lease just to get their hands on my machine.

A heavy sigh escaped my lips. Six months after pancreatic cancer killed him, I still missed my father's gentle humor and comforting presence. Especially when I was alone in his office. Sure, in reality, this was now my office with my name on the lease and all the bills. In my heart, though, Wainwright Financial, a small firm that handled local businesses and residents, would always be Daddy's kingdom.

These days, I employed a secretary, but she only worked part time: Monday, Wednesday, and Friday from ten am to two pm. During the first quarter of every year—when everyone and his cousin scrambled through receipts stuffed in drawers and coat pockets to satisfy the IRS—I hired outside help from a temp agency. In that crucial four-month stretch, the office buzzed like a stirred-up beehive. But after April 15th, the crowds disappeared, and my business slowed to simple quarterly records and the occasional financial plan. All work I could handle on my own.

I chose a chocolate raspberry flavored coffee and added a shot of raspberry syrup for extra fruity fortitude. Steaming cup in hand, I settled back in my leather chair for another slow, boring day of number-crunching. I was going to be so happy when my life turned around, thanks to this thirty day challenge.

Dara's guests hadn't said how long all their newfound good fortune took to materialize, but I was pretty sure nothing happened on the first day. So I prepared myself to suffer through this morning's ennui and focus on the big picture. Besides, maybe the Thirty Day Fairy was spreading her goodwill over Nia right now. Which would be worth my sacrifice.

Imagine that: me, the Mother Teresa of Snug Harbor. The thought of my pending sainthood gave me the warm and fuzzies.

As rejuvenated as possible thanks to my coffee infusion, I made the call to Captain Lou Rugerman, owner of two local fishing charter boats.

True to form, he answered on the first ring. "Captain Lou. What are you fishing for?"

"Lou, hi," I said. "It's Paige Wainwright."

"Paige, my little muffin crumb." Lou's usual Doberman growl softened to fluffy kitten mewl.

The poor man still hoped that eventually I'd see reason and marry his son, Evan. Unfortunately, Evan already had a serious love interest: our local veterinarian, Dr. Dominic Bautista. Not that Lou was homophobic. Just optimistic. As the father of an only son, he hated the idea that the family name would end here.

"How are you?" Lou asked. "More importantly, how's my tax situation?"

"You're up to date." I bit back the retort, *as usual*, which reminded me of Sam Dillon's comment regarding my smart mouth.

Seriously. Why did the man antagonize me every time we met? He should save that kind of animosity for criminals. Or a woman who'd done him wrong somehow. Because despite my checkered past with Mrs. J. and the M&Ms, I was a model citizen. Plus, Sam and I never swam in the same social circles, so I could hardly be seen as his *femme fatale*. Face it. The school math geek never broke the big bad quarterback's heart. Except in the movies. But certainly not at Snug Harbor's James Madison High School. Just talking to a nerd like I'd been would have killed his popular reputation faster than licking a petri dish full of Ebola.

Once, in tenth grade, Nia had confided that she thought

Sam was "kinda cool." I'd replied that her description of cool must have been the equivalent of "stinks on ice." Realizing my distaste for Sam Dillon ran deep, Nia had never brought up his name again.

Oh, good God. My mind conjured up a perfectly horrible scenario, and I nearly dropped the phone.

What if Nia really *liked* Sam? And what if Sam liked her, too? Nia, loyal Nia, would never go out with a man I despised so much. No matter what her heart wanted.

The idea, once planted in my brain, grew like kudzu. My Mother Teresa image shattered. The warm and fuzzies sharpened to cactus needles. Was I preventing my sister from finding true love? Was that why Sam sniped at me every time we met?

"Muffin crumb, are you listening to me?"

I jolted back to the man on the other end of the phone. "Of course," I lied.

"So you think it's a good idea, then?"

Idea? What idea? Unwilling to let Lou know I'd spaced out on him, I hedged myself. "Umm…why don't we table that discussion for now?"

"Because he wants an answer by next week."

He who? Okay. Deep breath. Try again. "Do you have anything in writing you can fax to me? For review?"

"What? Like a prospectus?"

A prospectus? What on earth had I missed? Time to rouse my daydreaming brain cells and regain some of my warmth—if not my fuzzies. I took another sip of coffee. I was in too deep to admit defeat, so I continued to play the game. "You're a savvy enough businessman to know better than to jump without a good safety net."

"Yeah, but he *is* my son-in-law."

Ah. Now I was getting somewhere. Lou had two sons-in-law. Brice Howell had married Lou's older daughter, Courtney, and owned the local auto body shop. I couldn't see him wanting to do business with Lou; the two had completely different careers.

On the other hand, Tony Boggs, Kristen's husband, was an arrogant, loud-mouthed jerk with more bile than brains. After Tony had lost his maintenance job at Snug Harbor's posh spa/hotel due to an altercation with a customer over the air conditioning unit in her room, Lou hired Tony as a first mate aboard the *Kristen Star*. Within three weeks, Tony had mouthed off to so many customers, the ship's captain threatened to make him walk the plank in the middle of the Atlantic. Lou reassigned Tony to a job on dry land. Five days as a booking agent resulted in four different fishing parties stranded at the pier. These days, Tony worked in the bait shop. While he cut and packaged squid, he griped to anyone who'd listen that his father-in-law kept him from a management position out of spite.

Tony was proof positive that Lou needed to be very careful in his business dealings. "*Especially* because he's your son-in-law," I assured him.

The old sea dog's sigh barked through my phone's receiver. "Yeah, that's exactly what I thought. It just makes me feel better to say no if I've got someone else to confirm my gut reaction. Thanks, Paige. You're a good girl."

He hung up before I could argue. Because the more I thought about Nia and Sam, the more I realized I was probably the most selfish woman on the planet. Well, no more.

Somehow I was going to find a way to give Nia her heart's desire. Even if her heart's desire gave me a terminal case of heartburn.

Sam Dillon.

I slugged down the last of my coffee and grimaced. *God, give me strength…*

~~~~~

Nia

Rainy days always brought crowds to the Main Street strip. If tourists couldn't sun themselves on the beach, they shopped. Ordinarily, I'd be thrilled with the bevy of customers the nasty weather blew into my store. But today, after the hit and run, followed by a visit from Prince Charmless and his evil stepmother, I'd already lived through more drama than a soap opera actress in her tenth season. My nerves were definitely shattered.

I managed to go through the motions all morning, showing off sea glass ornaments and ringing up pressed-flower greeting cards. But my head wasn't in the game. In fact, I'd go so far as to say my brain was temporarily sidelined. The downhill slide began when I taped my fingers together while trying to gift wrap a hand blown bowl. I overwound a music box for a curious browser and snapped off the crank mechanism. At least a dozen times over the course of the morning, I walked into the storeroom for an item, then stood there, my mind a total blank, with no memory of what I'd gone in to find. When I accidentally gave a customer change for a fifty instead of a *ten*, I could no longer deny the obvious. I needed a break.

I turned to Briana, one of the two teenagers who worked part time in the shop in the summer. "I'm done for the day. I've got a few things to take care of this afternoon." *Like rediscovering my mojo.* I untied my apron and folded it on the counter near the cash register.

Briana cocked her dark head. Her brown eyes, large in her teddy bear face, studied me, and a deep frown etched her Cupid's bow lips. "Are you okay, Nia? You seem kinda…" She looked past me to Andrew, who stocked a shelf with candlestick holders, as if seeking his support. When the skinny, blond boy with his sea blue eyes nodded, she ended with, "…frazzled."

Great. I was being psychologically analyzed by a pair of adolescents. Wasn't this the frilly toothpick in my crap sandwich? I offered a wan smile. "Bad day. Think you and Andrew can hold down the fort 'til Iggy comes in at three?"

Ignatz Zemski—Iggy—was my night manager, and a former classmate from James Madison High School. After graduation, he'd enlisted in the Marines. Ten years later, his kneecap shattered from a mortar shell, he'd returned to Snug Harbor to attend college at the nearby state university. His older sister, Irenka, worked part-time as Paige's receptionist while her kids were in school.

"Snuggies," the true locals in this town, the ones who hadn't bought or inherited million dollar beachside properties, tended to band together almost incestuously. We hired each other, dated each other, married each other. Even those who escaped our little town, like Iggy and Paige, tended to return to Snug Harbor to settle down and raise their own families. Once a Snuggy, always a Snuggy. Outsiders—tourists and townies alike—need not apply.

I glanced at the clock. A little after one. Maybe I should call Iggy and ask him to come in earlier. But I hated the idea of taking him away from homework or studying. Besides, what did I expect would happen during my absence? Briana and Andrew had proven themselves to be good kids, responsible and honest. I knew their parents. Heck, I knew all their *grandparents*. I was leaving my shop in very capable—Snuggy—hands.

"You need me for anything," I said as I ducked beneath the counter to grab my purse, "call my cell. Otherwise, I'll see you tomorrow."

Before I could second-guess my decision, I left the store through the rear door. The heavy rain and wind had disappeared as quickly as they'd come, but steely clouds hovered, lending a funereal pall to the air. Once again, I confronted the damage to my car. The dented bumper and misaligned trunk hit me with a new bolt of despair. My mood became as gray as the sky.

I took a deep breath to cleanse my battered soul. Okay,

no more self-pity. Time to regain control. First stop, the police precinct to get the accident report. Then to Snug Harbor Auto Body to see Brice Howell and start the ball rolling on repairs.

A short time later, I walked up the cement steps and into Town Hall. Even in our quaint little village, visitors passed through a gamut of metal detectors and armed security guards before getting farther than the marble and glass showcase lobby. German shepherds, tethered to their handlers by strong leather leashes, patrolled the area with ferocious dignity. After passing the safety precautions, I headed for the village police headquarters.

In the front reception area, a bulky uniformed police officer looked up from a waist-high counter littered with manila folders, a dirty coffee cup, the white paper wrap from a deli sandwich, and a ringing phone. The age-old odors of burnt coffee and stale grease seemed to come out of the air conditioning vent, permeating the room and its occupants.

"Can I help you?" The officer's lips dangled strips of red meat, dripping greasy yellow mustard onto the waxed paper below. Pastrami? Corned beef? Did it matter?

I swallowed my distaste around the same time he slurped up the meaty pieces. "I need to see Sam Dillon please?"

His dark brows knitted, hooding his eyes. "What about?"

"He has an accident report for me. From this morning. I'm Nia. Nia Wainwright."

He sighed as if I'd dragged him away from a murder scene to talk about the weather. "I know who you are, Nia-Nia Wainwright. Hang on." Rolling back from the desk, he stood, then adjusted his belt around his considerable midsection. He wore shorts with his uniform shirt, revealing hairy turkey legs, black socks, and clunky black oxford shoes.

Oh, my God. His identity finally clicked into place for me. Ronnie Bailey, once the star of the varsity track team. Looked like he hadn't run for anything but a beer in decades.

He pointed to a scarred wooden bench with a spindled back against the dark-paneled wall. "Have a seat. I'll see if Sam's available."

No way did I intend to risk permanent stains and God-knew-what sticky stuff on my skirt or bare legs by settling my posterior on that ancient contraption. Repressing a shudder, I said, "I'll stand, thanks."

My statement didn't seem to faze Ronnie whose expression remained a complete blank. "Suit yourself."

As he rumbled away, I glanced around the area. Past Ronnie's domain, there were at least a dozen desks, all in a similar state of disarray. The phone rang again, and Emily's voice echoed off the walls. "Snug Harbor Police. How may I direct your call?" From her post behind a complicated array of computer equipment, she caught my eye and waved, but never hesitated in her spiel. "Hold on, please, I'll connect you."

"Nia! Perfect timing." Sam's booming voice filled the open room a second before his larger-than-life presence appeared. "I was just about to call you."

I stiffened my shoulders, prepared for another unpleasant development. "You were? Why? What happened now?"

A broad smile lit up his face. "Relax. Nothing horrible, I promise." He jerked his head down the hall. "Come into my office. I'll fill you in on this morning's activities."

I followed him down the cream-colored hallway, each step heavier than that of a condemned man walking to the electric chair.

He stopped at the second door. "Sam Dillon, Chief" was etched in a brass nameplate above his head. As he pushed open the door, he swept an arm past the jamb. "Have a seat."

In contrast to the chaos in the outer area, Sam's office was an oasis of calm. The room was barely larger than a standard office cubicle, but no clutter or stale odors cloaked me as I sat in the clean, cushy chair across from his desk.

Sam closed the door and took his own seat. Clasping his hands, he steepled his fingers over an open folder on top of the desk blotter. "The owner of the car that hit you called me about fifteen minutes ago. Seems he let his father's fiancée borrow his Jeep for a few days. She, in turn, handed the keys over to her nineteen-year-old son from her first marriage…"

Father's fiancée? A tarantula of suspicion crept up my nape. No. It couldn't be. Could it?

"The kid brought the Jeep back late this morning with front-end damage and a cockamamie story about getting rammed by a renegade shopping cart at the supermarket. Owner's no dummy, though, and noticed the black paint smeared on the bumper. He called here to see if his vehicle might have been involved in an accident. I filled him in on your hit-and-run." He glanced down at his notes. "His name's Aidan—"

"Coffield," I murmured. The tarantula sank its fangs into my brain.

Sam nodded. "Yeah, that's right. Aidan Coffield. I didn't know you knew him."

"We've met. Briefly." I doubted Sam would care about my screwup with the vineyard heir and his stepmother. And I really didn't feel like rehashing that episode, thankyouverymuch. "Did you tell him it was my car?" *Oh, God, no. Please.*

The steepled fingers rose and bounced against his lips. "Well, now, here's the thing. He wanted your contact info to see if you and he could work out the particulars between you." Sam dropped his hands and leaned forward, eyes narrowed. "I'm guessing he means *without* legal interference. I told him I'd talk to you, but ultimately, the decision was yours. If you want to press charges against the kid, I'll back you up." He grimaced. "Rich tourists think they can buy and sell us poor locals. What kind of lesson is the kid learning if he gets bailed out without any repercussions every time he causes trouble?"

"So you think I should press charges?"

Sam shook his head. "I dunno, Nia. Honestly, this is your call. I gripe, but you and I both know what'll happen. The kid won't even see the inside of this precinct. A high-priced lawyer, some quick cash changing hands, and the little bas—the *kid* gets a Humvee free and clear from Daddy's unlimited coffers. Meanwhile, you're still going through your insurance, inconvenienced without wheels while Brice does the repairs, and your rates go up. So who learns the lesson?"

I thought back to Camille's rant in my store. *Do you know who my fiancé is?* I sighed. "I know. These are definitely people used to getting what they want."

Leaning back in his chair, Sam folded his arms behind his head. "I hate telling anyone to circumvent the law. But if you can get your car fixed without hiking up your insurance rates and with as little inconvenience as possible..." He shrugged. "Who am I to tell you not to?" Straightening, he passed me a Post-It note. "Here's the guy's contact info. Call him. Talk to him. Make no promises until you're sure you know what you want to do. If you decide you'd like to see the kid arrested for leaving the scene, I'll do it. If not, I'll file this under 'handled privately.'"

I took the bright yellow paper from him and stared at the name and phone number scrawled in red ink. The gods of mischief apparently had me in their sights today. Aidan Coffield. My personal demon.

Chapter 4

Nia

The morning's violent storm had blown out to sea, leaving gray skies and wet ground in its wake. The heat, however, had intensified so that I could actually see waves of moisture rising from the asphalt driveway outside Snug Harbor Auto Body.

Based on size and facial hair alone, Brice Howell resembled a golden grizzly bear. But in reality, he was a sweetheart to the max who did his best to put me at ease when I brought my damaged car in for an estimate of repairs. He strode around my poor Passat, bouncing the fender on one side and peering beneath the carriage on the other. "You going through insurance on this or paying out of pocket?"

"I'm not sure yet." From somewhere inside the repair area, a loud tool whirred—a sanding machine or some kind of buffing equipment. I had to shout to hear myself speak. "The guy who owns the other car wants to talk before I file any paperwork."

"He's not a local, I take it," Brice replied with a caterpillar brow quirked over his narrowed hazel eyes.

"No." Naturally, the whirring stopped just when the word left my mouth. I winced at my shrill shout in the sudden quiet.

Brice didn't even flinch. Expression bland, he held up a hand sheathed in a heavy work glove. "Got it. Say no more."

I had to. "To be honest, Brice, I don't know what to do. I'm in a lose-lose situation here. Sam Dillon says the choice is mine. I can press charges for the hit-and-run and report the accident to my insurance company. Or I can handle it privately. I'm not worried about my premiums going up since I've had a clean driving record for ten years. So, I'm leaning toward reporting the whole thing. Not because I want to teach the kid and his family a lesson like Sam wants. But because that's just who I am: by-the-book Nia, do-gooder."

"So do good and report it." He stroked his bushy blond beard. "Show the townies we're not cowed by their money."

I shook my head. "But, what if, when I call him, he tries to talk me out of it or gets nasty about it?"

"Who exactly is this guy?"

"Aidan Coffield. Of the Coffield Bluffs Coffields."

Brice whistled through his teeth. "Well, if you're gonna tick someone off, you may as well go big. How'd you manage to dive into that shark tank?"

If I didn't explain the Coffield run-in this morning with Sam, no way did I intend to share that shame with Brice. I simply shrugged and related Sam's phone conversation with Aidan about the delinquent stepbrother.

Brice kicked an errant pebble on the asphalt with a steel-toed work boot. "I'll tell you what. Give me fifteen minutes or so to provide you a complete estimate for the body work. Meanwhile, use the phone in my office to call Sam and your insurance rep. *Then* call Mr. Moneybags. This way, if he does try to coerce you, you can tell him it's too late. Let him think you contacted all the major players before he ever got hold of Sam. Then you can say…" He deliberately pitched his voice higher while his index finger rotated around a thick curl of his shoulder-length hair. "'Oh, golly, I wish I'd heard about your offer sooner. I guess your stepbrother will just have to face the consequences of his actions.'"

Ordinarily, Brice's impression of a girl would have had me giggling like an idiot. And boy howdy, I sure could have used a laugh by this time. Not today, though. Not on this topic. Instead, I frowned.

I might have been irked that Aidan Coffield thought he could buy my silence. Still, I was also savvy enough to know that *most* people would have probably done the deal. But my father had raised Paige and me with a strict sense of right and wrong. And the idea that I'd lie to Mr. Coffield to show him how honest I was? That reeked of hypocrisy. Then again, I didn't want to hurt Brice's feelings either.

"Well, that's certainly something to consider," I told him with the ghost of a smile. "But I don't think I could pull off the sweet and innocent act as well as you."

His lips twisted in a mock sneer. "Har-har."

I finally managed to muster up a chuckle, but it was weak at best. Time to get down to business. "Is it okay if I call Mr. Coffield from your office while you're writing up the estimate? I'd feel better knowing I have someone there to back me up if I need it."

"No sweat, Nia." With my car keys dangling from his fist, he pointed at the dented steel door behind me marked *Office*. "Dial nine for an outside line. And come get me if you feel yourself wavering." He opened my car door and slid into the driver's seat, effectively halting all further conversation between us.

I stepped inside his office, and the smell of paint thinners nearly knocked me to my knees. The room, with one lone window that opened onto the repair dock, received no natural light or ventilation. Here was a true man cave, the ultimate altar to all things automotive. Gray walls, gray steel desk, two gray metal folding chairs—separated by a pair of stacked milk crates piled high with magazines devoted to cars, trucks, and engines—clearly defined this masculine space. Adding to the bleakness, smears of grease and layers of gray dust coated every surface. Thick black cables tangled around engine pieces, reminding me of Hollywood's image of a post-apocalyptic world. Here I was, *Mad Maxine in the Temple of the Last Chrysler.*

Cheap plastic frames displayed stained certificates of courses completed in transmission and air conditioning repair, as well as the exorbitant hourly rate for labor in the garage. My personal favorite eye catcher was a white metal sign on the far wall that proclaimed in a bold, red, comic-style font: *"I couldn't fix your brakes so I made your horn louder."*

Averting my gaze from the cluster of big-busted, bikini-clad pinups on the corkboard, I skirted around the desk to the ripped leather chair poised in front of an ancient computer monitor. I found a sheet of blank paper on a shelf above the battered printer and used it like a potholder—a barrier between my hand and the filthy phone receiver. I held the chunky, black earpiece an inch or two away from my skin and punched in the numbers with my fingernail. At least I carried anti-bacterial hand gel in my purse. Did I have enough to bathe in if I spent too long in this room? Probably not, but after this I'd go home and take a long, hot shower to wash away the day's bad karma.

On the other end of the receiver, the phone rang twice, then, "Hello?" That sultry voice weakened my knees with its sweet syrup undertones.

"Mr. Coffield?" I sounded weird to my own ears. Like I'd sucked on helium. Breathy, high-pitched, and rushed. No doubt, the chemicals in the air took their toll on my throat. I wondered how Brice managed to work in this office for an extended period of time without becoming light-headed. I gulped and plowed on. "This is Nia Wainwright."

"Miss Wainwright? Wow. I didn't expect to hear from you so soon." His self-assurance, so apparent in his smug tone, raised my hackles. "Does this mean you've reconsidered going to dinner with me?"

Really? Had the man never heard the word no before today? I tightened my jaw, nearly grinding my teeth to dust. Before I spoke again, I took several deep breaths, relaxed

Duet in September

44

my muscles from the neck down to my toes, and counted to ten. Who knew my yoga classes would come in handy in my daily life? "No," I said, cool and elegant as a Siamese cat. "I'm afraid your car was involved in an accident with mine this morning."

Yes. Perfect poise. Let him try to get the best of me now. I drew out the silence, allowing him time to digest what I'd just revealed.

"Oh." That simple syllable told me I'd kicked the puppy love out of him. Mission accomplished. "There went all the goodwill between us, huh?"

"It's not about goodwill, Mr. Coffield." Not that we had any goodwill between us anyway. "It's a matter of someone using your car to drive recklessly, and then leaving the scene of an accident without concern for injuries or damage to other parties."

"He didn't hurt you, did he? If that scrawny brat left so much as a scratch on you, I'll make him sorry he ever took his first breath."

The passion in his voice took me aback. His reaction was so far flung from what I'd expected.

"No," I replied with hesitation. "The jolt wasn't pleasant, mind you, but I'm more concerned about the damage to my car."

"As long as you're unharmed, Miss Wainwright. I couldn't bear to think that I was even indirectly responsible for anything grievous happening to you."

I stared at the door that led outside, waiting for someone to jump inside and yell, "Gotcha!" and a bunch of guys to laugh at the surprised look on my face.

Aidan Coffield was putting me on. He had to be.

"Chief Dillon gave me your contact info. He said you wanted to speak to me." Doubts raced rampant through my brain, and my courage abandoned me. "If this is a bad time, I can call back later."

In contrast to my tentativeness, he became more self-assured. "No. That won't be necessary. Give me a minute, though, to get my thoughts in order."

"Sure. I guess." I winced at my own cowardice. Good God, if I kept up the shy maiden routine, I was doomed. I'd not only give in about reporting the accident, I'd probably wind up paying for the damage out of my own pocket.

From the corkboard, a nearly naked nymph bending under the open hood of a 1960's-era black Ford Mustang smirked at me. *Oh, honey*, her smile seemed to say. *You're gonna hafta do a whole lot better than that if you want to keep control of this conversation.*

Yeah, sure. Easy for her with her toned, tanned legs in sky high heels, her short shorts, and her Playboy centerfold looks. Unfortunately, some of us had to rely on our wits instead of beauty. And mine had suddenly fled the country, leaving no forwarding address.

"I hope this means you've already reported the incident to the police and your insurance carrier."

"Wait. What?" If his voice intruding into my debate with Miss Classic Car of February didn't jolt me, the words certainly did. "You do?"

"Does that surprise you?"

"Well, yes," I replied before I thought better of it. "I thought you wanted to talk to me about *not* reporting the accident."

"What happened, Miss Wainwright?" The change in his attitude plummeted the temperature in the office to sub-zero. "After we left the store, did you suddenly regret turning down Camille's generous offer? The stringent morals you displayed in your shop today only lasted until you found out who I was? Who my father was? I guess you were hoping for a large payout from this, huh? Sorry to disappoint you then. Because my father's the one with the deep pockets. Not me. I was actually hoping you might help me teach Camille's son a lesson."

As surprised as I was at the message in his diatribe, the

condemnation with which he attacked me boiled my temper. How *dare* he accuse me of calling him for some kind of payout!

"I called you out of courtesy, Mr. Coffield," I said through gritted teeth. "From this point on, however, all communication between us will be conducted through Chief Dillon or Mr. Howell at Snug Harbor Auto Body. If you haven't already done so, I suggest you contact your insurance carrier. I apologize for taking up your time."

With that, I dropped the receiver back on the cradle. Using the crinkled paper in my hand and a pen I found in an old filthy coffee cup, I scrawled a quick note to Brice. I told him my insurance agent would be in touch to arrange for the repairs and he could keep the car as long as necessary in the meantime. At least the rain had stopped. Because my mood at the moment could rival a hurricane's fury. With my purse hitched on my shoulder, I shoved open the door and stalked toward home.

~~~~~

Paige

For the rest of the day, my mind revisited the idea of Nia and Sam. The resulting nausea left me too sick to comprehend interest rates and write-offs. When the afternoon crawled past with no change in my condition, I decided to close shop a little early. One of the perks of being my own boss, no one made me punch a time card.

After leaving the office, I dashed home for my car and then headed for the local supermarket. Thursday was food shopping night. Living in a resort community, I didn't want to be caught in the mad crush on Friday night when the weekenders all showed up and stocked their pantries. Especially the Friday before a major holiday.

I raced through the aisles, filling my cart with single

girl fare. Once I'd accumulated a week's worth of Lean Cuisines, Diet Pepsi, and a pint of Ben & Jerry's for weak moments, I joined the end of the line at register number three.

In front of me, holding onto a cart overflowing with family staples: juice boxes, cereal, milk, fruits and vegetables, Emily Handler turned. "Paige, how *are* you? How's Nia?"

"We're good," I replied automatically. Most people here saw us as one entity so we generally answered as such. "How are you?"

"Busy." She jerked her head toward the four kids who ranged in age from fifteen to two years, loitering around her cart. "I'm glad to hear your sister's not hurt. Sam said the accident was minor. And she certainly looked okay when she came in to see him a while ago. But you never know with those kinds of impacts. You can be fine one minute, the next you're stuck in a hospital bed in traction." She whirled back to the parcel of children. "Lucas, put down that gum. Melissa, will you please watch your brother for me? For five minutes?"

With Emily distracted by her youngest son's attempt to swipe all the candy from the impulse shelves, I had a moment to digest what she'd just disclosed. Nia? An accident? And what did snide ol' Sam have to do with it? Why hadn't Nia called me?

Chills rippled over my skin. What had happened since this morning? More important, how soon could I pay for my groceries and get out of here? I glanced at my cart. Just a few items. Maybe Emily would let me jump her in the line? Then again, I'd still have to race home and put the frozen stuff away before it all defrosted.

Should I just leave all this crap? Head straight to Nia's house and find out exactly what happened and why she didn't call me? After all, what were a few diet entrees, compared to my sister's well-being? On the other hand,

Duet in September 48

how bad could this supposed accident have been? She'd gone to see Sam afterward.

Sam. Again.

What if I nearly killed myself getting to Nia's house and found her canoodling on the sofa with Sam? Ewww. My stomach churned.

One thing was for sure. I wasn't going anywhere near Nia's house until I'd made a phone call to make sure she was alone first. If Sam was there, I'd need a ring of garlic to wear around my neck.

Emily turned to me again, and I pasted a serene expression on my face. For a few more minutes, we made small talk, but what we discussed barely registered with me. Too many questions swirled in an eddy inside my skull. After I'd paid for my groceries, I sat in the driver's seat of my car, turned on the engine, and dialed Nia's house before pulling out of the parking lot. My hands-free device immediately forwarded the phone call through my radio speakers.

After three rings, her answering machine clicked on. "Hi, this is Nia. At the beep, speak."

I resisted the urge to bark, my usual greeting when I heard the recorded demand. In all fairness, since my message asked for the caller's name and number, Nia always replied, "Nia. Two," which signified her status as the younger twin—by a whole eight minutes.

Right now, though, levity wasn't an option. "Nia, what's going on? I just ran into Emily Handler at the supermarket. She said you'd been in an accident. What happened? Do you need anything? Are you hurt? Call me. I'll be at the house, but I can be at your place in twenty minutes if you need me."

I disconnected, headed toward home, and got as far as the next intersection before I reconsidered. Emily's voice echoed in my head. *You can be fine one minute, the next you're stuck in a hospital bed in traction.*

What if Nia was unable to answer the phone because she was hurt? Contrary to what some people thought, twins don't have a stronger psychic link than other close siblings. If Nia stubbed her toe in the middle of the night, I didn't suddenly bolt out of bed with sympathy pain.

What if, right now, Nia was lying on the floor waiting for help that would never arrive? I couldn't take that chance, regardless of my defrosting groceries. Who cared about twenty bucks' worth of frozen food when my sister might be unconscious or immobile?

The traffic light at Main and Maple flipped from red to green, and I popped a quick U-ie in the center of the intersection.

Whoop! Whoop! I'd barely straightened the wheels when red and blue lights excoriated my windshield, accompanied by the quick blasts of a police siren. As I slowed toward the curb, I slammed my hands on my leather-wrapped steering wheel. Without turning around, I knew who'd pulled me over because that was the way my luck ran today. Sure enough, when I dared a glance in the rearview mirror, Sam Dillon stepped out of the cruiser and swaggered toward the driver's door of my sporty SUV.

The minute I rolled down the window, his posture relaxed, and he exhaled a heavy sigh. "Paige. I should have known. Do you have some kind of death wish?"

"What's the problem, Sam?" I unclipped my seatbelt and glared out the window at Dudley DoRight. "I made a legal U-turn."

He had the nerve to quirk an eyebrow at me. "A U-turn in a major intersection with no regard for the possibility of oncoming traffic. Since when is that legal?"

"There *was* no oncoming traffic."

"This time." He shook his head like some disappointed parent. "Do you know Nia had an accident today no more than two blocks from here? What's the problem, Paige? Can't stand to see someone else get all the attention? Do you always have to one-up your sister? She has a little fender-bender, so you have to wind up in the emergency room? I have half a mind to slap the cuffs on you for first degree stupidity."

"Don't tax yourself, Marshall Dillon. You only have half a mind to begin with." Okay, so insulting a cop wasn't my smartest reaction. Even if he deserved it.

What made him think he could talk to me that way? Regardless of any emotional attachment he had to Nia, he had no clue about our sisterly relationship. Sure, as twins, we had indulged in some serious episodes of sibling rivalry over the years. But not since Mom had walked out on us twenty-some-odd years ago. Now, with Dad gone, we were all we had left. We treasured each other.

And Sam Dillon wanted to horn into our family. Well, I'm sorry but until he had a ring on my sister's finger, he didn't have a right to an opinion about me or Nia.

"Not that it's any of your business," I said curtly, "but I'm on my way to Nia's." Because now I knew that he *wasn't* there. I toyed with lying to him, telling him that Nia had called to say she desperately needed me. But not knowing the details of Nia's condition precluded me from inserting my foot into my throat.

Luckily, my intended destination seemed to calm the savage beast. He backed away from my car. "Okay. But drive more carefully."

"Yes, sir." I rolled up my window and pulled out again, even using my directional, although the only other car in sight was Sam's cruiser. I had to clench my thigh muscles to keep from hitting the gas with a stomp. I so wanted to spit gravel at him with some screeching tire action. Somehow, though, I managed to stifle the impulse and drive away with a sedate air.

Chapter 5

Paige

Nia lived in our grandparents' former house in Snug Harbor, a gingerbread Victorian on the outskirts of town, painted in a clapboard gray with lavender trim. The feminine lines and dramatic turrets suited Nia's personality. And of course, the detached carriage house in back was a perfect workspace for her glassblowing.

After Grandma passed away six years ago, her will left her home to both of us. Nia had immediately suggested we sell the house and split the proceeds equally. Living in Albany at the time, I'd told her to forget it. Aside from the fact that strangers living in her house would have had Grandma rising from the grave to seek revenge, I also understood that Nia needed her own place in Snug Harbor. She needed to get out of the broad shadow of our father's wings. If she sold her inheritance and gave half the money to me, no way could she afford a decent place of her own in this resort town. She'd be much better off keeping a house we all knew had been well-maintained, which would also keep Grandma resting comfortably in the hereafter. It was Dad who'd suggested our childhood home go directly to me after his death, so that each of us would have our own residences in Snug Harbor. The compromise worked perfectly, with Nia in walking distance of the beach and me near the marina.

I pulled into Nia's empty driveway and noted the dark house. No car. No sign of life inside. Where could she be? The hospital? Oh, God, no. I turned off my engine and opened my door. The unmistakable *thump-thump-thump* of my sister's bass-driven classic rock music nearly tossed me out of my SUV. Which meant Nia was in her studio, in creative mode.

Releasing a huge sigh of relief, I stepped out onto the gravel. Since her glass artwork required temperatures upwards of a thousand degrees, Nia wouldn't risk working with the excessive heat if she was even slightly under the weather. She always said, "One wrong move, and I could be incinerated." So whatever accident had befallen her, Nia was obviously unharmed. Thank God.

I took one last glance back over my shoulder and pressed the lock button on my key fob. The quick horn blast of my car alarm barely registered over the scratchy, raucous twang of some long-haired rock star's guitar. Guns n Roses? Van Halen? I never could tell the diff. My tastes always ran toward fun, quirky stuff that I could dance to or sing along with. At the top of my lungs.

Fumbling to drop my keys back into my purse, I carefully trod my way to the carriage house. Whereas the original building had been clapboard like the house, Nia had updated for safety precautions years ago. Now the ceiling between the first and second floors had been removed to create a large, vaulted space with lots of ventilation. The hot wall—where the furnace and other equipment stood—was constructed of sheet metal and cement board corrugated panels to deal with the extreme temperatures.

My wedge sandals challenged the flexibility of my ankles on the uneven gravel. With every crunch, I teetered first right, then left while I headed toward Nia's studio. Oppressive heat radiated through the doors when I got within ten feet of the building. How on earth did Nia manage to enjoy sweating buckets in this place, particularly on a humid summer evening? The music suddenly shut off, a signal that it was safe to enter. The walls, which reverberated from the speakers she had mounted in each corner, quieted to normal.

I reached for the door. Nia, coming through from the

building's interior, nearly barreled over me. "Oh, Jeez!" She jumped back, hand on her chest. "You scared me."

"Sorry," I said with deep breaths to get my own rapid heartbeat back under control. "Are you okay?" My fingers entwined around her wrist, and I looked her up and down carefully.

"Yeah." She offered a weak smile. "I told you. You just startled me, that's all. I didn't expect you to be out here."

"That's not what I mean. I ran into Emily Handler at FoodMart. She mentioned you'd been in some kind of accident."

"Oh, that." Wiping a long-sleeved arm across her shiny forehead, she grimaced. "Come on up to the house, and I'll tell you about the damage your thirty day experiment caused me today."

Damage? Aw, shoot. Hope trickled out of me.

Nia pulled a ring of keys from the back pocket of her jeans. "Give me a sec to lock up."

Frowning, I stood on tiptoe to peer around her toward the inside of the building. "Am I taking you away from anything important?"

"No. I'm toying with a line of decorative glass pumpkins and gourds for the autumn. It's good therapy for me. The accident was only the tip of my frustration iceberg today. I was actually just headed up to the house for dinner while I let my latest piece sit in the lehr 'til tomorrow. Wanna join me? Did you eat yet?"

"I've got Lean Cuisines in my car," I told her.

"Puh-leez," she said. "After the day I had, I'm up for homemade pizza. I took dough out of the freezer when I got home a few hours ago. Are you in?"

My forehead puckered in mock disbelief. "Are you *kidding*? You bet I'm in. Can I stow my cold stuff in your fridge 'til later?"

She shrugged. "Sure. I'll meet you on the porch."

While she fiddled with locking up her studio, I dashed
back to my car on my wobbly ankles to fetch my perishable
groceries. Once I had the two canvas bags in hand, I
climbed the stairs to the house's wraparound porch where
Nia waited beneath a hanging basket of vivid purple
petunias.

Her gaze followed the lines of my arms to the sacks,
and she smirked. "What flavor?"

Blood rushed into my cheeks. My sister knew my
weakness for Ben & Jerry's far too well. "Phish Food."

"I get to keep it," she said as she inserted the house key
into the lock on the lavender front door. "It's the least you
can offer me in penance."

Following her inside, I sucked in a sharp inhale. "That
bad, huh?"

"Oh, yeah." After flipping on a light, she stopped in
the foyer beside a dark wooden table inlaid with miniature
white and gold tiles. Atop the table sat a cobalt bowl with a
white rose in full bloom encased for eternity in the glass
bottom. This was one of Nia's creations from her most
popular handcrafted collection, a set of flower-inset
glassware she called Forever Summer. I always marveled at
how artistic she was. Somehow, that particular trait had
passed me by in the genetic lottery.

Nia dropped her keys inside the bowl with a *tink*, and
jerked her head at me. "Come on."

I followed her past the staircase and into the kitchen in
the back. Of all the rooms in this house, the kitchen was the
place where Grandma's presence lingered. Golden oak
cabinetry gleamed with orange-scented polish, creating a
warm and comfortable glow to embrace all who entered.
Pots of African violets still sat on the twin shelves of the
greenhouse-style window box above the porcelain sink.
Nia, always prepared for a possible burn, had added several
aloe vera plants to the purple flower jungle. A homemade
cross-stitch sampler mounted over the back door lintel

proclaimed the kitchen the heart of a loving home. I remembered when Grandma created that sampler, and how Nia had worked with her on the hundreds of teeny x's with multi-colored threads. Christmas vacation. 1997. While they stitched, I worked on an extra-credit project for my English class: reading *Animal Farm* by George Orwell and drawing parallels to the Russian Revolution. Good times, good times…

From one of the lower cabinets, Nia pulled out an extra-large wooden cutting board and set it on the center butcher block. "You know how I told you I would take First Avenue to work today?"

"Uh-huh." I stood frozen, my mind hopping from one bad case scenario to another.

"Well, there's a very good reason why I don't normally travel that route." She scooped flour out of a copper canister behind her and spread it across the cutting board. "Traffic's a nightmare. When I finally got to the corner of First and Maple—twenty minutes late, mind you—a bunch of teenagers in a Jeep rear-ended me at the light, jumped the curb, and raced off in the shoulder lane."

"Oh, my God." My shopping bags fell to the floor in front of the refrigerator. Fear coursed through me, leaving chills on my flesh. What if she'd really been hurt? God, I couldn't imagine. I opened my arms to squeeze my sister for dear life. "Nia, are you sure you're all right?"

"That's a matter of opinion."

She allowed me to cling for about thirty seconds, then stepped back to refocus her attention on the dough that sat in a sunny yellow ceramic bowl, covered by a pastel-striped dishtowel. One of Grandma's old dishtowels. Nia threw nothing away if she could help it.

"I'm not injured," she said as she plopped the dough onto the floured cutting board. "Although Sam tried to talk me into going to the hospital for some x-rays, just in case. He said sometimes spinal injuries can take a day or two to manifest."

And there he was: the invisible elephant in the room. I couldn't hold back the flood of sarcasm before it spewed from my mouth. "Sam said that, huh?"

"Yes, Sam said that." A definite spark of something lit up Nia's eyes when she grinned at me. And it didn't come from the high hat lighting set into the ceiling. She shook her head slowly as she picked up the ceramic rolling pin. "Honestly, Paige, after all these years, can't you soften up even a little? High school was a lifetime ago. And Sam's a really nice guy. You'd see that for yourself if you gave him half a chance."

If I bit my tongue any harder, I'd slice it in two. But I wanted my sister to be happy. So when I could finally get the words out without choking on bile, I said, "Yeah, I was thinking the same thing today. That he and I really got off on the wrong foot and maybe it was time to let bygones be bygones."

My suffering paid huge dividends instantly. Nia's whole face glowed. "You were? Really?"

Watching my twin's mood transform from shattered to hopeful, I catalogued a lifetime of moments stretched out before me. I'd just given Nia my blessing to date Sam Dillon. Every Thanksgiving, Christmas, and birthday might now have my arch enemy in attendance. Sucking face with my sister.

My stomach flip-flopped. What if she married him? Had children with him? Okay, they'd be super-good-looking, but—

"Good for you, Paige." Nia's enthusiasm interrupted visions of gorgeous offspring with Sam's stellar looks and her sweet personality.

"Yeah," I mumbled, one hand clutching my upset stomach. "Good for me."

~~~~

Nia

I will admit, I enjoyed watching Paige squirm when I honed in on her feud with Sam. Oh, I meant what I'd said. It was long past time both of them grew up. Snug Harbor was a small town, and these two ran into each other a lot. Best for all the innocent bystanders if their every meeting didn't turn into a bloody battle.

I also realized that, at the moment, my sister was just telling me what she thought I wanted to hear. If the insincerity in her tone didn't give her away, her sudden dive into my refrigerator to put away her groceries clinched my suspicions.

"So how bad is the damage to your car?" she asked from the vegetable crisper drawer.

"I don't know yet. Brice is handling the details for me."

Paige straightened and closed the stainless steel refrigerator door. "And the kids who hit you? Did Sam catch them at least?"

Ah, yes. Those kids. And that *man*. I pushed the rolling pin over the glob of dough on my floured cutting board. "Yes and no. The owner called Sam when his stepbrother brought the Jeep home with front end damage. He wanted to know if his vehicle had been involved in an accident."

"That was nice of him," Paige remarked. "He sounds like a decent, responsible guy—even if his stepbrother's an ass."

"You think so?" The memory of the odious Aidan Coffield filled my head. Unfeeling, privileged, arrogant...

"You *don't* think so?" She inched closer, bumping her hip against the edge of the counter. With her hands clasped near the dough, she leaned toward me. "I get the feeling there's more to this story than you're telling me."

I avoided looking directly at her, and focused on my

rolling pin. Forward, back. Forward, back. "No. Of course not. Why on earth would you think that?"

"Because you've pretty much pounded that poor dough into the butcher block."

I looked down and stifled a gasp. While thinking about Aidan Coffield, I'd taken out my frustrations on my dinner and rendered the dough too tough for use as anything but a door stop.

"Wanna try again?" Paige smirked.

"I can't," I said with a frown. "I don't have any more dough made. And it'll take too long to get another batch going."

"I meant about what happened today. What's got you so rattled? I mean, I know you had an accident, but you're not hurt, your car's going to be fixed, the owner of the other vehicle stepped up to take responsibility—"

"I'm stressed, okay?" To emphasize my emotion, I slammed the rolling pin on top of the ruined dough and sank against the counter's edge. "I had a really bad day, and if I have to go through twenty-nine more like this, you'll find me curled up in a fetal position in a padded room, babbling to myself, long before we reach October first."

"Oh, come on." Paige wrapped an arm around me and squeezed me against her side. "It's going to get better, Nia."

I eyed her with suspicion. "How do you know that?"

"I don't know. Because it can't get much worse?" she suggested. "Unless, of course, there's an axe murderer lurking in the backyard."

The giggle escaped before I could stifle it. Followed by another. Then another. Until we both collapsed to the floor in a puddle of laughter. I laughed until I couldn't catch my breath and my eyes filled with tears. I have no idea why, really. Paige's comment wasn't particularly witty or insightful. It just felt so good to let go with someone. And who better than my twin?

"Forget the dough," Paige said as she scrambled to her feet, then offered her hand to help me up. "Call Dino's. Order whatever toppings you want. I'll fly *and* buy."

She and I had a long-standing agreement when it came to pizza. One person flew: drove to Dino's to pick it up. The other person bought: actually paid for the pizza. If she was willing to fly *and* buy...? She must have been feeling mighty guilty.

I decided to push her a little further. "Can I get mushrooms on it?"

She flashed an exaggerated grimace and sighed. "Yeah." I must have gaped at her because she waved a careless hand. "I can pick them off."

A total lie. One of the things that made Dino's pizza so special was the way he chopped ingredients fine enough to be embedded in his tomato sauce. And Paige hadn't been able to tolerate mushrooms in her pizza since a slumber party when we were twelve where she came down with the flu two hours after consuming three 'shroom and sausage slices.

Enough of the niceties. Time to get down to the truth. "Why exactly are you being so generous tonight? Did you win the lottery today or something?"

Her brows arched in twin peaks of disbelief. "Compared to you? Yeah, I guess I did. I won the luck lottery. The worst that happened to me was getting caught in the rain this morning. Well...that, and a couple of run-ins with Snug Harbor's own Dudley DoRight."

"Paige." I offered her a warning glance and a wagging flour-coated finger.

"I know, I know," she replied. "I'm dealing with Sam. I promise." She pushed the cutting board to the farthest corner of the counter. "So, what do you plan to do differently tomorrow?"

This time I couldn't stifle my gasp of outrage. "Are

you kidding me?"

"Oh, come on, Nia. You're not going to give up after one bad day, are you?"

I gave her an exasperated look.

"Okay, a *miserable* day," she amended. "But still. We have to give this thirty-day thing a chance. Everything happens for a reason. I really believe that."

Remember in *The Wizard of Oz* when the Wicked Witch wrote "Surrender, Dorothy" in the skies over Oz? I didn't need a burning broomstick to get the message. I was fighting a losing battle. Paige wouldn't let me off the hook for this thirty day challenge if I was bleeding from my eyes. My muscles sagged beneath the weight of my capitulation.

"How about you pick me up for work tomorrow?" I suggested. "Since I don't have my car, we can kill two birds with one stone. Or better yet, spend the night tonight and drive tomorrow. That'll double our chances."

Paige frowned, then slowly shook her head. "I'm not sure. I mean, yeah, I'll definitely give you a ride to work until you get your car back, but I think we have to focus our challenges on new and different stuff, not just our everyday commute."

A chill zipped up my spine. "What'd you have in mind now?"

Was it my imagination or did my sister's smile grow devious? "After work tomorrow, let's skip the usual Friday night account settling in favor of specialty martinis and appetizers at The Lookout."

The Lookout?! That tourist trap attached to one of the priciest hotels on the Atlantic strip?

"You *did* win the lottery," I accused. "Either that, or aliens abducted my real, fiscally responsible sister and replaced her with a spendthrift lunatic."

"It's Labor Day weekend," she reminded me. "The Lookout's doing a last-week-of-summer blowout with two dollar mixed drinks and half-priced appetizers until ten p.m. tomorrow night."

"It's Labor Day weekend," I reminded her. "Meaning I work until ten p.m. tomorrow night."

"That's my point, sister-mine. You don't have to. Break the rules. Let Iggy close up, leave the credits and debits ledger for another day, and come out with me. We can ask Francesca and Terri to join us. Girls' night out. Drinks and appetizers, then maybe hit a dance floor. Just a teeny-weeny change to our routine, boring lives. Simple."

Simple. Again. I was soooo going to regret this. I knew it even before I sighed and said, "Okay."

Paige clapped like a four-year-old promised ice cream for dinner. "Yay! Now, let's order that pizza."

Chapter 6

Nia

Friday morning and afternoon passed without any unfortunate incidents. As Sam had predicted, my back and neck muscles ached whenever I sat or stood still for too long. Fortunately, despite a blistering sunny day—perfect for beachgoers—business inside my shop boomed, leaving me little time to feel any pain. Briana rang up so many customers, she broke three of her gel nails, which, apparently, was a major league tragedy requiring an emergency appointment with her manicurist immediately after work. Poor Andrew probably strode more miles than a runner in training for a marathon. He barely exited the storeroom with one box of merchandise before I sent him back for another. Items practically flew off the shelves. Even the wind chimes—not my most popular souvenir by any stretch of the imagination—sold out for the first time ever.

Ordinarily, I'd have been thrilled with the day's receipts. But I couldn't shake the feeling that something ominous loomed on my horizon. As if the universe was setting me up for a date with disaster. I feared the Fates planned to get me all calm, lull me into a false sense of contentment, then *whammo*! Hone in for the kill.

The great white shark of doom circled me all day. I kept looking over my shoulder and peering around corners while the *Jaws* theme played in my head on a continuous loop. *Da-dum. Da-dum.*

Yet, the bite never came.

Therefore, it was with no small trepidation that I prepared myself for Paige's Girls' Night Out event. Since this was the "thing we did differently" tonight, I suspected my shark would attack at The Lookout.

"I can stay 'til closing if you want to go home," I told Iggy as the clock inched closer to the moment when I'd have to leave the safety of my shop. "You could get a jump on your studies. Or start some of your homework."

Iggy stopped rearranging the last few glass Christmas ornaments on the tabletop artificial tree to stare at me. "Nia, it's the second week of school. I don't need a jump yet. I don't even have all my books yet."

"So, go get your books. There you are." Eagerness sped up my speech pattern. *An out.* Iggy needed books. I had an out. Even Paige would understand if I had to stay behind for Iggy's sake. "I'll close up tonight. You pop over to the university and take care of your study materials."

"You're being foolish." He rubbed a hand over his bald pate.

How the man could make a shaved head look downright sexy, I had no idea. But the ex-Marine had women—young and old—flashing doe eyes as they sighed dramatically when in his presence. The guy was textbook hunk, all six-foot, three inches of him. An action figure come to life. Throw in silver-hued eyes with lush, sooty lashes, and that rock-hard physique, and Iggy could have any female he wanted with one heart-stopping smile. But Iggy didn't want *any* female. Raised by his uber-romantic Polish mom, Iggy waited for his soul mate. Oh, he wasn't celibate by the loosest interpretation. He shopped around for his soul mate, sampling the goods whenever possible. He just hadn't found The One yet.

"You wait," he chided me with a wagging finger. "Tomorrow morning, you'll stroll in here to tell me you had a great time and can't wait to do it again."

He meant Girls' Night Out. He had no idea what "it" really was. I hadn't told anyone about the thirty day challenge. I mean, I wasn't insane. Imagine the daily ribbings and probing questions from my well-meaning friends who'd wonder if anything exciting had happened every time I did something different. No, thank you.

"The Lookout's a fun place to kick back on a Friday night," Iggy continued. "Well, the bar area's fun. That's where you're going, right?"

I couldn't muster up an iota of enthusiasm. "Uh-huh."

"Then relax. You'll have a blast."

Da-dum. Da-dum. The *Jaws* theme echoed louder, drowning out Iggy's happy prediction. With a defeated sigh, I pulled off my apron and grabbed my purse seconds before my sister strode into the store.

Paige wore a purple tank top embellished with embroidered silver butterflies and sequins over a black tube skirt and sky-high needle heels. I took a quick look from my royal blue silk t-shirt and white crop pants down to my flat sandals with chunky plastic jewels across the toe band. Clearly, one of us was inappropriately dressed. But I'd bet my whole store my ensemble better fit in with the bar's regular clientele. I couldn't outshine her enthusiasm, though.

My sister's face glowed with excitement. "Ready to go?"

No. But I didn't have much of a choice, did I?

Fifteen minutes later, at precisely six o'clock, we walked into the waiting area of The Lookout. A crush of other dining parties milled in the lobby. Some dressed to impress; others couldn't care less. Easy to discern Snuggies from tourists in this crowd.

Gleaming expensive sports cars that halted beside the curb of the front door to discharge their designer-clothed and accessorized passengers all belonged to the visitors. The wealthy tourists sashayed inside on a breeze of exotic cologne and strolled to the podium, where the snooty maitre'd confirmed their reservations. A waitress would then escort them to the high-priced dining room, past a wall of windows overlooking the ocean. For extra ambience, a tuxedo-clad pianist tickled the ivories of a white Baby Grand. Entrees were a la carte, and dinner for two generally cost more than I took home in a week. Seriously. The least expensive menu item was a ten-dollar cup of coffee. Coffee. Not a latte or cappuccino. Plain old ordinary brewed coffee.

Locals, like us, poured out of late model vehicles parked in the rear lot. Most of us still in our work clothes, we bypassed Mr. Stiff and his clipboard of exclusivity on our way to the bar area, which had a spectacular view of the hotel's maintenance garage. There, a jukebox thumped out classic rock and the latest Top Forty hits to whomever dropped in a few coins. The same cup of coffee in the bar cost three bucks. Well, not exactly the same. Restaurant patrons sipped their coffee out of delicate bone china cups with matching saucers. We consumed ours from sturdy ceramic mugs or Styrofoam cups to go.

Terri and Francesca were already seated on high stools at a corner table when Paige and I walked into the bar area. They were hard to miss. Terri's cinnamon-colored hair, cut in a choppy bob, bounced as she bopped to the song blaring out of the jukebox. I recognized it as a Top Forty song about feeling sexy on the dance floor, overplayed on the local radio station. Francesca, who looked like she just stepped off an old lady's cameo pin, sat across from Terri, her dark hair a storm cloud of curls around her perfect face. The four of us had been friends since elementary school.

Francesca Florentino was the oldest child of five noisy siblings. Years of being surrounded by crises made her the perfect emergency room physician: calm, level-headed, and smart. She'd come inches close to the altar five years ago, only to have her fiancé accept a job offer in Oregon without consulting her first. Despite the Pre-Cana classes they'd attended as a requisite for their church wedding, Francesca had never realized Michael didn't value her career or that he expected her needs to take a back seat to his. So, rather than flying off to Hawaii for a honeymoon, she drove Michael to the airport for his flight to Portland. Only her three closest friends know she'd come home from JFK and cried herself into near-dehydration. Typical Fran, "never let them see your worries." Nowadays, she focused solely on her patients. To be honest, I was surprised she'd agreed to attend tonight's soiree. Then again, she'd probably say the same thing about me. Which only proved my sister had some mighty powerful methods of persuasion.

The last member of our quartet, Terri O'Mara, had arrived in Snug Harbor at the age of twelve to visit her aunt and uncle. She'd never gone home again. Only years later, as adults, did Paige and I learn that her parents had died in a murder-suicide during her fateful respite in our sleepy town. Even after two decades of therapy, she still had a tendency to numb her pain with a little too much alcohol and food. I worried about her sometimes.

"Looks like they started without us," Paige grumbled and grabbed my arm. "Come on."

We meandered our way through the noisy crowd of local bargain diners to their spot. A gigantic round platter filled with fried calamari, bruschetta, and stuffed mushrooms sat front and center on the table, between a pair of brightly colored drinks in martini stemware.

"Hey, girls!" Terri lifted her Pepto-Bismol pink cocktail in salute as we neared the table. "You better catch up. We're two ahead of you already."

"What *is* that?" Paige asked as she jumped up onto the stool on Terri's right.

One of the benefits of my height: I only needed to stretch on tiptoe to slide onto the leather-cushioned seat of the high bar stool between my sister and Francesca.

"A cotton candy martini. It's the coolest thing ever." Terri's overly bright green eyes glittered like wet marbles, and I stifled a wince. Her glassy eyes did not bode well for the evening's festivities. "After the vodka's shaken with ice, Gary actually pours it over a tuft of cotton candy. The candy melts and changes the clear liquid to a bright color. He can do pink or blue, if you want. Or both, maybe. Or would that make purple?" She held up the glass, tilting it toward the track lighting overhead. "Isn't it pretty? Like babies in a nursery. Yummy boy and girl babies." She tickled the bowl of the glass with her index finger. "Koochie-koochie-koo."

I took a good look at my inebriated friend, then turned to Francesca. "We're only *two* drinks behind?"

She offered a shrug, hands outstretched, palms up. "Well, that depends on who's doing the math. See, between four and six o'clock, the drink specials here are two-fers. Since Terri and I got here about a half hour ago, I've had one Diet Coke. The other drinks were all hers."

I blinked once, twice, and a third time while realization sank into my brain. "You mean she's on her second round of double cotton candy martinis in thirty minutes?"

"Actually, those are drinks five and six. She's already two rounds *ahead* of you. I ordered the platter of appetizers before you got here, hoping I could get Terri to put something besides alcohol in her stomach." Placing her chin in her hands, she sighed. "No such luck, though."

Well, Terri definitely needed to eat, if for no other reason than to absorb all the vodka she'd swallowed. I speared a plump brown mushroom with a fork, set it on a white plate, and passed it to Terri. "Here. Crab stuffing. Your favorite."

Much to my relief, Terri picked up the mushroom and took a small bite. A sharp inhale later, she spit it out onto the plate. "This is ice cold," she exclaimed and flung the untouched portion across the room.

The mushroom landed in Ted Gadsen's lap.

"Hey!" On a screech of chair legs against scarred wooden floor, Ted shot to his feet. "What the—?"

Hoping to smooth things over quickly, I immediately

Duet in September
68

stood, hands raised in surrender. Pain sluiced down my spine, but I stifled a wince and kept my expression placid. "Sorry," I told Ted. "It was an accident."

My apology might have had a more positive effect if Terri hadn't burst out laughing. "Omigoddidyouseethat?"

"Terri," Francesca whispered fiercely. "Shush. It's not funny."

"You're right. It's not. It's hysterical. I hit him right in the gonads." Terri's laughter turned raucous—the sound of a braying ass—and she pounded a palm on the table.

Of course the jukebox chose that particular moment to go silent. Conversations halted, and all eyes turned toward our table. Paige and Francesca simply stared at each other helplessly.

Great. Tonight was quickly becoming a three ring circus. "Okay," I said with more calm than I felt. "I think we're done here. Time to go home, Terri." I reached to take her arm, but she shook me off.

"No fair," Terri exclaimed. "You guys just got here. If Deadhead Ted can't take a joke, that's his problem. Let *him* leave. I'm having fun."

I clenched my teeth, but the easy smile never left my face. "I think you've had enough fun for one night."

"Screw you, Nia," she shouted back. "You think I don't know you're only my friend because you feel sorry for me? Screw you!" On the last word, she picked up her martini, turned, and hurled it against the wall behind her.

Crash! The glass collided with the dark wood paneling, splintered into hundreds of shards, and sprayed drops of pink liquid all over Terri's white shirt.

"Screw you," she repeated as the tears streamed down her face. "Screw all of you."

"That does it," Gary announced from behind the bar. "I'm calling the cops."

Da-dum. Da-dum. Dum-dum-dum-dum...

The *Jaws* theme grew louder and picked up tempo,

just like in the movie—right before the great white sank its teeth into its next unknowing victim.

Chapter 7

Paige

Nia, Francesca, and I managed to wrangle Terri into the ladies room before she could do any more damage. At least, she couldn't do any more damage to others. Her esophagus, on the other hand, received plenty of burning punishment when she started puking.

I gotta admit, nothing gets to me like the sound of someone else throwing up. Just the retching noise is enough to pitch my stomach into free fall. So while Terri prayed to the porcelain god in the first stall, I doubled over, lips tightened and hand clutching my abdomen to keep my own dignity intact.

Lucky for me, Nia knew my infirmity all too well. "Go ask Gary for some ginger ale," she ordered brusquely.

Gladly. Even facing Gary the Scary Bartender held more appeal for me than lingering in this vomitorium. I yanked open the door and raced into the hallway, where I barreled into a rock-hard chest. A pair of brawny arms encircled my waist, and firm hands landed on my butt. The sensation was actually kind of pleasant. The hair on my arms feathered, and a delicious shiver rippled across my flesh. Until he spoke and broke the spell.

"Whoa, easy there."

Me and Sam Dillon. In a dark hallway with his arms around me. With me, thinking I liked it. Awkward.

Even now, I couldn't say who recognized whom first. I prefer to think the realization was simultaneous. I do remember we both stiffened at the same time and stepped away from each other as if jerked back on Bungee cords.

I'd also like to think I behaved with grace, but I know better.

"Oh, for God's sake," I snapped. "Isn't there *any other* cop in this whole rinky-dink town?"

"Paige," he replied flatly. "I should have known you were involved in a drunken brawl. How much did you have to drink, sweetheart?"

How much did I…? Sweetheart? A red mist descended over my eyes. "Wow. Three insults in one statement. Even for you that's ambitious, as well as overly hostile. In the first place—" I stopped in mid-tirade as my promise to Nia echoed in my head.

Give the man a chance.

Okay. For my sister's sake, I'd try. After a deep breath to calm my outrage, I said in a much more sedate tone, "Never mind. Nia's in the ladies room with Terri so she's in good hands."

"Nia?" Sam's eyes widened, taking on a luminous glow beneath the bare bulb over our heads. "Are you saying *Nia* is the out-of-control drunk I'm here to arrest?"

"Of course not! Terri's the dr—"

I halted again. Arrest? Did he say arrest? Sure, Terri had become drunk and a little belligerent, but it wasn't her fault. Not really, anyway. I couldn't imagine having to live with the knowledge my father killed my mother, then himself while I was on vacation at the beach for a week. If she chose to dull her guilt, along with her senses, every once in a while rather than deal with that horror, who was I to judge her?

But most people didn't know the truth. So of course, they just saw Terri as a troublemaker, the town drunk who needed an intervention. Or, in this case, a stretch in the local hoosegow.

Thank God I hadn't gone on the full-frontal attack when Sam and I crashed together in this hallway. Because Terri needed the lawman on her side. And apparently, I had just taken on the role of liaison. Of all the sucky luck. The one man in this whole town I couldn't talk into helping me was the one man in this whole town whose help I needed.

"Look," I said, my hands outstretched, palms up, in the typical *I'm-not-carrying-any-concealed-weapons* pose. "She broke a glass against the wall and threw a stuffed mushroom at Ted Gadsen. There's no need for an arrest. Really."

Sam sighed. "That's not up to me, Paige. It's up to Gary. And Ted, apparently. If they want to press charges, there's not much I can do to change their minds."

Oh, for God's sake! Did I have to draw him a diagram? "You could *help*. Soothe their anger, minimize their attitude. Tell them I'll pay damages. I'll buy Ted some new jeans. The man probably hasn't bought a decent pair since 1986 anyway. And tell Gary I'll do his taxes for free this year. Please?" I actually clasped my hands in prayer on that last word. Like I was pleading with God Himself.

God Himself, however, simply frowned. "Look. I know you mean well and you think you're helping her, but the plain truth is your friend's in trouble. She needs professional help."

Yeah. I think we were all beginning to see that Terri's drunken binges were more than just Girls' Night Out, let loose fun. "Maybe. But she's not gonna find salvation in a holding cell."

This time I got a head shake in response. "I'm not so sure about that. Sometimes an addict's gotta hit bottom before she'll crawl out of the madness. Terri will never hit bottom if her friends keep bailing her out."

"She's not an addict." My voice lacked any fury under the weight of Sam's comments. Were we really making things worse for Terri?

He arched that brow at me. But this time rather than making me defend my argument more vehemently, his expression forced me to consider the implications. Still…arrest her? That was like going after a mouse with a flamethrower.

"She's in pain, Sam," I confided on a hoarse whisper. "Nia and I, we know stuff about Terri that no one else knows. And it makes a difference. A *huge* difference."

He stared at me, as if he could suddenly see the secrets Nia and I were privy to. I dropped my gaze to my strappy silver sandals. Much as I wanted Sam on our side, I had no right to reveal Terri's past to anyone.

Finally, he sighed again. This time I was pretty convinced the sound smacked of surrender. "You said she's in the ladies room with Nia?"

Hope flourished, and I snapped my head up to grant him my mute appreciation. "Uh-huh. Nia and Dr. Florentino are in there with her."

"Excuse me." He strode around me, aimed for the rest room.

"Wait! You're not going into the ladies room, are you?"

"Yeah." One hand on the door, he turned to me again. "Don't worry. I'm a professional."

"No, it's not that. It's just…" How to put this delicately? "Terri's… indisposed... right now."

Sam grinned.

Holy cow, the man had a thousand watt smile. Why I had I never noticed that before?

"Still can't deal with someone getting sick, Paige?"

I sputtered. "How did you…?"

"Senior class picnic. Remember? Bobby Shaw drank too much rum and tossed his cookies in the weeds. You walked by where he crouched on his knees and *boom*. Hit the ground like a cannonball."

I grimaced, recalling that sunny June day when I fainted in the school athletic field. "Definitely not one of my stellar moments."

"Oh, I don't know," Sam replied. "I think it was the first time I ever considered you human."

The insult hit me right between the eyes, and I blinked.

How much more could I possibly take? "Human?" I asked pointedly.

"Yeah." My obvious umbrage was lost on Sam, who still grinned without shame. "Before then, you always seemed like this living computer, full of facts and numbers with no emotion. But that afternoon, you looked *vulnerable*. It was actually kinda cute."

My jaw dropped. Vulnerable? Kinda cute? What cave did this man crawl out of? Before I could utter any logical response, he pushed his way into the ladies room.

A split second later, he popped his head out again, and I stifled a smug *I told you so*. Apparently, even the big, bad police chief had his vulnerable moments.

"Hey, Paige," he called to me. "Make yourself useful and ask Gary for some ginger ale, would you?"

Make myself useful? Oh, he did *not* just say that to me.

Give the man a chance. Once again, Nia's plea echoed in my head.

Gritting my teeth, I nodded at Sam and stalked toward the bar. Make myself useful, I grumbled. Lucky for him Nia had already sent me on the same errand. She was probably wondering what was taking me so long anyway. My rush to fetch the ginger ale now had absolutely nothing to do with the fact that he sent me so I could be *useful*. Jerk.

I had to elbow my way past a throng of men and women clamoring for service around the polished bar. And since the three mixologists handling customers had all witnessed Terri's earlier meltdown, I wasn't going to be their top priority. Time for Plan B. I scanned the dozens of faces around me, seeking out a friendly compatriot. My gaze settled on Evan Rugerman, who had one elbow on the bar's curved edge while the other hand waved a twenty at Gary. I smiled. Target acquired.

"Hey, Evan." I left my Siberian corner and wound my way through the crowd to my new best friend's side. "Fancy meeting you here."

"Paige. You believe this? It's a madhouse here." He gestured at the crush of people, then leaned in to peck my cheek.

If I hadn't known about his boyfriend, I might have snuggled closer. Evan had eyes the color of a perfect summer sky and lustrous, thick, black hair. His full-lipped smile was the stuff of forbidden fantasies. No doubt about it. Evan Rugerman was a walking advertisement for sex, which was one of God's greatest jokes on the female of the species, considering Evan's gender preference. In fact, Evan had been crowned Miss Fire Island at Cherry Grove three years in a row. Alas, our loss was mankind's gain. Literally.

"Can I buy you a drink, sweetheart?"

His hot breath tickled my nape, and the clean citrus smell of his cologne tempted me to lick that delightful hollow below his Adam's apple. Who cared if he didn't get turned on? I'd enjoy the hell out of it.

Focus, Paige. Terri needs you.

"I just want a ginger ale, thanks," I replied.

"You the DD tonight?"

"Something like that." DD, designated driver. I didn't feel the need to enlighten him about the events currently unfolding, or rather…coming up…in the ladies room. Better to change the subject. "Where's the dashing Dr. Bautista tonight?"

Evan's eyes clouded. "An emergency with the McDonnells' dopey dog. Again."

"Uh-oh." The rottweiler had a reputation for ingesting anything left within reach of his mouth. Since rotties weren't exactly petite, anything lower than…oh, say, the top of the refrigerator…was fair game to the canine. Last month, he'd required emergency surgery to remove two Hot Wheels cars and a baby sock. "What did Boomer eat this time?"

"An entire tray of fudge brownies."

I sucked in a sharp breath. "Yowza. That dog has a real death wish."

"So do you, Paige," Gary growled as he stopped in front of where I stood with Evan. "Haven't you and your friends done enough damage tonight?"

There went my intention to fly beneath his radar. I'd have to switch to Plan C. Or X. Or whatever letter I was up to at this stage. Unfortunately, I didn't have another plan prepared at the moment. Lucky for me, though, Evan Rugerman opted to play white knight.

"Oh, come on, Gary, that's not fair. Everybody knows Terri O'Mara is a hot mess."

Hmm... My white knight might be closer to beige.

"You should have cut her off earlier," Evan continued. "She was already blitzed by the time Paige got here. And once Terri became nasty, Paige hustled her into the ladies room. So be a nice guy and say thank you by giving our fair maiden a ginger ale, okay? And a summer ale for me."

The bartender grumbled something I couldn't decipher before reaching overhead for a clean glass, which he then slammed on the bar. A quick push of a button on a gooseneck spigot, and he handed me an ounce of ginger ale. No ice.

"Gee, Gar, why not let her suck on the bar rag?" Evan took the glass from my hand and thrust it back at the bartender. "Fill it up."

"Why? She'll be outta here as soon as the cops show up. Along with the rest of her drunken entourage."

"You called the cops?" Evan demanded. "For four girls who, combined, probably don't outweigh you?"

"Terri damaged restaurant property."

"She dropped a glass," Evan replied with a careless shrug.

"She also assaulted a customer."

"With a mushroom. Did you tell the 911 operator that she's armed and dangerous? I mean, after all, she could start hurling Maraschino cherries. Imagine the mess. You might want to advise them to bring in a SWAT team." He shook his head. "Let it go, dude. Fill up Paige's ginger ale, give her and the others a chance to take Terri home, and they'll never patronize this establishment again." He squeezed me up against his side. "Will you, Paige?"

I held up my right hand. "Never again."

I could almost hear the hamster wheel turning in Gary's mind. Wrenching the glass from Evan, he slammed it on the bar again. The spigot came up and filled the tumbler. Still no ice, but I was wise enough to keep my mouth shut before my foot fell into the gaping maw.

"Here," Gary said in his gruffest tones. "Now get that sot out of here, or I'll have her arrested."

Before hightailing it back to the ladies room, I planted a loud kiss on Evan's perfect peachy cheek. "You're my new hero."

"Pshaw. Now, get outta here, kiddo. Fast."

Ginger ale in hand, I took off. Who needed Sam Dillon? Evan had finagled our release with one conversation, and I didn't even have to offer Gary free tax prep.

Feeling smug, I pushed into the ladies room and entered mayhem. Terri lay supine on the dirty tile floor wedged between the first stall and the bank of sinks. Nia sat on her haunches, Terri's head cradled in her lap. On one side of this interesting tableaux, Francesca fussed with wet paper towels pressed to Terri's face.

Meanwhile, Sam crouched on the other side, talking into his radio. "She's coming in with Dr. Florentino."

Terri coughed suddenly, jerking away from her friends, and I saw what I'd missed on my first view of the situation. Blood. Lots of it. All over Terri's blouse.

My stomach revolted. The way I reacted to puke? Was ten times better than the way I reacted to blood. And the sight of red wetness streaking white cotton boiled bile in my belly. To fight the pending nausea, I carefully sipped the ginger ale I'd brought in with me, then choked as my throat closed around the liquid.

"Get outta here, Paige," Sam growled at me. "Go out front and wait for the ambulance."

I looked from him to my sister and back again. "Am...ambulance?" Good God, what had happened? I'd only left them alone for ten minutes. How on earth had Terri managed to hurt herself so badly in ten minutes that she needed an ambulance?

Only Francesca was kind enough to answer me. "Terri passed out in the stall and slammed her head against the toilet. She broke her nose and maybe fractured a cheekbone."

"Oh." I looked down at the glass in my hand. "I guess she doesn't need the ginger ale then."

Stupid. I knew it was a stupid thing to say. I knew it before Sam glared at me in disgust, before Nia groaned and looked away as if I'd just humiliated her with my idiocy.

Once again, the ER doctor took pity on me. Rising, she patted my shoulder with her damp hand. "Terri's going to be okay, Paige. But I need you to flag down the EMTs when they arrive and get them in here as fast as possible. Can you do that for me? For us?"

This time, I kept my mouth shut. What had Abraham Lincoln said? "It's better to remain silent and be thought a fool than to open one's mouth and remove all doubt." This fool would remain mute for the rest of the evening.

I nodded, set the glass of ginger ale on the counter near the last sink, and fled the room before I lost my lunch. For the briefest moment, I thought of Dara Fitzsimmons and the guests on her talk show. By the end of this thirty day stint, Nia and I would be lucky to still be alive.

Chapter 8

Paige

Ah, Saturday.

I rolled over and stretched with the languor of a pampered Persian cat. Toes first, then legs, hips, and arms. At last, I splayed my fingers and sighed. Deeeee…licious. Lucky me, I didn't work weekends in the summer so I could loll among my Egyptian cotton sheets with my air conditioning on high and a thick quilt. Unlike poor Nia who—

Nia!

I shot upright in the bed. Dang. I was supposed to pick up my sister this morning to take her to work. Cursing, I scrambled out of the tangle of bedcovers and glanced at the clock on my nightstand. 8:28 am. I had two minutes to get to Nia's house.

Yeah. Like that was going to happen. Oh, God, she was gonna *kill* me. Especially after last night's disaster at The Lookout. All the way home last night, she insisted she was done with our thirty day challenge and refused to consider giving it one more day. Well, like it or not, she was going to participate at least today. Because ever-punctual Nia was about to be late to work. Probably for the first time ever. If I'd intentionally tried to sabotage her, I'd pat myself on the back right now. Instead, I zipped to the bathroom to take care of my personal needs, then back to the bedroom.

Next to the clock sat my cell phone. Should I call or just bolt and blame my lateness on traffic?

Both.

I grabbed a brush and elastic tie from my dresser and pulled my hair into a ponytail. My shortie pajamas served as underwear as I yanked on a pair of loose workout pants and an overlarge t-shirt. Sliding my feet into cheapie flip-flops, I swept up my cell. I dashed downstairs for my purse and keys, then raced out the door, the phone to my ear.

The phone on the other end barely rang before it was answered. "I knew you'd forget."

Since she couldn't see me, I screwed up my face at Miss Know-it-All. *I knew you'd forget,* I mouthed, acid scorching my tongue. I dove into my car and used the subterfuge of starting my engine to sigh out of Nia's earshot. God, sometimes my sister could be more uptight than a boa constrictor.

"I didn't forget. I just overslept. I must have lost power during the night, and my alarm clock got all screwed up." Why waste a perfectly good traffic excuse when she wouldn't believe me anyway? "I'm on my way now."

"Uh-huh. Terrific."

I didn't have to see her face to know her expression when she hung up seconds later. No doubt my sister paced in her foyer, teeth clenched, fists at her sides, mumbling my list of faults: unreliable, flighty, careless. Which was so not true. Normally.

Okay, in all fairness, she had every right to be furious with me. I would have to do some major league mea culpas to atone for all the bad juju she'd experienced the last few days. And I had a pretty good idea how to go about my penance.

As I drove past the sign post at the corner of Moby Lane and Seawatch Court, I smiled. *First Annual After Season Clambake* blared at me in bold red print. The Chamber of Commerce had announced this event at the last town meeting. After the frantic months of summer tourists, the clambake—for locals only—was intended to drum up support for the village politicians, although they claimed it was a chance for the community to create stronger ties. I had no clue who planned to attend this shindig—except for *one very important police chief.* Sam would be there to represent the town's law enforcement community. Therefore, I had to convince Nia to make an appearance. Get these two together in a social situation. Let the music of the night take over. Or, in this case, the music of the quahogs.

Not an easy task with my sister's current attitude toward my ideas. Still, I thought as I took the left that would bring me to her house, not impossible. I'd have to use a little finesse, maybe a bribe. Worse come to worst, I wouldn't discount a bit of subterfuge. After all, my evildoing was for the greater good.

I pulled into Nia's driveway and spotted her on the porch, standing beneath the hanging basket of petunias. I was surprised the poor flowers didn't wilt from the steam coming out of her ears. She practically flew down the steps as my car crept toward the house. I hadn't even come to a full stop before she yanked open the passenger door and jumped into the front seat.

I attempted an apology, but she held up one hand while buckling her seatbelt with the other.

"Save it," she growled. "Just drive."

Yes, Your Majesty.

I drove out of her driveway and off her block, allowing her time to cool off. Then, I decided to open with, "Francesca called me last night. She said Terri's okay, just a few cuts and scrapes and the broken nose."

"Yes, I know. I got the same phone call." Nia kept her gaze pinned out the passenger window while I pulled out and headed for Main Street.

"Sam thinks Terri needs help. And that we're doing her more harm than good by putting up with her drunken antics."

No answer. Ouch.

My air conditioning was no match for the heat of her anger, and in no time, perspiration beaded beneath my t-shirt. I squirmed against the leather carseat and drummed my fingers on my steering wheel. On the radio, the same song that had played when Terri blew her gasket yesterday—*Sexy on the Dance Floor*—drifted from my speakers. I quickly changed the station to something less volatile, but the best I could find was political talk radio. Hardly soothing.

Once again, I passed the sign at Moby and Seawatch. I took a deep breath before diving into the abyss of my sister's rage pool.

"I was thinking we should go to that," I said as casually as I could create when barely awake and facing a sibling firing squad without benefit of caffeine. A totally inhuman condition, by the way, that I do not recommend as the harshest punishment. Even Death Row inmates got their choice of last meal, for God's sake.

Nia whirled toward me, her expression baleful. I'd never seen "baleful" before—from Nia or anyone else—but I'd certainly read the description in books. Whenever I stumbled over the word, I always translated it as exactly the way Nia looked right now: frigid, furious, and joy-sucking.

"I already told you," she said, though I never saw her lips move. "I'm done with this thirty day nonsense."

I swallowed hard. *Courage, dear heart.* "This isn't about the challenge."

Her eyes hardened to flint. "No?"

"No," I imitated with an edge, then flashed a quick smile to ease the tension between us. "I just thought it would be fun. And good for the community." Oh, I was on a roll now. "Good for business, too."

"Maybe for *your* business. Not mine. So you go."

"I intend to," I lied. "But not by myself. I'd feel…" My mind scrambled for the right description to drum up empathy. "…adrift."

She cocked her head, but her expression didn't soften. "Adrift?"

"You know what I mean. It's not the same unless we're together. We've always been Nia and Paige, one entity. If I show up without you, it'd be like…I don't know…showing up missing a leg. Everyone's gonna stare and ask why you didn't come too. And then the rumors will start. 'Why didn't Nia stop by?' and 'She thinks she's too good for us, I guess.'"

Okay, so according to Sam, I was the one everyone thought acted high-and-mighty. What had he called me the other morning? The perfect Princess Paige? Even now, the insult stung. That particular nickname popped into my head at weird times. In bed at night, in the shower in the morning, sometimes at my office when I was on hold or deep in thought about something entirely unrelated. What a crummy thing for him to call me. And if he called me that, did everyone else, too? Why? I mean, I didn't *think* I came across that way. Evan Rugerman didn't give me any kind of attitude problem. And his dad loved me. Maybe it was just Sam who thought so harshly of me.

"You're not even listening, are you?" Nia's sharp question popped the bubble of my self-consciousness. Thank God.

What were we talking about? Oh, yeah. The clambake.

"Would you at least think about going with me?" I pleaded.

Nia harrumphed and folded her arms over her chest. "Maybe."

I'd kinda hoped for more enthusiasm, but I'd swallow this dish in small bites. I had until the end of next week to convince her. A lot could happen between now and then. In the meantime, I'd dream up other ways to get my sister and Sam together as often as possible.

I flashed a beaming smile in Nia's direction. "That's all I ask."

~~~~~

Nia

From the storefront window, I watched Paige drive away. Questions buzzed in my head. What bizarre game was she playing now? And what inspired her new obsession with the town clambake? Only a week ago, she and I had laughed ourselves silly during our morning coffee, joking about the obvious political manipulation. Now she planned to attend? And wanted me to go with her? Why?

When her tail lights disappeared over the hill in the road, I turned my attention to getting the shop open. With the lights on and the sign flipped to "Open, Come In Please," I dug in my tote bag for the piece I'd designed the other night. I placed the glass gourd on a shelf adjacent to the window, then stepped back to scrutinize the setting. Morning sunlight, resembling dew at dawn, streamed inside and sparkled on the rich golden orb with its thick, brown vine and dark green leaves. Perfect. I could picture two full shelves, like a miniature glass farm stand, lined with all kinds of fall décor: pumpkins, jack o'lanterns, Indian corn, apple pies, maybe even a black cat if I could figure out the dimensions and shaping.

Creative juices flooded from my brain to my fingertips, and I strode to the counter with my imagination zipping from one idea to another like mile markers on the Autobahn. Once I'd tossed on my apron, I pulled a sketchpad from the lowest shelf and settled down on the stool behind the register with a pencil. I wanted to jot down as many of the images as I could before they disappeared from my consciousness. I started with the cat, drawing an arched back, erect tail, and stretched haunches. The face stayed blank for now; details could be enhanced later. I then moved on to apple pie, right down to the little vents in the top of the crust.

I don't know exactly how long I perched there, my hand flying over the pages. I only looked up when the bells on the front door jangled to announce someone's arrival. After putting the finishing touches on a scarecrow, I rose from the stool and tossed the sketchpad where my butt had been. "Good morning. Can I help you?"

Only after I'd spoken the greeting did I focus on my customer. I stiffened.

Aidan Coffield stood in the store, a cellophane-wrapped vase full of lavender roses, eucalyptus stalks, and English ivy in his hands. My jaw must have dropped, or maybe I gasped or something, because he hefted the bouquet a little higher and shrugged. "I have trouble seeing you as a standard red rose kind of girl. Now, purple, in my opinion, says you're a little complicated, but in a good way."

If he'd wanted to get technical, I could've told him lavender roses signified love at first sight. But I kept that translation to myself. I didn't move toward him or the flowers. I simply stood, aloof and unapproachable. "What do you want, Mr. Coffield?"

"To apologize for starters," he replied. "I was pretty hostile to you the other day. You didn't deserve that."

My icy reserve thawed to a nonchalant cool, but I stood my ground. "Okay, fine. Apology accepted. If there's nothing else, I'm rather busy."

"Really?" His gaze swept the empty store.

"Not everything I do here revolves around customers," I retorted.

He inched closer and placed the flowers on the counter next to me. I had to admit, the bouquet enthralled me. I'm a girly-girl, and a man who brings me roses—particularly unusually colored roses—will always make my heart melt. Once again, Aidan Coffield turned my insides to goo. Even in faded jeans and a well-worn dove gray t-shirt, the man exuded sex appeal. Of course, he also radiated arrogance,

Duet in September

which should have minimized my attraction. Too bad my heart refused to heed my head's advice.

I could feel myself crumbling into itty bits of want. I wanted to like him. I wanted him to like me. I wanted to hear him say my name. I wanted to push that stray wisp of hair off his forehead. I wanted to cook him breakfast.

I wanted the roses, too. And the ittiest bit of me wanted to believe he'd known their color signified love at first sight when he chose them for me.

"That's new." He gestured to the glass gourd on the shelf to my right. "When did you make that?"

"How did you…?" No. I wouldn't let him know he'd surprised me. Again. "I finished it yesterday."

"It's incredible." He strode to the shelf and stretched out a hand. "May I?"

I nodded, granting him permission to handle the piece.

His fingers delicately traced the lines of the vine and leaves. "Such beautiful detail," he said, his voice husky with appreciation. "Exquisite. Almost delicious in its perfection."

The words wrapped around me like a naked embrace, seductive and heady. I couldn't breathe. The air grew dry, and I licked my lips. He didn't even turn in my direction, yet the heat of his gaze warmed my flesh.

"You've got quite a talent."

"Th-thank you." With my knees wobbling, I backed up and attempted to use the stool for support.

Thunk. The sketchpad slid off the top and fell to the floor. I scrambled to pick it up.

"You okay?" His voice came from above. Like a god's.

Crouched on my haunches with the book of drawings in my hand, I looked up. He'd transferred his attention from my glass sculpture and now leaned over the counter, his arresting gaze totally fixated on me. My knees gave up the fight, and I landed on my butt on the floor.

"Whoa. Easy there."

My cheeks burned. Both sets. Could I be more of a klutz? I managed to pull myself up, but by the time I got to my feet, he was beside me. He had one hand on my arm and the other in the small of my back. Nice. He smelled good, too. Soapy and clean. Which, naturally, sent my imagination into Sexual FantasyLand, where I pictured him stepping out of the shower, wet, draped in a towel, leaving a tantalizing peek of muscled golden skin.

"You okay?" he asked again.

"Unh." Words stuck in my dry throat.

"Are you always here by yourself?"

I understood what he was asking and why. He'd only come to my store twice, and both times I was alone. But with my current vocal handicap, I couldn't wrap my tongue around the explanation that Iggy and I took turns opening and closing the shop. I settled for a shrug.

"Someone should take better care of you."

Annoyance sizzled through me, and I yanked myself out of his hold.

"Uh-oh," he remarked with a crooked grin. "I screwed up again, didn't I?"

I simply glared at him.

He stuffed his hands into his back pockets. "I'll take that as a 'yes.' So you tell me. How do I get a second chance with you? I know you probably don't believe this, based on our track record, but I'm a nice guy—honest, hardworking. You want character references? I'll get them. A note from my fourth grade teacher? A credit report? Want to strap me to a lie detector? Whatever you need, name it."

"I'm not making the grape lamps for you, no matter what you offer."

Eyes wide, he laughed. "Grape lamps? You think I'm here about grape lamps? God, no. And before you mention it, I'm not here about your car, either."

"Then what *do* you want, Mr. Coffield?"

"Well, for starters, I'd like you to call me Aidan. But more important, I want you to consider going to dinner with me."

Dagnabbit, he took me by surprise *again*. "Dinner?" I croaked.

"Yes, dinner. Traditional first date stuff. Or lunch, if that makes you more comfortable. I'd settle for a twenty-minute coffee break, but I'd really prefer at least an hour in your company, if you can spare it. Just name the day, time, and locale, and I'm yours."

I stole a glance at the beautiful roses on my counter, then gazed up into his face. For the first time in all our interactions—few as they were—I had the upper hand with Aidan Coffield. I had never before considered myself power hungry, but this particular shift boosted my confidence. I casually flipped through the pages of my sketchpad, seeing nothing, but determined to draw out this delicious moment.

"Nia." My name came out of his mouth on a whisper of warm air that melted any resolve still left inside. "Please."

The "please" did me in. "Okay," I said with a sigh of surrender. "Next Friday is my first day off."

He beamed as if I'd just told him he won the Irish lottery. "Then Friday night, it is. What time should I pick you up?"

Oh, no. No way did I intend to transfer control into his hands by putting myself in his passenger seat. "I will *meet you* at the Beach House. It's a restaurant in Amagansett. I'll be there at seven." I said a silent thank you to the fates that I'd already arranged with my insurance agent for a rental car until mine was repaired. I wouldn't want to have to borrow Paige's. She'd want a reason, and no way did I intend to tell her about Aidan Coffield. Another reason for this rendezvous to occur outside of Snug Harbor: I'd be less likely to run into someone I knew.

His expression shifted slightly, as if he fought an inner battle against attempting to change the rules. *Tough luck, buddy*. He'd ceded all the decisions to me, and I wasn't about to give an inch on this. To reinforce my position, I folded my arms over my chest and kept my gaze steady on his. I didn't blink until my eyes stung.

Thankfully, he looked away first as he nodded. "Okay then. Friday night. The Beach House. Seven pm. I'll see you then."

Before I could gloat over my victory, he leaned forward and kissed me. Full on the lips. And not a quick peck, either, but mouths parted, our breath mingling. No tongue, thank God, since I wasn't ready to play tonsil hockey with a man I barely knew. He probably realized he'd gotten as much out of me as he was going to, at this juncture. When he pulled away, he drew a finger down my cheek, sending pleasure rippling through my bloodstream.

"Enjoy the flowers," he murmured in my ear.

"Uh-huh," I said stupidly. I was amazed I managed to say anything at all. Intelligence had fled from my brain.

Only after he'd left my store on the jangle of bells did I return to my senses. My first coherent thought was I'd somehow managed to continue the thirty day challenge, by agreeing to a date with Aidan Coffield. Next came the realization that Friday night was the night of the town clambake. Paige would have to muddle through that fiasco without me. *That* thought kept me smiling for the rest of the day.

The memory of Aidan's yummy kiss, still tingling on my lips, was just a bonus.

Chapter 9

Paige

After dropping Nia off at her store, I considered my options. Going back to bed was out of the question. But if I planned to forgo my usual Saturday morning routine in favor of an early start to the day, I would need coffee. Stat.

As I cruised down Main Street, I sought out a quick spot for a caffeine infusion. My mistake. This was the Saturday of Labor Day weekend, one of the peak times for tourists in Snug Harbor. I passed the block where Mama's Hen House served breakfast and confirmed my worst fears. Crowds of tourists loitered outside the restaurant on the three park benches, window shopping at the realtor's next door, or chatting with the others waiting for one of the two dozen tables inside. Their children zipped up and down the sidewalk or slouched beside their parents. Strollers, which were not allowed inside due to the cramped interior, sat parked in rows near the entrance. Strike one.

Two blocks later, the line at the local bakery snaked the length of a football field. Really? These people were willing to wait over an hour for a few Danish? Sorry, I didn't have the kind of patience needed to infiltrate that mob scene. Strike two.

One last place to check. And I couldn't even squeeze into the parking lot at our local convenience store, thanks to the multitude of beachgoers buying ice for their coolers, twelve packs of canned soda, a quick breakfast, or all of the above. So much for my getting coffee to go. I'd have to wait until I got home for my morning jolt. Which, when I took my sweatpants and giant t-shirt into account, was probably a very good idea.

I made a beeline for home and soon enough, sat at my

kitchen table with a toasted English muffin and my longed-for coffee. Once I finished breakfast and washed my few dishes, I stared at the clock above my sink. Now what? It wasn't ten o'clock yet, and I had an entire day stretched out in front of me with nothing to do. I couldn't hit the beach for the same reason I had to come home for breakfast: the plethora of tourists. Ditto for the shops, which would be jam-packed with those seeking that last-minute souvenir of the summer they'd spent in Snug Harbor. I should probably throw some laundry into the washer, but I cringed at the idea of spending my day off doing *housework*. Besides, it was far too beautiful a day to stay cooped up indoors.

A bike ride might be nice. And…I sneaked a peek at my thighs in my shortie pajama bottoms…beneficial. Yes. A little fresh air and some cardiovascular exercise. This excursion would also serve as my "something different" today. Win/win/win.

I quickly dressed in shorts and a t-shirt, before my lazy side could convince me if God wanted us to exercise, He wouldn't have invented the Lifetime Channel. In the garage, I found my bike penned in by my artificial Christmas tree, the snow blower, and my ski equipment. Okay, so it'd been a while since I'd opted for two-wheel transport rather than four. When I first came home from Albany, Daddy's deteriorating health had kept Nia and me running back and forth to the hospital. After his death and the funeral, I'd invested all my time into becoming the new Wainwright at the helm of Wainwright Financial. Such a dismal time…

Enough. I shook off the memories and wrestled the poor bike free. Once I rolled it out, I checked the tires and noticed the front one was flat. I ventured back into the garage for my manual pump and filled the tire with air. Fifteen minutes later, I sailed down my driveway, aimed for the circular road that ran around the marina. A salty breeze kissed my cheeks as I rode leisurely through my neighborhood.

I waved to Mrs. Seifert as I pedaled by where she knelt, weeding the garden of red and white impatiens around her mailbox. "Good morning."

"Morning, Paige," she called after me. "Enjoy your ride."

I would.

Snug Harbor earned its name because the town bordered large water on two sides. On the southern coast, the Atlantic Ocean offered miles of pristine beach with soft white sand, ideal for the tourist trade. The rocky northern coast sat at the edge of the Long Island Sound, creating a perfect waterway for fishermen. Whereas the south end of town prospered due to multi-million dollar properties, five star restaurants, and upscale boutiques, this side—the north crescent—catered to a very different clientele. No-frills motels, bars, delicatessens that opened at four in the morning to serve breakfast for early rising mariners, bait shops, and takeout restaurants ruled here.

The north side also had a wilder beauty than the south, thanks to less development and a more rural flavor. At least, that was my opinion. Buildings were erected farther apart, with lots of open space between. Bulrushes caught the breeze and rustled. Seagulls hovered, squawking as they sought leftover food to scavenge. Across the rocky inlet, the Coast Guard station stood sentry with its lighthouse and flapping flags.

The one exception to this pristine homage to Mother Nature was Coffield's Wharf, a miniature version of San Francisco's Fisherman's Wharf. Our replica boasted a popular clam bar where tourists and locals could grab fresh-caught seafood and pitchers of frosty beer while dining outdoors at picnic tables. For higher end clientele, there was also one five-star restaurant with spectacular water views. The various outbuildings housed a few souvenir shops, an old-fashioned ice cream parlor, an expensive toy store, and of course, a Coffield's Bluff wine store that offered free tastings on weekends. When Nia and I were kids, our parents often took us to the wharf in the evenings for ice cream or fried clams, or just to walk over to the docks next door to see the party boats sailing back with the day's catch. At ten on a Saturday morning, I figured most of the crowds would be elsewhere: the beach, breakfast (obviously), aboard party boats, or wherever else tourists went on beautiful sunny days.

The simple joys of childhood echoed around me as I cycled toward the wharf. I passed the old elementary school Nia and I had attended. Behind the school sat the playground where I'd had my first kiss from a boy. Darren Simmons had been eight and I was seven. His family moved to Texas a few weeks later and for a while, I thought my scandalous behavior was the cause of their abrupt departure from Snug Harbor. When I'd finally confessed my deep dark sin to my mother, she'd laughed and explained Darren's father had been offered a transfer from his company. The peck on the lips I'd shared with Darren was probably his way of saying goodbye. Of course, only a year later, my mother became the poster child for "scandalous behavior," but at the time, her comments made perfect sense.

On the next block, I rode past the public library, a frequent hangout in my school years—before the existence of the Internet.

Everywhere I looked along my route sparked a memory to make me smile.

Why hadn't I done this before now? My legs pumped for an uphill climb, then relaxed my feet on the pedals as I coasted down the other side. I felt exhilarated, powerful, and a little bit sexy. No wonder people raved about the endorphin rush that came from exercising. This was amazing!

A higher hill came into view, and I shifted gears to

prepare. I had to pedal a bit harder than I'd anticipated, but I pushed myself, knowing I could coast down the other side. Once I *reached* the other side. Funny how I never noticed how steep this road was when I drove it every day in my SUV. My thigh muscles ached, and I actually rose off the seat to get more power into my pedaling. Sweat broke out on my forehead. Still, the bike and I climbed. My pace slowed with my exertion, making every motion harder to complete. At last, I crested the hill, but only found a plateau. No downhill break to catch my breath. I had to push on.

A few yards ahead of me, a man walked a large, lean dog near the curb that ran along the shoreline. The man had a great build with broad shoulders packed into a tight t-shirt and long, muscular legs in khaki shorts. Nice buns, I contemplated as I drew closer. A good handful, but no excess.

Beeeeeeep! A car horn blared from behind me, and I swerved to keep the front tire straight. The bike veered onto the road's shoulder and slid on a patch of sand, nearly upending me.

The expensive convertible roared past me at a speed I surmised was double the town's limit. The blond driver, her long hair whipping with the wind, flipped me the bird as she sped on down the road.

"Nice," I shouted after her. "I hope you get arrested!" Where was a cop when I needed one?

"Paige, is that you?"

Oh, good God. Mr. Yummybuns looked at me over his tasty shoulder, and I groaned. Why had I wished for a cop right now?

"Hey, Sam." I tried to play nonchalant as I braked my bike next to him. "Did you see that moron?"

He shrugged. "Yeah, but I'm off-duty right now. If it makes you feel any better, though, Tonya's at the top of the next ridge with a radar gun."

Imagining the blonde's upcoming surprise, I laughed. "No lie?"

"Nope." Sam's grin sparked fireworks in my belly.

In the dim hallway last night, I'd found his smile dazzling, but in the light of day, I could easily understand Nia's attraction to the rest of him. He looked like a sun-bronzed god, all sinew and golden skin with eyes the color of honey and the lushest lashes I'd ever seen on a man.

If only he were mute...

As if to introduce itself, the fawn-colored dog suddenly lurched forward to sniff at my sneakers.

"Daisy, get down." Sam yanked on the leash.

"Hi there, sweetheart. Aren't you a love?" I bent to rub the pooch between its folded ears, then looked up at Sam again. "I didn't know you had a dog."

"Daisy won't hurt you. She's big but loveable."

"Daisy?" I quirked my eyebrows. "You named this huge beast Daisy?"

"Not my choice. She's a rescue from the Greyhound Liberation. Her full name is Daisy Chain of Love."

"Wow." I slipped my hand under Daisy's angular jaw, and she snuffled. "I'm impressed."

"Don't be," he replied. "All the racers get goofy names."

Actually, I was referring to the fact that he had a softness for any living thing. But I wisely bit back the insult. "How long have you had her?" I asked instead.

"Two years." Daisy licked his hand, and he patted her fondly. "If you're thinking about a pet, I could probably hook you up with the rescue group. They're always looking to place retired greyhounds."

Me with a dog? I shook my head. I couldn't even keep a houseplant thriving. "I don't think I'd have the energy for a former racing star."

"The keyword there is 'former.' They're retired so they actually don't do much running. And you've got a decent-sized yard for a dog to get out his ya-yas. Besides, you look like you could handle anything." He glanced at my bike, then the road ahead, as if he didn't want me to see the smirk on his face from his attempt to compliment me.

Yeah, sure. Suddenly he's worried about hurting my feelings. Get a grip, Paige.

"Where you headed?" he asked, gaze still fixed on the horizon.

"The wharf, then home again."

He whistled through his teeth. "Oh, right. But you don't have the energy to keep up with a greyhound. That's like…what? Eight miles round trip?"

Eight miles?! I swallowed a gasp and forced a casual smile. No way did I want him to know I had no idea how long a trek I'd planned for myself. "Yeah, something like that."

"You training for some kind of marathon?"

"Sort of," I lied. "The 10K Twin Fork Ride is next month. I figured I might as well start getting ready." Wow. Could I get any more ridiculous? No way I had the slightest intention of participating in that torturefest.

"Where's your water?" He gestured to my bike frame, then looked up at the sun and shielded his eyes with the flat of his hand.

Water? My gaze followed his to the empty wire rack where a water bottle should rest beneath my seat. Oops. I forgot about bringing something to drink on my morning trek. I wasn't about to let him get the better of me, though. "I'll pick up a bottle when I get to the wharf," I replied with a dismissive air.

His brows rose in twin arcs. "The wharf is still two miles from here. You'll dehydrate long before you get there." He jerked his head in the direction of the side street. "Come back to the house with Daisy and me, and I'll grab you a coupla cold ones to go."

If this were a movie, the creepy music would start

building right now. What should the naïve heroine do? Go home with the monster so as not to hurt his feelings?

Lucky for me, this wasn't a movie. I had no qualms about turning him down. "No, that's okay. I'll be fine."

"Do I scare you, Paige?"

I snorted to hide my surprise. "Puh-leez." He thought I was *afraid* of him? Or was he actually *daring* me to come to his house?

"Good. Then you've got no good reason to decline. And the break will give you time to reapply your sunscreen, too, since it looks like your face is starting to burn."

"My…" Sunscreen. Of course. Something else I forgot. Jeez, I was a moron. But I'd committed to this stupidity and wouldn't give Sam Dillon the satisfaction of catching me in my lies.

"Forgot that as well, huh?"

"I didn't forget," I retorted. "I just ran out and decided to pick up more when I got my water."

"Uh-huh." His knowing grin raised hackles on my nape. *Note to self: don't try to lie to a cop.* "Come on. Let's get you properly outfitted for your 'training.'"

"It's really not necessary," I said lamely.

"Yeah, it is. Your sister would never forgive me if you wound up in the hospital and I could have prevented it."

Nia. Again. I sighed my defeat and pushed my bike forward. "Then I guess I'll take you up on your hospitality. Thanks, Sam."

As I followed him and his dog, I had the uneasy feeling I'd just agreed to visit the devil in his private circle of hell.

Chapter 10

Nia

Now that I'd agreed to meet Aidan Coffield for dinner, I decided to do some reconnaissance. Sure, I should've researched him before giving in, but he'd taken me by surprise. *This time.* He wouldn't ever take me by surprise again. While I was still alone in the shop, I pulled my tablet from my purse, logged on, and looked up his information online.

Unfortunately, I didn't find as much fodder as I would have liked. In contrast to his father's addiction to fame, Aidan seemed to keep a low profile. There were a few mentions of him in connection with a property located a few miles outside of Snug Harbor, a newly established vineyard called Piping Plover. That explained his obsession with my grape lamps. Apparently, he planned to follow his father into the winemaking business.

Ogden Coffield had been the heir to a vast Manhattan real estate fortune when he'd caught the wine fever that ran rampant through Long Island's east end in the 1980s. Nowadays, millions of gallons of wine were produced every year from the thirty or so local vineyards. And Coffield's Bluff was one of the most successful in the country.

Do you know who my fiancé is?

I shoved the memory of the obnoxious Camille's snide remark into a dark corner of my mental attic. I didn't care about Ogden Coffield. And I cared even less about his bride-to-be.

Digging deeper online, I found several articles in the local newspaper's archive. The oldest was from more than twenty years ago when Coffield's Bluff Vineyards presented their first varietals to the public. The article included photos of Ogden Coffield, his first wife Luisa, and their then pre-teen son, Aidan, who looked a lot like his mother, now that I scrutinized the images. Thank God. Ogden Coffield had one of the most misshapen faces I'd ever seen on a man—like a rotten potato with jowls.

"Wow. Where'd the flowers come from?"

I looked up to see Briana rubbing the pale purple petals of my roses. "Don't touch," I scolded. "The oil in your fingertips will kill them." I had no idea if that were true or an old wives' tale, but I didn't want anyone touching *my* roses.

Briana moved her hands away from the bouquet, head tilted at me like a curious owl. "Have you got a boyfriend, Nia?"

Embarrassment dried my mouth to the moisture level of a jar full of cotton balls. "They're from a customer," I managed to croak out.

"Really?" Briana's expression turned dubious. "For what?"

"For a project I'm working on for him." Every word I spoke rasped. I needed water. Desperately.

"Uh-huh."

"It was just a thank you gesture." I realized the more I denied the boyfriend angle, the more ridiculous I sounded. I kept up the charade anyway. My social life wasn't Briana's business, or anyone else's for that matter.

"Roses," the teen remarked. "That's a weird choice, don't you think? I mean, these look really romantic. I wish some guy would give me an arrangement like this." She bent closer to the blooms and inhaled. "God, I *love* the smell of roses. And the eucalyptus is a nice touch, instead of the usual baby's breath. Gives them an edge. Roses with an attitude." She looked up at me, eyes narrowed in open speculation. "I bet these cost a fortune. I hope you're doing something amazing for him."

Did agreeing to dinner count as something amazing? It certainly did in my opinion, considering the idea went against all my principles. But that wasn't an avenue I intended to pursue at the moment. "Briana, did you come in to talk or to work today?"

"Sor-*ree*," she retorted with a sly grin. "Gee, somebody didn't get enough sleep last night. *Must* be a new boyfriend."

No matter how much she needled me, I would not discuss Aidan Coffield with her. Glancing down at my tablet, I zeroed in on a photo taken at some award ceremony in his father's honor. The man sure knew how to wear a tux. In contrast to his father's severe black on black ensemble, Aidan wore midnight blue with a pale pink shirt and dark blue tie—a touch of whimsy that made me smile. I still couldn't believe I'd agreed to a dinner date with him. Had I lost my mind?

"Hey, Nia, think I can leave early tonight?" she asked.

My head shot up from the image of Aidan Coffield. "Didn't you leave early yesterday?"

"Yeah, but that was an emergency. Although, technically, tonight's an emergency too. Drew Pruchik asked me out, and I need time to redo my face and hair before he picks me up. I mean, this is *Drew Pruchik*. I gotta look absolutely perfect for him."

I wondered if Drew Pruchik launched the same butterflies in Briana's stomach that Aidan Coffield did in mine. But now was not the time for us to share some camaraderie over a few good-looking men. "Oh?" I said instead. "Where's this guy taking you? Someplace special, I hope."

"To the movies."

I blinked. "Let me get this straight. You have to look perfect to sit in a dark theater for three hours?"

"And for afterwards. When he takes me home." The sharp edge to her tone, the way she rolled her eyes, and her exaggerated sigh all conveyed her opinion that she was speaking to the world's biggest idiot—which, maybe she was.

Defeat crept into my managerial psyche. "Exactly how much time do you need?"

"Well, the movie starts at seven, so..." She tilted her head to stare at me, no doubt gauging how much slack I'd allow her. "Maybe four, four-thirty?"

"You need two and a half hours to get ready?" I might have faltered as a boss, but I hadn't totally lost my mind. Yet.

She shrugged, but if she hoped to show nonchalance with that action, the way she bounced on the balls of her feet gave away her excitement. "Only because I need a shower. I don't want to smell like this store when he picks me up."

Smell like...? The verbal slap stung, and I sucked back a gasp. "What exactly does this store smell like?"

"I dunno. Kinda old ladyish. Like potpourri and cardboard. It's not a bad smell, it's just not how I want Drew to think of me."

I stifled the urge to turn my head and sniff my shoulder. Did I smell old ladyish? Like potpourri and cardboard? I cringed.

Then sanity returned.

Briana was overstating her case, and I was buying into her bullcrap because an extremely good looking guy—an extremely good looking *townie*—had asked me out and I'd agreed. So naturally, I needed to find something wrong with him. Because, otherwise, I might discover something wrong with me, some gene I'd inherited from my mother that would compel me to turn my back on everyone I loved for some pretty boy with a wallet full of cash.

Paige and I had been eight years old when Mom left. I could still recall every minute of that horrible day. Snapshots filled my head. On his way to work, Daddy took us to Grandma's because Mom had complained of a headache. Her third of the week, and probably tenth of the month. I had worried that my mother was seriously sick. Grandpa had suffered from lots of headaches before a massive stroke killed him. What if Mommy had a stroke and no one was home to help her? I remember every tick of the big clock in the hall as I sat in Grandma's living room that day. I stared at the brass pendulum, willing time to speed up so Daddy could finish work and come for us. We *had* to get to Mom!

At last, I heard his car in the driveway, and I yanked Paige away from the television to meet Daddy on the porch. Then came the ride home—minutes that seemed to take hours. When we finally reached the house, I knew something was very wrong. The front door was closed, a rarity. Snug Harbor wasn't exactly a hotbed of crime. There were times we didn't even lock up at night before going to bed. Worse, there was a desperate quiet to the whole property that tore my heart to shreds.

"Mommy!" I screamed as I raced from the car to the house. To this day, I can hear the blood rushing in my head and the thunder of my rapidly beating heart. "Mommy! Mommy!"

"Nia," my father scolded. "Stop that. Mommy's probably asleep."

But I knew better. Shoving open the front door, I stumbled into the living room. "Mommy!"

Of course, I didn't find her. Instead, I found the note. The note intended for my father. The note that started with *I'm sorry* and revealed her frustration over her boring life as a wife and mother in a sleepy Long Island town. The note that ended with the bombshell that she'd escaped Snug Harbor with a stockbroker from Greenwich she'd met earlier that month. The note written on pale pink stationery with bluebirds flying in the corners. As if her life was some bizarre Disney movie, where Bambi's mom wasn't shot by the hunter, but ran off with him instead.

Mom didn't even look back. We never heard from her again.

"So?" Briana's nagging question shook me out of the memory. "Can I go early?"

Unfortunately, the bitterness from that memory remained. "You can leave at six," I said firmly.

Briana's posture slouched. "But that only gives me an hour."

Tough. "Take it or leave it, kiddo. I've got a business to run."

"Jeez," she murmured as she strode toward the counter where the employee aprons were stored. "I would've thought a dozen gorgeous roses would put you in a better mood."

"Yeah, well, they didn't, so let's get to work."

~~~~

Paige

Daisy Chain of Love loped at my side as I followed Sam up the driveway toward his house, a dopey grin on her canine mouth. No one should look that happy—not even a dog. And especially not Sam Dillon's dog.

Like me, Sam lived in his parents' former home. Unlike me, however, he'd bought the house outright when the older Dillons retired and moved to Florida. I have no idea how much he paid, but I'd bet the price was way below market value.

At the edge of the lawn, Sam unclipped Daisy's leash, then bent to pick up a tennis ball and toss it toward the front door. "Go get it, girl."

Daisy bounded toward the ball at top speed. The blur of neon yellow bounced in the grass, but the dog stayed on course. At last she stopped beside where it finally came to a halt, her tail wagging furiously.

When she made no attempt to pick up the ball or bring it back to him, he sighed. "Once again, I'm reminded by my dog that greyhounds are *not* retrievers."

I smiled, but not with any real humor. Oh, the dog was cute. And Sam's comment would have normally entertained. But the weirdest sensation had washed over me as I cycled up the driveway.

I saw myself at fourteen, riding my bike past this very house where fourteen-year-old Sam and a half-dozen friends tossed a football around the front lawn. On the steps near where Daisy stood, I could still picture Annabelle Sutter, Sam's then girlfriend, with her perfect hair, perfect teeth, and perfect skin. As opposed to my adolescent self with a mouth full of braces, zits puckering my forehead, and a few extra pounds around my middle. When Annabelle spotted me that day, she shouted, "Geek alert. Quick! Someone toss her a bag to cover her face." A chorus of hoots and laughter erupted—until Sam drilled the football in Annabelle's direction. I heard her disgruntled, "Hey!" before I pedaled away.

I don't know why that particular memory came back to me while I followed Sam now. Maybe because it was the one and only time he had come to my rescue. Although, to be honest, he only helped me out because the ball went awry from his intended receiver.

Shaking off the vision of that long ago day, I squeezed my hand brakes, pulling to a stop. Once I got off the bike, I popped down the kickstand.

"Come on," Sam said, gesturing me forward. "Let's get you set up properly for your ride." He strode forward a few steps, then stopped and turned to me, his face alight with keen interest. "Unless you'd like to stick around for a while…?"

The words came out before I could stop them. "With you?"

His expression hardened to stone, and I couldn't spit out an apology fast enough.

"I didn't mean—"

"Forget it," he bit out. "Stay here. I'll get your water."

He stomped to the house with as much angst as the petulant teen I remembered from high school.

Yeah, I know. I screwed up. But it wasn't like he and I were such close pals that we'd hang out together on a Saturday morning.

So, okay. If I planned to give him a chance like I promised Nia, I probably shouldn't think of him as some bonehead without a scintilla of human emotion. Old habits, however, were hard to break. Especially when those habits involved Sam Dillon, the heartthrob of Snug Harbor.

From the day we first met in kindergarten, when all the other girls in our class clamored for his attention, I kept my distance. Even at the innocent age of five, I didn't trust a pretty face. My mother had been a beautiful woman, but I knew her ugly side long before she left us. Nia and Dad only learned about Mom's vices when she left us. But me? I'd seen the cracks in her perfection, although I hadn't really understood them at the time.

When I was in college, I was forced to take a psych course. One of the lesson plans dealt with the sins of the parent, a study on how much impact a child's view of his/her parents affected his/her adult life. The corresponding data-based report I prepared as part of my mid-term exam, based on my personal family dynamics, earned me an A grade in that class. I barely remember the details now except for my *coup de grace* closing paragraph: *Perhaps sins of the parent can be forgiven, provided there is an act of contrition for closure. When wounds are left unresolved, however, scars can become malignant, resulting in irreversible damage to the heart.*

Or something like that. I'm paraphrasing, of course. I gained an additional benefit from that paper—a catharsis or something that allowed me to move on from Mom's transgression. Oh, it was always in the back of my mind, but I never let *her* sin rule *my* life. Unlike Nia who carried the shame and guilt of that sorry episode to this day.

The screen door clacked, and Sam strode back outside with two bottles of water in his hands and a large orange tube tucked under one arm. "Here," he grumbled. "Take this crap."

It was at this moment, as he shoved bottles at my chest, I realized I might have sincerely hurt his feelings. Go know. The big bad police chief had a soft underbelly, and maybe even—gasp!—a heart. Which, apparently, I just crushed with one careless remark.

Juggling the bottles in my hands, I told him, "Look, I'm sorry. That came out wrong."

"Forget it," he said with enough ice to freeze my water.

"No. Really."

"No. Really," he repeated with a large dose of acid in his tone. "Forget it."

Oh, for crying out loud! Would I need to grovel to get him to forgive me? "You took me by surprise, that's all. You've always said my fast mouth would get me into trouble, right?" I paused, waited for God to strike me dead for my hypocrisy. When the sky remained a clear blue with no lightning bolts spearing in my direction and no fiery vortex opening at my feet, I added, "Hey, I've got an idea. Do you want to come with me? I mean, if the ride's too much for you, we don't have to go all the way to the wharf. But if you're up for it, maybe we can have an early lunch at the clam bar if it's not too crowded."

I stifled the urge to turn my gaze to the heavens and hoped my silent prayer would still reach past the stratosphere to The Big Guy's ears. *Please say no, please say no…*

"You're on. Let me just put Daisy back in the house."

Sam grinned, and I felt the impact in my weakening knees. The man really did have a killer smile. "And I can do the full ride, no problem."

Oh, you vengeful God.

"Great." I slid one of the water bottles into my bike rack holster and tossed him the other with as much joy as I could summon up from my inner basement. "This should be a lot of fun."

Chapter 11

Paige

By some miracle, Sam and I managed to ride alongside each other for most of the trip to the wharf without my alienating him or him getting my back up. Once or twice, I even mustered up a smile at something clever he said. I'd never realized Sam had such a wicked sense of humor—or, maybe it was funnier when his zings were not aimed at me. In any event, I admit, I was beginning to enjoy myself. When we took the final turn on Shore Road, the twenty foot open steel archway with "Coffield's Wharf" scrolled in some fancy gold script came into view. That's when it happened.

With my gaze focused on the stupid arch, I never saw the tree branch until my front wheel's spokes caught in the twigs that jutted out. The thicker part of the branch came up, hit the back of my pedal, and I faltered. Okay, "faltered" is an understatement. The bike went down, tilted to the left, and I went with it, landing smack-dab in the center of the branch on my knees. I distinctly remember a quick "Paige!" coming from Sam before the impact of my kneecaps crashing into wood erased all senses except the excruciating pain, like starbursts exploding in my leg.

Before I drew a second sharp breath, Sam stood above me, lifting the bike off my hips. "You okay?"

I nodded, but with no sincerity. "God, how stupid am I?" I muttered.

Once he had my bike propped on its kickstand, he knelt by my side. "You're not stupid, Paige. Never have been. You and I both know that."

He pushed the branch of doom into the sandy underbrush where it could do no further damage. I lay there on the hot asphalt, too stunned to move. Sure, partly thanks to the fall, but more because Sam Dillon had just paid me a compliment. Then he touched me. My ankle, to be precise.

"You've got a nasty looking cut on that knee," he said. "And you'll probably have one heckuva bruise before the day's out."

The heat of his fingers branded my skin. I pushed up on my elbows and stared at him blankly. Maybe the jolt from the fall had loosened something in my brain. Because I, Paige Wainwright, always immune to Sam Dillon's charm, found myself dumbstruck the minute the man held my ankle in his hand and looked at me with his warm, golden eyes.

"Can you get up or do you need help?"

I opened my mouth, but nothing came out. Until he ran his hand up my calf, and then I sucked in a sharp breath. Shivers of delight rippled my skin, leaving goose bumps in their wake.

"That hurts?" Sam asked, all paternal-style concern.

Meanwhile, I couldn't reply, couldn't do more than stare at him, at his face so close to mine. What would he do if I just pushed forward and kissed him?

Wait. What? Me? Kiss Sam? Why on earth would I want to do that? What was *wrong* with me?

"I-I'm fine," I managed as I pulled my leg from his clasp. I had to get away from him before I did something stupid. Like kiss him. With that crazy thought rattling around in my head, I scrambled to stand and get some distance between us. "Let's hit the road."

"Whoa. Easy there, Paige. Give yourself a minute. You're bleeding into your sock, for God's sakes."

I looked down at my feet and finally noticed the stream of bright wet blood that ran from the massive scrape on my right knee, all the way down my calf. Dirt caked the wound itself and circled my kneecap, a filthy halo. My left knee, although not as severely injured, bled in thin strips surrounded by another ring of dirt. I took a step toward my bike, and sucked in a breath as pain rocketed from the middle of my right leg to my hip.

Sam must have noticed because his next statement was, "At least let me walk you down to the beach. You can take off your shoes and socks and wade into the water. The salt will stop the bleeding and dull the sting."

I wanted to say no, wanted to tell him I didn't need him mothering me. But the facts remained the same: (a.) I was bleeding like wet newspaper, and (b.) the scrapes, particularly the one on the right knee, hurt deep down to the bone when I put any weight on my feet. I couldn't imagine climbing back onto my bike and pedaling until I'd done something to stop the bleeding and maybe even close up the wound a bit. Salt water really was the best curative in my current situation. Of course, the added bonus would be a chance to put a little more distance between me and Sam until I came back to my senses.

"I can do it myself, thanks," I told him, polite but firm. "Stay here with the bikes. I'll be back in a few minutes."

"You gonna be okay walking over the rocks?" he asked.

"I'll manage." I had to. Having him with his arm around my waist, helping me down to the water, would make my current confusion worse. So I limped across the street and to the wide expanse of various rocks that led to the vast blue-gray water of the Long Island Sound. Every crunchy step on the uneven bed of cream-colored pebbles and stones, which created the shoreline, sent new adventures in pain to my knees, but I persevered. At last, I got close enough to the water's edge, and I sat to remove my socks and shoes. I stepped into the cool water, also layered with rocks. Wading in deeper, I felt the rocks give way to the muddy bottom of the Sound. When the salty water hit my poor injured knees, wet lightning zapped through me, and I let out a soft cry of, "Ooh, ooh, ooh!"

Lucky for my pride, this portion of the beach was virtually empty, and those around me hadn't heard me. One family, two parents and two young boys, picnicked about ten yards from where I stood. The children's screeches of delight pierced the air as they merrily plucked and flung rocks into the Sound from their place at the shore's edge. Another man, even farther away, tossed a stick into the surf, and a chocolate Labrador bounded after it, kicking up water like spray from a fountain.

Once my scrapes were totally immersed, I crouched and gently splashed the water around my kneecaps. I didn't want to linger too long here. Sam waited at the top of the road for me. I couldn't stop my heart from flipping in my chest at the very idea. He'd looked so sweet, so concerned, about my fall. When he touched me, I practically went stupid on him.

The dog barked, which seemed to snap me out of my sugar coma. Dang. I had to keep reminding myself this was *Sam Dillon*, the man who'd tormented me since kindergarten. The man who'd, only a few days ago, called me "the perfect Princess Paige." Then again, only minutes ago, he'd said I'd never been stupid, which was kind of a compliment.

Wasn't it?

God, this whole Sam thing really drove me crazy. Why all of a sudden did I find myself falling prey to his sweet words and warm eyes? I was so much smarter than that. So when had I stopped seeing him as a big, noisy mosquito and started thinking of him as romance material?

Maybe I needed to expand my social circle. After all, my last date, Kevin the Cretin from Hampton Bays, had been a disaster. Not only had Kevin taken Darlene the waitress's phone number during our first dinner together, he'd actually rushed through the meal at NASCAR speed. Before we could order coffee or dessert, he got the bill, paid in cash, and whooshed me out the door. He actually dropped me off home by eight o'clock—some kind of dating record—then probably returned to the restaurant to finish the evening in Darlene's company.

So it was entirely possible I'd fixated on Sam because he'd actually been nice to me. A new routine for both of us.

Or could there be another reason? My stomach somersaulted as my mind traveled a new road.

The day Nia had been in that car accident, when I ran into Sam before I drove to her house, he'd hit me with another of his jibes. *What's the problem, Paige? Can't stand to see someone else get all the attention? Do you always have to one-up your sister?*

Did I? Is that why I now kept noticing how attractive Sam was? Because I knew how much Nia liked him and I wanted him for myself? No. That was stupid. Nia and I never really competed with each other. We never had to. Daddy—and even Mom when she was still with us— always treated us as separate people, but showered us with the same amount of love and attention.

So why on earth did I find myself being drawn into the Sam Dillon Fan Club? Maybe it was because I wanted to understand Nia's attraction? Yes. That made sense. I was simply finding reasons to like Sam to make my sister happy. Hadn't I promised to give him a chance? Noting his kindness, his sense of humor, and the rich honey color of his eyes was clearly my subconscious way of complying with that promise.

Feeling much better in both my knees and my heart, I left the water and grabbed my footgear. I walked barefoot over the smooth rocks to where Sam waited, but not because I was in too much of a rush to get back to him to put my shoes and socks on. My legs and feet were still pretty wet, and the walk would give them a chance to dry.

I managed to get to the roadside, and there he stood, concern etched in his forehead. "You okay?"

I nodded. "Better. That's for sure. Thanks." I sat down

on the curb and slipped my socks onto my slightly damp feet, then pushed into my shoes. The air around us crackled, and I struggled to say something lighthearted to short-circuit the electricity. "I hope you brought your wallet. You're buying the beer."

His expression eased to that devastating smile. "I wouldn't have it any other way."

"Excellent." My knees protested a bit when I straddled my bike yet again, but I forced myself to move forward. From the moment I'd run into Sam at the crest of that hill, this ride had evolved into some kind of chess match. And I didn't intend to lose. "Ready?"

"You bet."

"Then let's do it." I rolled into the street's bike path and pedaled toward Coffield's Wharf.

Ten minutes later, we parked our bikes on the racks at the edge of the walkway, and Sam produced a lock from the leather satchel behind his seat. Snaking the flexible red tube through both our front tires, he clicked the pieces together, then spun the combination dial. Once the bikes were secure, he strode back to the satchel and pulled out a black leather wallet. Waving it toward me, he said, "All set. Let's go."

There was something nice about a man who was so well prepared. Particularly since I hadn't thought to bring water, sunscreen, a bike lock, or money. We strolled up the wooden walkway to the first row of gray clapboard buildings where the souvenir gift shops hawked their wares.

I stopped in front of the large display window of a shop called Captain Christmas, where delicate glass holiday ornaments gleamed beneath the mid-morning sun. Among the trinkets were several glass globes filled with beach sand and tiny multi-colored shells. Did Nia know about this place? Not that Captain Christmas's mass-produced junk could compete with my sister's handblown art. Still…

I frowned.

"Your sister's stuff is much better."

"OhmyGod!" I nearly jumped out of my skin at the sound of Sam's voice so close to my ear.

"Sorry," he said from beside me and took a step back, leaving another half-inch of space between us. "I didn't mean to scare you."

While I waited for my heart to return to its normal rhythm, I nodded then pointed to the storefront. "Has Nia seen this place?"

Sam shrugged. "I guess. Larry's had this store for a couple of years now. I'd imagine they've run into each other once or twice." He cocked his head at me. "You're angry?"

Yes. But how did he know that? "No," I lied. "Of course not."

"Yeah, you are. You get these little sparks in your eyes when you're angry. God knows I've seen that look enough times over the years to recognize what it means."

I sighed. Naturally, he knew my expressions too well by now. "It's just…it's not right. Like you said, Nia's stuff is much nicer, and because it's not created by slave labor in some overseas sweatshop, it's a lot more expensive too. This guy could run her out of business."

Sam took my hand in his. "Why don't you let Nia worry about that? Come on. Let's go grab an early lunch at The Pier."

Lunch? I pulled up short. Was this a date? I mean, normally, I'd let a guy know exactly where he stood with me by insisting we split the check evenly. But I didn't have any money to do that at the moment. And I couldn't turn him down altogether. I had invited him on this trek, after all. Besides, he'd been so sweet when I'd fallen off my bike. I was enjoying the new Sam Dillon. Sam Dillon, nice guy. I really didn't want to see the return of Sam Dillon, arrogant jerk.

His fingers squeezed mine, drawing my attention to him. "Paige. You're overthinking this. For once, do something spontaneous. Just relax and say yes. Okay?"

I inhaled deeply. "Okay. I mean, 'yes.'"

"Great." That smile reappeared, and I swear the sun shone brighter just to compete with his brilliance.

His hand still enclosing mine, he led me to the order window of The Pier Clambar. Two teenage boys stood behind the counter, triangular paper hats covering their dark hair. The aromas of garlic, fried fish, and French fries cloaked the sea air.

"Hey, Chief Dillon," one of the teens greeted him with a head jerk sort of nod. "What can I get you today?"

Sam turned to me. "What would you like?"

I glanced up at the menu chalkboard mounted on the wall above the boy's head. When did all their prices get so...pricey? No way would I allow Sam to blow that much money on a casual lunch after a casual bike ride. He might think I owed him something spectacular—like a kidney. "Umm," I hesitated. "Maybe just a diet cola?"

One of Sam's eyebrows arched. "Un-unh. Not good enough. I owe you a beer, to begin with. And I wouldn't be a responsible public officer if I allowed you to drink alcohol without something hearty in your stomach. So unless you want me to order for you, you'd better revise that diet cola nonsense."

I opted for a fried clam strip basket with French fries. Somehow I'd find a way to pay him back. Maybe I could take a mortgage on my house.

Sam ordered the same. "And a pitcher of beer," he added to the boy.

I nearly choked. "A *pitcher*?"

"Bike riding's thirsty work." He nudged a gentle elbow into my ribs.

He must have noticed the dubious look on my face because he chuckled, a sound I had never before heard from him. At least, not like this. In the past, he'd laughed at me with derision or sarcasm. But this time, the sound came out more indulgent, *warmer*.

"Relax, Paige. The pitchers equal about a glass and a half for each of us. If you don't want to drink all of it, you don't have to. But you did insist that I buy the beer. After lunch, we can walk around a bit—give you a chance to work off the alcohol and prepare those damaged knees of yours for the bike ride back." He led me to an empty white plastic picnic table shaded by an open navy and white-striped market umbrella. A few other early morning lunch patrons sat chatting and eating. A dozen seagulls squawked as they picked their way across the red flagstones, waiting for someone to drop a tasty tidbit.

Not once during this entire exchange did Sam release my hand. That alone got my guard up. The rest of the day's interactions just added to my suspicions. "Umm…" I began as I sat in one of the plastic chairs. "I'm going to regret asking, and I apologize in advance if I offend you, but why are you being so nice to me all of a sudden?"

He shook his head slowly, his smile still dazzling. "Don't get it yet, do you, Paige?"

Nia. My sister's name flashed into my head like a bolt of lightning. Of course he was charming me, trying to win me over so he could date Nia without any roadblocks. He probably considered me the Mount Vesuvius of roadblocks: impassable and liable to spew without warning.

Okay, I'd play. "Yeah, I think I do get it."

The boy from the counter brought over a small plastic pitcher filled with icy beer and two clear plastic party cups. "Enjoy. Food'll be out in five minutes."

Once the teen left us alone, Sam expertly poured beer into the two cups, creating a thin head of creamy foam on top of the golden pilsner. He handed me one of the beers, and when I took it, he lifted the other toward me. "To new beginnings."

"New beginnings," I repeated and tapped my cup against his.

~~~~

Nia

I wasn't off the hook with the roses once I'd set Briana to work. In fact, every person who came into the store, employee or customer, remarked about them. This renewed Briana's speculation, and she began collecting opinions from everyone.

Did I have a boyfriend? And if so, who? Why did I keep him a secret? Was he married? Hideously deformed? Or just some loser I was embarrassed to be seen with?

When there were no customers in the store, Briana and Andrew spent the downtime one-upping each other on the flower-giver's identity. The theories ran from Quasimodo to Mr. Needham, our seventy-plus-year-old high school principal, who made the Crypt Keeper look like Ryan Gosling.

I finally stowed the roses in the back room to gain some peace. Aidan had included a card with the bouquet. On the tiny white cardboard rectangle with "I'm Sorry" in fancy blue script, he'd added a personal message.

Nia,

I hate knowing my harshness offended you. I truly didn't mean what I said. Truce? Please?

A.

As apologies go, it wasn't exactly a sonnet. But in all fairness, the size of the florist cards didn't allow room for more than two sentences—unless the message was printed in a five-point font on a PC, cut out, and taped to the wee bit of cardboard. Still, the last thing I wanted was to give my employees more gas for their rumor motor so I had surreptitiously removed the card, with its teeny envelope, and stowed it in my pocket. Once or twice during the day, I'd suddenly remember it was there, and I'd reach into my apron to run a finger over the edges. The memory of Aidan Coffield standing in my shop, waiting for me to agree to a date, made my head swell.

When Paige appeared to pick me up, Andrew immediately moved from stock boy into chief interrogator mode. "Hey, Paige. Who's the new boyfriend?"

If I didn't know any better, I would have sworn my sister blushed. Her lashes fluttered, shielding her wide eyes, and she looked around, her expression almost panicked. "Huh?"

Iggy jerked a thumb at me. "Nia got flowers today," he told Paige. "Roses. Won't tell us who they're from."

"Really?" Paige's scattered focus honed in on me.

"It's no big deal," I insisted for probably the thousandth time of the day. "They're from a client I'm doing a project for."

"Client?" Paige persisted. "What client?"

"No one you know," I replied with a shrug. "Just some guy. He liked my grape lamps and ordered a few. The flowers were just his way of saying thank you."

"Where are they?" Paige asked. "Can I see them? What did the card say?"

"No card," Iggy announced with the fervor of a prosecuting attorney grilling the defendant.

"No card?" My sister's eyes narrowed at me, gleaming with speculation. "Then how do you know who sent them?"

I reached a hand into my pocket to trace the edge of the tiny envelope yet again. "He dropped them off this morning right after I opened the store. What's the big deal? Enough already."

Paige let the topic go then and there, but I knew we weren't finished with the discussion. Sure enough, as soon as we sat alone in the car, she zeroed in for the kill. "So?" she said as she pulled her seatbelt across her chest. "Who's the guy?"

"It's not like that," I insisted as firmly as I could. I'd transferred the card from my apron pocket to my purse, and I glanced down at the car floor to be certain no telltale pink glow emanated from its hiding place. "He's just a really nice, *old* guy with old-fashioned values."

I tried picturing Ogden Coffield as a reference point, but couldn't envision that austere, stony-faced Mr. Potato Head as the kind to send roses to a potential contractor.

"Awww..." Paige cooed. "I'll bet the old coot's sweet on you."

"Maybe." I rolled down the car window, allowing the breeze to cool the sudden burn in my cheeks.

"Nia's got a boyfriend," my sister sing-songed. "Nia's got a boyfriend."

"Knock it off," I grumbled and glared at her. "What did *you* do today?"

She wriggled in the seat, peeling her thighs from the hot leather. "What do you mean?"

"You had the day off," I reminded her. "Did you do anything special?"

"Oh, not really. I took a bike ride to Coffield's Wharf."

Did I detect some caginess in her response? I realized she was driving, but she hadn't taken her focus off the road since the topic switched from my flower-giver to her day. Or did my guilty conscience color my insight? "You had a nice day for a ride."

"Yeah." A long pause, then she added in a tighter voice, "And you'll never guess who I ran into."

"Who?"

"Sam."

"Uh-oh."

"Oh, Nia, stop." She clucked her tongue. "You'll be happy to know we were both on our best behavior. He rode with me for a while, and we had lunch at The Pier."

Paige? And Sam? Well, this was encouraging.

"And…?"

"And nothing. We shared some fried clams and a beer or two. It's not like we started making out or anything. Jeez, Nia, what do you want from me?"

"Nothing." Her quick mood change left me no doubt how she really felt, but I guessed she wasn't ready to admit it yet.

"We made a fragile peace with each other. He actually got me to laugh a couple of times, and I kept a civil tongue the whole afternoon. Satisfied?"

No doubt about it. I'd ruffled Paige's feathers. I bit back an indulgent smile and returned my attention to the scenery outside the SUV. "Sure. Why wouldn't I be satisfied?"

Chapter 12

Paige

Sunday morning, I woke up on time to get Nia to work, which was no small feat. I'd spent a good part of the night awake, with the ingredients of a delicious plan bubbling in my head.

Once I had my sister trapped in the car with me, I set Operation Matchmaker into action. "Hey, I was thinking," I began, feigning spur-of-the-moment inspiration. "How about we have a barbecue at my house tonight? Nothing big. Just you, me, a friend or two, a bottle of wine, and some grilled marinated mako. I noticed yesterday that shark steaks are on sale at the fish market at Coffield's Wharf."

I'd assumed Nia, scrolling through messages on her BlackBerry, was too distracted to pay much attention to my invitation. But boy was I wrong!

Her head snapped up so fast, she risked a case of whiplash. "What'd you say about the Coffields?"

"Nothing. I said the fish store at Coffield's Wharf had mako steaks on sale. So what do you say? You in?"

Distraction dulled her expression, and she returned her attention to her BlackBerry. "Yeah, sure," she said half-heartedly. "Sounds nice."

Purrrrfect. All I needed was a lukewarm agreement. "Great," I exclaimed. "Leave the details to me. You just go to work, have a good day, and when I pick you up later, we can go straight to my house."

"You don't have to pick me up today, remember?" Nia said, still focused on the day's schedule she routinely plugged into her phone. "The rental agent is dropping off a car this morning so I won't be inconveniencing you anymore."

Right. I *had* forgotten that detail. Even better, though, for my plan so I wasn't about to argue. "Okay, then, after work, come straight to my house. Sound good?"

Her gaze never left the BlackBerry as she said, "Uh-huh. Sure. Whatever."

Laughter bubbled in my throat, but I swallowed hard, which initiated a coughing fit. Once again, Nia's head jerked up. "You okay?"

Too incapacitated to speak, I nodded.

"Here." She reached into her tote bag and pulled out a bottle of water. "Drink something."

With my eyes tearing and my throat raw, I took the bottle and uncapped it. The second we stopped at a red light, I swigged the icy liquid until I'd regained control of my voice. "Thanks."

The traffic light switched to green, and I dropped the bottle in the cup holder in my console as I hit the gas. When I reached the Nature's Bounty parking lot minutes later, Nia climbed out of my Cherokee, still engrossed in her phone.

"Be at my house by six sharp," I called after her. "Tonight's gonna be great. You'll see."

"Uh-huh," she repeated, walking toward the shop's back door.

I waited half a heartbeat after she entered before putting the Jeep in drive and shooting out of there. I had lots of plans to make. First, a call to the Snug Harbor Police station. I'd looked up the main switchboard number in the phone book and programmed it into my cell this morning.

Turning off Main Street, I ordered my dash-installed mobile phone system to "Call Sam Work."

The digital voice replied from my radio speaker, "Dialing Sam Work."

After two rings, a man announced, "Snug Harbor Police Department."

I tried to say something, but my tongue thickened in

my mouth, and my brain shut down.

"Hello?" the guy prompted.

"Umm, hi," I said stupidly. "May I speak to Chief Dillon, please?"

"What's this in reference to?"

"It's a personal call."

The man on the other end sighed. "Hold, please."

I used the ensuing quiet to get my breathing under control and reboot my overloaded brain.

Too soon, Sam's voice erupted through my stereo speakers. "This is Chief Dillon."

"Sam?" God, was that *my* croak? Frogs with head colds sounded silkier. I quickly gulped more water and tried again. "Hi, Sam. It's Paige." Not as smoothly confident as I'd hoped for, but better.

"Paige? Is everything okay?" The question came out in an urgent rush. "What's wrong?"

"Nothing," I hurried to assure him. "I'm sorry to call you at work, but it's the only number I have for you."

"Well, we'll have to remedy that, won't we? Got a pen?"

"No, not now, I'm driving. And before you say something about my risking life and limb, I'm on my hands-free device."

"Still not a hundred percent safe, but okay. I'll let it slide for now. So, what's up?"

"Umm…" The frog returned, and I slugged down the last of the water.

"Paige? Are you okay? Where are you? What's going on?"

"I'm fine. Really. Just got something caught in my throat." I gave a loud "ahem!" for effect. "Anyway, I was just calling because…" I stopped, started again. "I was wondering…" *Get to it already, idiot. Do it for Nia.* "I wanted to know if you have any plans for dinner tonight."

"Tonight? Well, I get off work at five—"

Duet in September

"Perfect! How would you like to join a few of us for a barbecue? My house. Six o'clock. Marinated mako steaks, corn on the cob, salad, totally casual."

Silence greeted my invitation, and a rivulet of sweat ran down my back.

"What's the catch?" he asked at last.

He had every right to be suspicious, I reminded myself. If *he* invited *me* to dinner, I'd be sniffing for arsenic in every course. Hoping to keep my tone light and sunny, I spoke through a forced smile. "No catch. New beginnings, remember? It's my way of saying thank you for lunch yesterday." I kept my fingers crossed he'd buy that lame story.

"In that case, what can I bring?"

Thank God.

"Absolutely nothing but yourself," I said. "This is all on me. You get the next date." Oops. Before he could pick up on my slip, I added, "Don't forget. Six o'clock, my house. See you later."

"Don't you—"

"Gotta go." I quickly hit the disconnect button on my steering wheel, effectively cutting off whatever he planned to say.

Next stop, Coffield's Wharf for two mako steaks and the ideal complimentary bottle of wine. Maybe even some decadent chocolate goody for dessert. With the perfect meal in the perfect setting, I would push Sam and Nia firmly on the path toward true love.

~~~~

Nia

The most exciting part of my day was when the rental car agent showed up with the keys to a shiny silver two door Iota, or whatever that teeny box on wheels was called.

Still, at least the car gave me back my independence. I'd no longer have to rely on Paige or anyone else to schlep me wherever I needed to go. That in itself made me happy.

With sales slow all day, I sent Briana and Andrew home before four o'clock, much to their delight. Because the shop was only open until five on Sundays, Iggy wouldn't be in at all. Not that it mattered. Absolutely no one had stepped inside in the last two hours. By 4:45 I was antsy to close up.

I decided to busy myself by rearranging some of the shelves in the storeroom. Naturally, the minute I began wrestling with a crate of unwieldy felt hand puppets shaped like sharks and dolphins, the bells on the front door jangled.

"Be right there," I called out.

"Take your time, Nia."

I froze. It couldn't be. Leaving the crate balanced precariously on the top of a step stool, I sped out of the storeroom. There he stood near my counter.

Aidan Coffield wore a collared, short-sleeve blue and black striped button-down shirt tucked into sleek black trousers. His hair gleamed under the row of high-intensity spotlights intended to showcase my glass art. Apparently, Aidan Coffield was an entirely different work of art. The lights definitely enhanced his star quality. He might as well have stepped off a magazine cover.

"What…what are you doing here?" I lifted a hand to smooth my hair, but stopped in mid-air. Some touch-ups required a special effects crew.

He grinned, his masculine features becoming youthful beneath the twinkle in his eyes. "A couple of things occurred to me after I left here yesterday."

My heart softened in my chest. "Oh? Like what?"

"For starters, I underestimated you. A mistake you took full advantage of."

I bit back a smile of my own. Here I thought I'd gotten away scot-free. "I have no idea what you're talking about."

"Yes, you do." He pointed an index finger in my direction. "I can see it in your eyes, even if you're doing your best to hide it. When I asked you out to dinner, you told me when you had the next *day* off. Now, unless your boss is a real slave driver, which I doubt because you're your own boss, you don't spend twelve hours a day here, six days a week. Since you open this shop every morning, you must have another employee to close up at night. Therefore, I don't need you to tell me about your next day off for a casual dinner date. Any evening after work should be fine."

I tapped my temple. "Very clever."

His eyebrows arched, reflecting how pleased he was. "Yes, I know. But, wait. There's more. Factor in the thought that your car is at the auto body shop for an undetermined amount of time."

"Yes, that's true. So?"

"So you're relying on someone else to drive you back and forth to this store every day."

"That would be my sister. But I just got a rental this afternoon, so she's off the hook. You're two for three. Go for the bonus question and tell me why you're here." I folded my arms over my chest, projecting an image of stubborn defiance. At least I hoped that's what I projected. My insides were quickly turning to Jell-O.

"I also mentioned that you always seem to be alone in here." He looked around to ascertain that yes, indeed, I was alone again. Receiving confirmation, he quirked a brow at me. "With a holiday weekend and a drawer full of cash, that's not safe."

"Trust me. There isn't much cash in my drawer today."

"Business is slow, huh?"

I shrugged. "Do you want to risk the prizes you've already won to take a shot at our big winner round, Mr. Coffield?"

He immediately caught on to the game show joke

because he pretended to question an imaginary audience before he added, "I'm going to go for the big prize because I put all the facts together and came to an interesting decision."

"Which is?"

"Since it's my soon-to-be stepbrother's fault you're so inconvenienced, I should be helping you out."

"Oh, no, you don't—"

"Please, let me finish. I'm here to drive you home. *After* we have dinner together."

Surprise. Again.

"That's very nice of you, but we've already established I don't need a ride home," I said smoothly.

"Then just have dinner with me anyway."

Panic swirled inside me, and I looked around the store for some means of escape. I wasn't ready for this. My palms dampened, and my heartbeat kicked up in tempo. *Think, Nia, think. Get rid of him.* And then I remembered Paige's discussion this morning.

"I can't. My sister and I have plans for dinner."

"Cancel them."

I shook my head. "She's hosting a barbecue at her house with some of our friends."

"Then she's not alone tonight. She'll never miss you." He took a step closer to where I stood in the doorway to the storeroom. My breath shuddered in my lungs. "Which, if you turn me down, is more than I can say for myself."

My mouth dried to sawdust. I teetered on very dangerous ground here. I liked him. Too much, truth be told. He was handsome, charming, and my pulse danced the cha-cha every time he came within two feet of me. With one look, he made me feel as if I stood on the edge of a mountaintop. I could push off on my toes, spread my arms, and soar.

Was this what love felt like? Had my parents felt these fluttery feelings when they were together? Or had my mother only experienced this rush with her tourist from Greenwich? My joy screeched to a dead stop at the thought.

What did I know about this man anyway? That he came from a monied background and probably learned to charm women while still in his designer nursery? Was he another rich jerk who wanted to fool around with a local for a weekend before heading home to Miffy and their kids?

I'd never even asked if he was married! For all I knew, he had a wedding band shoved into his pocket. I stared at his left hand, looking for a telltale strip of white on his tanned ring finger. Not that anything short of a private investigator's report would put me at ease on this issue. Married people cheated; my mother was undeniable proof of that fact.

The gooey center of my heart hardened to stone.

"No, Mr. Coffield. Thank you anyway."

He arched a brow. "Mr. Coffield? I thought we'd progressed past that. I told you to call me Aidan. Remember?"

"Yes, but I don't believe I know you well enough to call you by your first name."

"And whose fault is that?" he snapped, then immediately mellowed. "I'm sorry. Every time I think I have you figured out, you confuse me again. So why the cold shoulder? Are you married? Engaged?"

"No." I couldn't stop the words erupting from my lips. "Are you?"

His lazy smile reappeared. "Ah, that's it. No. I'm not married. Never came close. But if you'd bothered to research me online, you'd probably know that. The biggest problem with being Ogden Coffield's son is that nothing in my private life is very private."

Warmth crept into my cheeks, but if he noticed, he didn't remark on it.

"Does that help you make up your mind? I'd ask what else you want to know about me, but then we'd have a lot less to talk about over dinner."

I had to stifle my smile. No doubt about it, this man kept finding the chinks in my stony heart, crawled through, and melted me to a pool of warm liquid. He must have read the hesitation in me because he pressed his case by taking my hand, my fingers loosely clasped in his palm. "Put me out of my misery and have dinner with me tonight."

My entire skeleton sagged with defeat. "Let me call my sister first."

As I picked up the shop phone, his words from moments ago echoed in my head like a death knell. *The biggest problem with being Ogden Coffield's son is that nothing in my private life is very private.*

On the other hand, while my life wasn't as public as his, in Snug Harbor, my family history was an open book. The last thing I wanted was for anyone I knew to see me with the heir to the Coffield fortune. Twenty-five years may have passed since my mother's departure from Snug Harbor, but the minute it became known that I was seen with a wealthy out-of-towner, the scandal would be regurgitated everywhere. I was *not* my mother and wouldn't allow anyone to compare me to my mother.

"Two conditions, though," I said, the phone's dial tone buzzing near my ear.

"Name them."

"First, I drive myself. You follow in your own car."

He arched a brow. "Still not sure you can trust me?" Before I could justify my request, he held up a hand. "No, that's fair. And smart. We only met a few days ago. I could be anyone. So I agree to that. What else?"

"I want to go someplace casual and out-of-the-way." I gestured to my capris and t-shirt. "I'm not dressed for any of the fancy places around here. I do know a great little bistro in Water Mill, if you don't mind going that far."

"Sounds perfect."

I narrowed my eyes. "I haven't said anything about the

place yet."

His thumb traced my cheek, and I shivered.

"You said yes. That's perfect enough for me."

The edge of the mountaintop came into view in my head. My toes curled, ready to take flight.

My stony heart was doomed.

Chapter 13

Paige

I stood on the deck overlooking the yard, delighted with the day's labor. Since I'd only moved home six months ago, the house's interior still left a lot to be desired, but I'd managed to transform the backyard into a pastoral homage to all things romantic without being obvious. The bistro-style table, ringed by four chairs, was set as if we were expecting at least one more guest. All the ratty patio furniture Dad had kept for decades now sat piled in the garage, out of sight. I'd found our old white Christmas lights in the attic and strung them into the thick, leafy branches of the maple trees, hidden until darkness fell. Not quite the fairy lights I'd hoped to achieve, but they'd still be pretty. Besides, by the time the lights clicked on, Sam and Nia should be well on their way to Smooch City and unconcerned with petty details.

China plates and crystal goblets sat atop a burgundy tablecloth. The ice bucket stood sentinel in the sterling stand, a bottle of Sauvignon Blanc chilling inside. My iPod, set to a homemade playlist, wafted party music into the honeysuckle and lilac-scented air. In two hours' time, the playlist would subtly switch to nothing but R&B love songs: soulful and suggestive.

To all outward appearances, I'd created the setting for an intimate outdoor dinner party. Only after the quarry entered the trap would I change the scenario from party for four to romantic rendezvous for two. I could almost smell love in the air.

Eat your heart out, Cupid!

Pleased with my machinations, I returned to the kitchen where the mako steaks swam in citrus marinade

Duet in September

and the triple chocolate torte hid inside the refrigerator. Now all I needed were my participants.

I craned my neck under my armpits. And maybe a shower before my guests showed up. All the preparation for this event had me smelling like a barnyard animal. I headed toward the staircase to go up to my bathroom, but my cell phone sang from the dining room table where I'd left it. "We Are Family." Nia's ringtone. Speak of the devil. I grabbed the phone in mid-song and hit the connect button.

"Hey," I said as a greeting. "I was just about to jump in the shower. I've been busy getting everything ready. Wait 'til you see the backyard. You won't recognize it."

"Umm…yeah, about that. Change in plans. I completely forgot Iggy and I have to go over the inventory for the upcoming week. I'm sorry, but I'm not going to make it tonight. You guys will have to enjoy the barbecue without me."

My hopes froze, along with my happiness. "Nia, no. You can't. I mean, it's a holiday weekend. Can't the inventory wait? I've got mako. And wine. And chocolate for dessert."

"Unfortunately, it can't wait. I'm sorry."

"But I've got a special night planned."

"I know, and I'm sorry. Tell everyone hi from me. I'll talk to you tomorrow. Bye." *Click.* The phone went dead in my hand, and my heart sank to my toes. I wanted to throw myself on the floor and indulge in a good old-fashioned pity party.

No, no, no! This was so not fair. All my plans, all my hard work, all gone with one twenty-second phone call. And *Sam*! He'd be here in a half hour. Unless I could stop him. I scrolled through my cell's contact list until I reached "Sam Work" and pressed the connect button again.

"Snug Harbor Police." This time, a woman answered, but I had more important things to take care of than identifying the voice's owner.

"Sam Dillon, please." I bounced from foot to foot as I spoke, too antsy to stand still.

"I'm sorry," the woman replied. "He's gone for the day. I can transfer you to the night officer or to Chief Dillon's voice mail."

"Neither. It's vital that I reach Sam…er, Chief Dillon. A personal matter. Urgent. I'll try him at home. Do you have that number? Or even better, can you give me his cell phone number?"

"No, ma'am, I can't. I can either transfer you to the night officer or to Chief Dillon's voice mail."

"But Sam and I are friends," I argued. "I promise he won't mind that you gave me the information."

"If you and Chief Dillon are friends, you should already have his cell and home phone numbers. I'm sorry I can't be of further assistance to you. Have a good evening, ma'am."

Again, the person on the other end of the phone suddenly disconnected. *Well, thank you very much.* What had happened to manners? Didn't anyone use proper etiquette anymore?

Meanwhile, time ticked away from me, looming ever closer to the moment Sam stood on my doorstep, expecting a party in full swing. Good God, what a disaster. What could I do now?

The phone book. A long shot, but maybe he was listed in the phone book. I sped into the kitchen and flung open the cabinet door where Dad had always stored the White Pages. The book hit the counter with a *thunk*, and I madly flipped until I hit the Ds.

Da, De, Di, Dic, Die, Dig, Dil…

The rapid knock at my door stopped me cold before I passed the surname, "Diller."

I groaned aloud. I was only expecting one person, and he was a half hour early. Naturally.

Sure enough, when I crept to the foyer, Sam stood

outside on my front porch with a twelve-pack of beer cradled under one arm. "Hi," he greeted me through the screen. "I know I'm early but I thought you could probably use some help setting up." Before I could move, he opened my storm door and stepped inside.

"Umm…gee…" I stammered. "That's…umm…that's sweet. But…umm…there's kind of been a change in plans…I tried to call you…I didn't have your cell number…and whoever answered the phone at the precinct is a real...Wait! Where are you going?"

While I'd fumbled through my explanation, Sam had strolled past me, set the twelve-pack on my kitchen counter, and now stood by the French doors leading out back.

"The backyard," he replied. "That's where everybody's going to be, right? How's everything going? You need someone to do any heavy lifting? I'm betting you didn't tell any of your guests that you hurt your knees yesterday. Admit it. You planned to do all the dirty work yourself, didn't you?" He pulled on the latch and stepped outside.

I had no other option except to follow him.

"Wow," Sam said, glancing around the backyard. "You've been busy."

He didn't know the half of it. I'd even weeded the garden, or what passed as a garden these days—three rose bushes and a spiky hedge. Dad had lost interest in landscaping after his diagnosis. The kneeling had nearly killed me, but Sam didn't need to know that either.

"Who else is coming tonight?"

At last, he'd given me an opening to explain. "See, that's the thing. Nia's stuck at work and…" I stopped there. I couldn't admit I hadn't invited anyone else but him. He'd suspect some kind of setup.

"…and everybody else already had plans," he finished for me.

I grabbed the verbal rope he'd tossed and clung with both hands. Sighing dramatically, I shrugged. "That's what I get for waiting 'til the last minute to plan a party."

He nodded. "I'm guessing we won't need the beer then."

"Don't worry. You can take it home with you." I turned to go back into the kitchen. "Come on. I'm sorry you made the trip over here for nothing."

"Whoa, wait a second." He grabbed my hand and stopped me with one foot on the threshold. "Does this mean you're not planning to feed me now?"

I sputtered. Was he kidding? "I already told you. No one's coming."

"*I* came. And it would be a shame to let that mako go to waste." He shot his index finger, pistol-like, at the stainless barbecue on the patio. "I'm an excellent grill master. Why don't you bring those steaks and the corn out here?"

No. This was all wrong. Nia was supposed to have dinner with Sam tonight. Not me. I had to make him leave, make him come back another time. "Maybe we can try again tomorrow."

"I've already got plans for tomorrow. Remember? The fireworks show in the village? I'm on crowd control. Come on, Paige, I'm starving. We'll create a feast that will make everybody sorry they missed tonight's dinner."

"But we can't." *Oh, powerful argument there, sweetheart.*

"Why not?" Sam trampled right over my defenses without moving a muscle. "You have a better offer? Besides, you and I are supposed to be trying a new beginning, right? Isn't that why you invited me tonight?"

"Yes, but—"

He took a step toward me, and I automatically took a step back. One sooty eyebrow quirked in my direction. "Don't tell me you're afraid of me, Paige."

"Me? Afraid?" Actually, I was terrified. Every time he came too close, my insides quivered and my brain flew off on vacation. But I forced an easy smile. "Ha."

His grin infused me like a warm bath. "Prove it. Let's have dinner out here on the patio. Just the two of us."

Oh boy. I was in deep trouble.

Stop it, I told myself. Stop reading signals that aren't there. Sam and I had enjoyed a pleasant enough afternoon together yesterday. So what could one dinner hurt? After all, in case he and Nia ever became an official "couple," I should probably get used to having him around.

I pointed to the wine chilling in the ice bucket. "Are you any good with a corkscrew?"

"Skip the wine," he told me with a wave of his hand. "And the beer. A party's one thing. But for just the two of us, how about something non-alcoholic?"

"Sure. I've got iced tea, lemonade, or soda."

"Soda's perfect, provided it's not diet. If that's all you got, I'll go with iced tea. You get the drinks and the food while I light the grill."

Before I could argue, he opened the barbecue lid and fussed with the attached propane tank. One thing I'd learned in my thirty-four years: never attempt to come between a man and his need to "provide fire" to the female populace. Dad was the same way. I think it's some kind of leftover caveman instinct. The way my luck ran these days, if I argued with Sam, he'd club me over the head and drag me to his lair by my blond locks.

Better to save my energy for a more meaningful disagreement in the future. Which could be any time between five minutes from now and a day or two from now. Trouble never stayed away for more than forty eight hours when it came to me and Sam in close proximity.

He and I had been adversaries for nearly thirty years now. Those days, however, were quickly coming to a close. We were on our way to a new beginning. A *friendship*. As bizarre an idea as it was, there was something almost comfortable in the way we talked these days. *Almost*. If only my heart and brain would cooperate.

So I went to fetch the fish and soft drinks—no argument. For the moment.

~~~~

Nia

Valera's Pub in Water Mill lent me the anonymity I wouldn't have anywhere in Snug Harbor. Back in the 1930s, the building had housed a dinner theater where live shows, rivaling Broadway's best, were performed nightly. Valera's paid homage to that illustrious history with framed black and white photos lining the walls, the original bar still serving drinks, and the curtained stage remaining in use for private parties or corporate events.

Although this was the Sunday night of a huge holiday weekend, we had no long line to fight. Few vacationers ate dinner at 5:30 pm so most of the tables sat unoccupied. With ten miles separating me from my hometown, I didn't need a table in a dark corner when Aidan and I arrived, but we were escorted to a private spot in the back anyway.

Once we sat down, a perky blond waitress, wearing the traditional red and gold usher's uniform and with "Chloe" on her red name tag, handed us leather-bound menus and asked to take our drink orders.

I opened my mouth to order a club soda with lime but Aidan stopped me with a gentle touch on my hand. "If it's all right with you, I'd like to choose a wine based on your dinner preference."

I hesitated, my gaze fixed on his fingers resting on the back of my hand. Was this his way of taking control? How should I respond? I didn't want to play mind games. Honestly, I've never been very good at them. But I had no idea if this "allow me to choose your wine" gimmick was for real or some kind of test.

"I'm sorry if that sounds high-handed," he said as if I'd spoken my concerns aloud. "It isn't meant to. I want you to enjoy your meal to the fullest tonight." He shrugged. "The wine thing is an occupational hazard, I'm afraid."

Chloe the Waitress's enthusiastic sigh whistled between us. She sounded impressed, not annoyed. I made a quick decision to follow her lead. "By all means, but I'd like to start with just a club soda with lime," I said to both of them.

When Chloe turned to Aidan, her entire demeanor switched from "server" to "predator." She licked her lips, stood up straighter, and turned on the full wattage of her smile. She practically shoved her chest in his face as she leaned closer to him. "And for you, sir?"

For a second or two, I thought of Paige and Kevin the Cretin. I remember how hard I'd laughed when Paige told me about the waitress flirting with her date. Through an excess of giggles that made my stomach hurt, I'd told my sister that if Kevin had been *my* date, I would have tossed my ice water in his and the waitress's faces, and then called a cab to take me home.

Now, however, sitting catty-corner to Aidan with a similar situation about to break, I sucked in a breath and waited to see how he'd react to our prowling waitress.

"That sounds good actually." Despite Chloe's best efforts, to his credit, he didn't even glance at her, but kept his eyes completely locked on me. "I'll have the same."

The blonde fluffed away, and I released my breath.

"Relax, Nia," he murmured. "You look like you're waiting for someone to sneak up behind you and stab you in the shoulder blades. Trust me. I don't bite. Let's just have a pleasant meal and get to know one another."

I tried. Really, I did. I almost succeeded, too. Until I saw Mr. and Mrs. Bergen seated at a table directly across the room from us. With my shoulders hunched to my ears, I quickly whipped open my menu to hide behind. What if they saw me?

Mrs. Bergen and my mother used to be good friends, regulars at PTA and Tupperware parties. When my mother left town, the Bergens stopped socializing with the Wainwrights. In our senior year in high school, though, their son, Glen, asked Paige to the prom. I'd been so happy for her. Poor Paige hadn't exactly been the queen of popularity in high school. Glen, on the other hand, moved in all the right social circles. Two weeks before the big night, Glen started shooting off his mouth in the gym locker room, announcing to all who'd listen that he'd only asked Paige to be his date because his mother had said "the Wainwright girls were, no doubt, as loose as their mother." Too bad for Glen, Sam Dillon was in the locker room that afternoon. He beat the snot out of Glen, earning himself three days of in-school suspension and revocation of his prom tickets. Glen immediately cancelled his date with Paige, and I wouldn't go without her. On prom night, Dad took the two of us out to dinner and the movies so we didn't have to witness our classmates in their formal wear and limos.

Sixteen years later, my cheeks heated with that familiar flush of shame as I watched Mrs. Bergen lift her wineglass and sip the ruby liquid. When she swallowed, she tilted her head up, and in my direction.

I dove even deeper into the menu. "What looks good tonight?"

"Nia?" Aidan's fingers curled around the top of my menu, lowering it slightly until our eyes met. "Are you all right?"

"There's someone over there I don't want to see," I said through clenched teeth, then immediately wished I could bite the words back. Oh, God, why had I told him the truth? Now he'd think I was some kind of psycho.

With a deep frown etching his features, he turned to scan the restaurant. "Your boyfriend? Or your husband, maybe?"

"No," I said quickly. "God, no. Just a snooty old couple I don't like."

"Do you want to leave?" He started to rise. "We can go somewhere else if you prefer."

"No!" I grabbed his wrist. "Sit, please. I don't want to draw attention to us."

"Okay, then, how about this?" He slid his chair away from mine until his broad shoulders completely blocked my view of the Bergens. And vice-versa. "Does that work?"

It did, but this whole scene was ridiculous. I'd lost my appetite and my good mood. Worse, he probably thought I'd lost my mind. Shaking my head, I dropped the menu on the table. "I'm sorry. You don't have to stay here with me if you don't want to. I can wait 'til they leave, then slip away."

He slapped a palm on his closed menu. "Are you kidding? You think I'd leave you here because you ran into someone who made you uncomfortable? After all the obstacles I cleared to get you to agree to have dinner with me? Lady, you're worth a little inconvenience. You're worth *a lot* of inconvenience. Who are those people anyway?"

"No one important."

His lips tightened, and for a fraction of a second, I saw a slow tic appear in his cheek, but it disappeared beneath his placid expression when I blinked. "Uh-huh. I get it. None of my business. Just tell me they aren't your husband's parents, and I'll drop it."

On a deep exhale of relief, I smiled. "Nope."

"So we're good?"

I nodded.

"Excellent. Then pick up your menu for real this time, tell me what you want for dinner, and I'll choose a wine to perfectly complement your entrée."

"What if I want a hotdog?" I teased.

"Especially if you want a hotdog. The wrong wine could completely ruin such a fabulous dinner choice."

"Lucky for me, then, I have you here to avert disaster."

His fingers traced the back of my hand, a gentle caress that whispered of tenderness. "Lucky for me you've decided to stay."

I wasn't so sure he'd continue to voice that opinion all night. "We'll see."

Chapter 14

Nia

Despite the dubious start to our evening, Aidan's charm soon won me over. I'd chosen a duck breast with sweet cherry glaze for dinner, and he'd recommended a Cotes du Rhone wine, a delicious combination that kept my taste buds tingling. Conversation flowed between us easily, perhaps because we stuck to neutral subjects: movies, books, beach conditions, and the traffic that snarled Snug Harbor's roads all summer. The fact the Bergens left without ever noticing me also went a long way toward putting me at ease.

By the time Chloe the waitress set dessert menus in front of us, the delicious food, the single glass of wine, and my dinner companion's easygoing style had broken through my defensive walls. I was flexible, flirtatious, *fluid.*

"I'll have the brownie a la mode," I told Chloe, passing back the menu. Yeah, I was *that* relaxed. Tomorrow, I'd have a chocolate hangover and rue the damage to my waistline, but tonight I planned to indulge my hedonistic side.

"How about coffee?" Aidan asked.

What the heck. Why not? I nodded. "Regular please," I said to Chloe.

"What can I say?" Aidan grinned, once again keeping his focus on me as he handed the menu to our waitress. "The lady has exceptional taste. I'll have the same on both."

Clearly, Chloe was not happy at how my date continued to ignore her not-so-subtle interest. She practically stormed away from our table, her heels thumping over the hardwood floor with more violence than a rabid rhino.

When we were alone again, he cupped my hand in his. "So, tell me about glassblowing."

I didn't try to pull away, the sensation too pleasant to withdraw. "What exactly do you want to know?"

"How did you get involved in something so unusual?"

"School trip. I was nine. It was a pretty bad time in my life. We went to this historical village. You know the type? Where the employees all dress in period costumes and show the tourists how colonials used to churn butter and shoe horses and stuff?" At his nod, I continued, "Well, this particular village had a glassblower. He told us how the craft hasn't changed that much over the centuries and explained its significance to history. Then, while we watched every step, he created the most beautiful bowl I'd ever seen. Thin and fragile-looking with a wide curved lip. The whole thing was decorated with swirls of purple and blue…God, to this day I can still remember every detail of that bowl."

I dared a glance at him, expecting to see some odd expression aimed at me for waxing poetic about a bowl from twenty-five years ago, but he never blinked, never looked away. His obvious interest spurred me on.

"I was hooked. Of course, since I was only nine, I was far too young to actually work as a glassblower. The heat, the tools involved, it's too dangerous for any child. But I constantly talked about learning the trade and someday having my own hot spot—to anyone who'd listen. The following year for Christmas, I got my first glassblowing kit."

"A kit?" His eyes widened in surprise. "They actually sell glassmaking kits for kids?"

Wincing, I sucked in a sharp breath. "Yes and no. This thing must have been from the 1950s. I don't know where my dad found it—a garage sale, maybe—and compared to the real thing, it was pretty lame, but still extremely dangerous for a child."

"Your mother must have had a fit when she saw it."

I shrugged. "She was already gone by then, which is probably why Dad bought me the kit. I told you it was a bad time for me."

A deep flush stained his cheeks. "I'm sorry."

"Don't be. It was a long time ago, and I'm not the least bit sensitive about my mom's loss anymore." Now I had to change the subject before my nose grew like Pinocchio's. "I don't suppose your dad bought you a winemaking kit for Christmas when you were a kid, huh?"

"Hardly." His lips twisted for a moment, then eased into placidity. "I bet your father's pretty proud of all you've accomplished since you started with that lame but dangerous kit at Christmas."

"He *was*. Dad passed away six months ago."

He slapped a palm to his forehead. "Cripes. I'm sorry. Again. I just keep sticking my foot in my mouth tonight."

With gentle pressure, I squeezed his fingers. "It's okay. Really. Why should you know so much about my private life? Unlike you, I'm not Googled that often."

My joke brought the smile back to his face.

"Now, obviously," I said, "I know about your parents. You've got quite a pedigree. Dad's the vineyard king of Long Island, and didn't your mother marry some Italian duke or something?"

"A count, actually." He lifted his glass of club soda, grinned at me over the rim. "The Conte de Petroni."

"Would I be showing my ignorance if I asked what the difference was between a duke and a count?"

"As far as you and I are concerned, very little. To my mother and the Conte de Petroni, all the difference in the world. Dukes are usually closer relations to the royal family. Counts are a bit lower on the nobility hierarchy."

"It's still impressive," I replied. "Do they live in a palace?"

He laughed. "They live in his 'ancestral home.' I have no idea what it looks like, so don't ask."

"You've never been there?"

"Nope. Their wedding took place in Manhattan before the lovebirds flew off to the conte's estate in Italy. Since then, I've barely seen my mother. We talk on the phone, but—"

"Excuse me." Chloe reached between us with two coffee cups. She managed to dither with the china server that held the assortment of sugar packets, effectively becoming a wall between us and cutting off our conversation.

Aidan, however, didn't allow our waitress's antics to go unchecked. Rising, he slid his chair around until he could sit right next to me. "You know what?" he said as he settled beside me and draped an arm across my shoulders. "This is better anyway. Now, where were we?"

"You were telling me about your mother's wedding."

"No, I wasn't."

Huh? Of course he was.

Before I could correct him, though, he leaned close to whisper in my ear. "I was just about to kiss you." His thumb brushed my chin, and he pressed his lips to mine.

The kiss landed soft as a kitten's fur, and with the same melting effect on my heart. By the time he pulled away again, Chloe had disappeared.

"That was only a temporary fix, I'm afraid," I told Aidan. "She'll be back any minute with our brownie sundaes."

"Good. More fun for me."

Then he kissed me again, and I had no arguments left.

~~~~

Paige

"Tell me about Albany."

I took a sip of iced tea before answering Sam. As promised, he'd grilled the mako and corn to perfection. My contribution, a chilled pasta salad with bleu cheese and bacon, added just the right tang. Food-wise, we made an unbeatable team. Our empty plates were proof of our culinary expertise. "What do you want to know?" I asked.

"Do you miss it? Living there, I mean."

I gave a half-hearted shrug. "Sometimes. It's a different world from here. Albany is bigger, noisier, busier. Not as big, noisy, and busy as New York City, but definitely more bustling than Snug Harbor."

"You worked for the state, right? Did you like it?"

"Uh-huh. I worked in the comptroller's office. I loved it. I didn't always *like* it, but I really loved it."

"Why?" He actually sounded confused.

I squirmed in my chair. What was this? An interview? Toying with my silverware, I stifled my impatience. Eating had given us an excuse not to talk. Now with dinner over, conversation seemed necessary. Sam was probably seeking common ground between us.

"I don't know. Maybe because there was always something going on. Think about it. The state coffers hold more than fifteen billion dollars in payroll, nearly a hundred fifty million in retirement benefits, and nine billion in unclaimed funds. That's a lotta scratch. Then there were the routine audits, local government spending, taxes. For a finance geek like me, every day the circus was in town. I never knew what I'd walk into on any given morning." I flipped up my right hand. "Now I've come home, and the most activity I see on a daily basis is when Lou Rugerman calls to make sure his quarterlies were paid on time or Lisa Bloomfield asks if she can write off the cost of central a/c on her taxes because her son has asthma."

He started to say something, but I held up a hand to stop him.

"Don't get me wrong. I don't mind helping everyone here. It's just…Wainwright Financial is so much more…" I struggled for the perfect description and finally settled for, "…low-key. It's a huge adjustment for me."

"So why do it?"

An excellent question. One I toyed with whenever I was bored with my day-to-day rut, which of course, had been the reason behind my enthusiasm for Dara's thirty day challenge. "I came home because Nia and Dad needed me. Now I stay to run the business. Someone has to keep my father's legacy alive. It's not fair to ask Nia to do it."

"That's not very fair to you, though, is it?"

I offered a weak smile. "Don't get upset on my account. I like being here, too. I just wish my job was a little more exciting. And I miss all the people in Albany."

"What, like your friends? You didn't keep in touch?"

That actually got a laugh out of me. "No, silly. I miss the *amount* of people in Albany. There were too many to keep count. Everyone was a stranger to everyone else. Do you know I lived in my apartment for five years and still didn't know everyone on my floor?"

He arched a brow. "That's a good thing?"

"Sure. I mean, maybe not to you, but to someone like me, with a past to live down, it was *heaven*. I didn't constantly get compared to my sister. No one knew about my weak stomach or my high school nickname. Best of all, I could walk into a drug store without being told to keep my hands where the clerk could see them." Dropping my head, I rested my chin on my cupped hand and sighed. "I guess I miss being able to get lost in the crowd."

"I can't imagine you *ever* get lost in a crowd."

My head snapped up. "Oh, please." I sat up straighter and leaned across the table toward him. "Remember high school?"

"Do *you*?" He leaned closer to me. "I always knew where you were in high school. No matter how many other people were around."

Our faces were now breaths apart, and if I stretched a little closer, I'd be kissing him. The air between us hummed with anticipation.

Coward that I am, I pulled back enough to allow us some emotional distance. Then, to be sure I broke any sensual spell the night might have conjured, I laughed. "Got that prickly feeling on the back of your neck when I was in proximity, huh? Like when there's a mosquito in your bedroom at night. Turn on the light, the pesky bug disappears. In the dark, though, it's constantly buzzing in your ear."

Frowning, he slapped a hand on the table. "Why do you do that?"

His disappointment shook me. Whatever test he'd just conducted, I'd apparently failed. "Do what?"

"You always put yourself down. I don't think of you as a mosquito or a spider or any other kind of bug. There's nothing bug-like about you. Never has been."

This conversation was becoming far too intense, but I sloughed off the warmth coiling in my belly and stabbed my index finger near his nose. "You're forgetting my eyeglasses."

"What eyeglasses?"

"Hell-*o*?" I rolled my eyes with more exaggeration than I'd used as a teen. "Ninth grade? Before I got my contacts I had those big black clunky frames with magnifying lenses that made my eyes look huge? Everybody called me Fly Eye. Ring a bell?"

It should. He was the one who first gave me the nickname. The minute he said the insult aloud, it became my talisman for the rest of the semester.

He waved off my sharp reminder. "You wore those god-awful glasses for…what? A month?"

"*Three* months," I corrected. "Which in ninth grade time equals seven years."

"I think you're confusing yourself with a dog."

"I think you're forgetting what I looked like in those days."

"There you go again." He pointed his iced tea glass at me. "That's exactly what I'm talking about. Why must you always insult yourself? Poor Paige, the math geek. Poor Paige, the M&M thief. Poor Paige, the *other* twin. We were all a mess in high school. Even worse in junior high. The difference is, the rest of us don't dwell on it or beat ourselves up over it the way you do."

"Yeah, well, the rest of you weren't social pariahs, thanks to your mother's hijinks."

He grimaced. "Now you sound like Nia."

I didn't want to talk about my sister right now. Quite frankly, I didn't want to talk about my mother, either. "Let's change the subject. Why didn't you ever leave Snug Harbor?"

"I never saw a reason to." He shrugged. "I've got everything I need right here."

Of course he did. Sam was the town's Golden Boy. I imagine one day, the chamber of commerce would erect a statue in Sam's honor. After he'd saved a dozen kittens from a burning building, or got an old lady out of a tree, or some other heroic act.

Before they moved away, his mom and dad were pillars of our little seaside community. Happily married almost forty years now, they had hosted charity functions, served on the school board, volunteered at civic events. Jonathan and Sophia Dillon were the closest Snug Harbor came to a society couple, our very own Kennedys. Except, no scandals were ever attached to the Dillon name. Perish the thought.

"How are your parents doing? Do they like living in Florida?"

Sitting back, he stretched his legs out away from the table, toward me. "It depends on the season. In winter,

Duet in September

when I call them with our latest snowfall accumulation, they chuckle and 'casually' mention they're sitting by the pool while I'm shoveling the sixty-foot driveway. In the summer, they complain the sun is so strong, they can't go near the pool until night falls. That's when they start reminiscing about the ocean breeze up here and dropping hints about flying up for a visit."

"Maybe you should invite them to come up here in the summer. I'm sure they'd love to see you and all their old friends."

He groaned. "Please! Don't give them any ideas. Whenever we're together, whether I go to them or they come to me, I suddenly revert to a nine-year-old in their eyes. It's always, 'Did you remember to go to the bathroom before we left, Sam, honey?' And, 'Let's go buy you some new clothes.' Or, 'When are you going to get a haircut? I can't see your gorgeous eyes.'"

"Well, they *are* nice eyes," I told him with a smirk.

"Funny."

I shook my head. "You know what? You don't know how lucky you are. You still have both your parents, and they dote on you. I'd trade places with you in a heartbeat."

"Great. Next time they're here, I'll let them stay at your place. Then, when they're not reminding you to wash your hands before dinner, you can listen to them harp about how your refusal to get married denies them a bevy of grandchildren to spoil."

"They have a point." I held up a hand. "Don't get me wrong. I'm not advocating you get married to provide your parents with entertainment in the form of mini-Sams, but…well…you aren't even seriously dating anyone. Maybe that's why your parents still treat you like a child. Aside from your job, you don't seem to have any adult responsibility. Isn't there anyone in this town—or even a neighboring one—you're interested in dating?"

Thwap! That put the ball firmly in his court.

"Oh, I have someone in mind," he replied with a ghost of a smile. "But she isn't willing yet."

Whoosh! His reply flew past me, almost too fast, but I reached for it anyway. "What do you mean 'she isn't willing'? Have you told her how you feel?"

"No."

"Why not?"

A deep frown etched his features. "Because she doesn't see me as anything more than a friend right now."

Poor Nia. At this rate, she and Sam would *never* get together. Thank God these two had me to play matchmaker for them. "Whoever she is, you should go for it, Sam. You'll never get her attention if the poor girl doesn't have any clue you're interested in her."

"I'm working on it. Soon, I hope, I'll convince her otherwise. But now it's my turn to change the subject. Did you leave some broken-hearted guy back in Albany?"

I snorted. "Are you kidding? I left a dozen of them. Men threw themselves off bridges when they learned I planned to come home for good. The entire city closed down the day I left. The governor coined it 'the new day that would live in infamy.'"

His full wattage grin returned. "I knew it."

We lapsed into a comfortable silence, and dusk closed in around us. The music switched from up-tempo party songs to sultry rhythm and blues. Fireflies danced on the warm evening air. My white lights twinkled in the trees, creating a mystical world where only we existed.

We. Me and Sam.

The idea sent butterflies flitting in my stomach. "I should clear the table before we attract bugs," I blurted as I shot to my feet.

"I'll help," Sam offered in a similar rush.

I leaned toward his plate at the exact moment he leaned toward mine. The result was inevitable. We wound up with our faces breaths apart again.

"Go for it, right?" he muttered, and then his mouth claimed mine.

A rush of emotions flooded through me, and my head spun. His lips were firm but soft, sweet with a lingering hint of lemon from the fish and the iced tea. We fit together perfectly, two halves becoming one whole.

Somewhere, in the loneliest corner of my brain, a voice cried out a warning. Something about Nia.

Nia! Oh, God, what was I doing? Encroaching on the guy my sister loved. This was bad. And *wrong*. So very wrong.

I broke away, breathless, and more than a little ashamed of myself. Because for the first time in over a decade, I was bitterly jealous of my twin.

Chapter 15

Nia

Daylight still hadn't relinquished a hold when we left Valera's. I had to shield my eyes with my hand until I adjusted to the difference from dim restaurant to bright outdoors. I'd forgotten that dinner at 5:30 in the summertime meant that, even after a three-course meal, early evening retained the light of late afternoon. In fact, the sun sat on the waterline by the shore next door, fully prepared for a glorious, colorful exit. Dozens of people milled on park benches, waiting to view another spectacular East End sunset.

Aidan took my hand. "Come on."

As he led me over the rocky beach, closer to the water's edge, a crazy thought burst into my head. *I could get used to this.*

Wait. What was I thinking?

Do you know who my fiancé is? This time, I couldn't ignore Camille's voice in my head. Because not only did I know her fiancé's background, I had also become familiar with her soon-to-be stepson's pedigree.

Aidan Coffield was practically royalty with his rich, successful father and an Italian noble mother—even if that noble title came through a second marriage.

What on earth did he see in me?

I didn't need a psychic to figure out the answer to that question. For him, tonight was nothing more than a fling, a walk on the low side of town. And he couldn't get socially lower than one of the Wainwright girls, with their floozy mother and poor, cuckolded father. I'd heard a radio deejay use the term, "cuckold," one morning and thought how descriptive it was. In just seven letters, "cuckold" summed up all the adjectives associated with what my father became: distrustful, miserable, lonely, a laughingstock. A loser.

I shivered.

Aidan stopped walking and turned to me, eyes narrowed with concern. "Are you cold? Here, come closer." He pulled me in front of him, wrapped his arms around me, sharing his warmth and allowing me a front row view of the sun sinking into the horizon.

Just for tonight, I told myself. Just for tonight, I'd forget he and I came from two very different worlds. Just for tonight, I had no sordid history. I deserved one night with a Prince Charming. Tomorrow, this Cinderella would go back to her small-town existence, and her storybook romance would be a memory.

Resolved, I shoved my dismal thoughts aside and focused on the blood orange sun disappearing inch by inch, minute by minute. "God, that's beautiful," I exclaimed.

"Yes, you are," Aidan murmured, his breath warm against my ear.

Just for tonight, I insisted again.

Although the night was still in a newborn stage, I knew my time with him would come to an end the minute that fiery ball disappeared into the sea. If tonight was all I had, I wanted to make my time with him as enjoyable as possible. I twisted in his arms, craning slightly so we were face-to-face. The evening had turned out so well, I didn't want silence to bring the slightest discomfort between us. I racked my brain for something to talk about, then remembered the news articles I'd discovered online earlier when I'd researched his name.

"When's your new vineyard scheduled to open?" I knew the answer, of course, but he didn't know I knew.

He turned his attention away from the sunset, giving me the full impact of those gorgeous espresso-colored eyes. "Officially? Next month. That's when I'll introduce the first bottles and host a tasting event for the press. I'm particularly proud of our Sauvignon Blanc and Chardonnay. I think those two are going to be the crowd-pleasers."

"And unofficially?" I asked.

"Unofficially, we've been working behind the scenes for nearly four years now."

Wow. Four years? I had no idea. "Is that how long it takes to make wine?"

"It's how long it takes to get a new vineyard up and producing. I suppose if I'd started with an existing winery, I might have cut that time in half, but I'm not a halfway guy. Something my father discovered too late..."

His lips tightened, and I sensed an undercurrent of tension. Strange how every time the topic of his parents came up, he seemed displeased. While I didn't know the reason, I fully commiserated with the reaction. Therefore, I wouldn't pursue an avenue that might land me in an unpleasant conversation neighborhood.

"I've never been to a vineyard," I said.

"Never?"

I shrugged, admitting nothing. Until now, I'd never had the slightest interest in vineyards or winemaking.

"Would you like a private tour of Piping Plover? I happen to know the owner pretty well."

I smiled. Of course he did. So did I. He was cradling me close against his chest, and I never wanted to leave his embrace. "Do you think the owner will mind? I don't want to be a pest."

He kissed the top of my head, another unusual benefit to a woman of my height. Yes, Aidan Coffield was definitely my prince. *Just for tonight.*

"You, sweetheart, could never be a pest. I'll take you there on Friday, if you like. That's your next day off, right?"

"Uh-huh." A frisson of delight tickled my flesh,

whether from the invitation or the way he called me sweetheart, I didn't know. Cinderella, however, heard the first chime of the clock striking twelve. "I should head home. I've got a few things to take care of before bed." Yeah, like returning to real life.

He tightened his hold on me. "Stay, please. At least until the sun sets. I'm not ready to say goodbye yet."

Honestly, neither was I, but I knew I was playing a very futile game. I surrendered easily.

"Okay."

Just for tonight, my conscience reminded me. And maybe for Friday, too, my heart shot back.

Then we would say goodbye. He'd go back to his life, and I'd return to mine.

~~~~

Paige

After a completely sleepless night, I finally crawled out of bed at six-thirty on Monday morning and grabbed the first of many cups of coffee. Images danced in my head like Radio City Rockettes, each one kicking my bruised conscience: Sam when he showed up on my doorstep, Sam grilling the fish on my barbecue, Sam sitting across from me at dinner, Sam telling me he always knew where I was, Sam kissing me...

Okay, I replayed every minute of my evening with Sam, but interlaced with those memories, I saw Nia, an expression of shock and anger on her face that drove a knife into my heart.

I had to tell her. She was going to ask about last night's so-called party the next time I saw her. I couldn't avoid the conversation for more than a day, at best. What on earth could I possibly say to her? That maybe my animosity toward Sam had revolved one hundred eighty degrees into attraction?

Yeah, that would go over well. Especially if she blamed me for keeping *her* apart from Sam for all these years.

Telling her the truth would only hurt us both. I'd have to lie.

Facing a day lined with possible life-altering disasters, I hit the button on another cup of coffee, then decided to tackle my laundry. At least, if Nia killed me, she'd have plenty of clean outfits to choose from for my burial. I imagine since it worked for clean underwear in the hospital, the rule was doubly important for funerals.

At 12:30 pm, I strolled into Nature's Bounty with a large white paper bag filled with yummy goodness. I spotted Nia immediately. She wore a sundress the hue of egg yolks, a perfect complement to her coloring and sunny mood. I had no clue what kind of morning she'd had, but it must have been a doozy. My sister beamed brighter than sunshine, which only enforced my decision to prevaricate about last night. How could I intentionally break Nia's heart when she looked so happy? She stood by the cash register, counting out money, totally oblivious to me.

"Lunchtime, Nia!" I announced and held up the bag. "Behold, I bring you food of the gods: a double cheeseburger from America's Drive-In, sweet potato fries with fabulous maple dipping sauce, and for irony's sake, a diet soda. It's a beautiful day outside, and you and I are going to take advantage for an hour. I paid Tommy and Monica Kelly five bucks each to hold the bench in the gazebo for us. Let's go."

At last, she looked up. When she spotted me, a frown pinched her features. She groaned, "Oh, God, Paige, after last night's feast I couldn't possibly eat all that food."

Wait. What? "I thought you and Iggy did inventory last night."

"We did." Spots of color appeared in her cheeks. "But

you know Mrs. Z. God forbid her son doesn't get a decent dinner. A good stiff wind might blow him over."

"Yeah, sure." I stifled a snort of amusement. "Only if that wind knocks down the water tower when Iggy's standing underneath."

She shrugged, a silent agreement, then went back to bundling her money.

"So what did you eat last night?" I persisted.

Her head snapped up. "Huh?"

"What did Mrs. Z. bring in last night? What has you so full?"

"Oh, umm, ham in rye crust and pierogis."

Briana, hovering near the storeroom, chimed in. "Iggy was here yesterday? How come?"

"Inventory," Nia replied quickly.

The teen's eyes nearly bugged from her head. "But we did inventory last week."

Really? I switched my attention from Briana to Nia and back again.

"Yes," Nia said softly, "but we missed a shipment that came in late, so Iggy and I had to do a recount."

Briana frowned. "You should have said something before you sent Andy and me home yesterday. We would've stayed to help. Especially for homemade pierogis. I wonder if Iggy will bring in the leftovers when he comes to work today."

"I don't know if there are any leftovers." Nia shoved the cash into a drawer beneath the register and locked it, pocketing the key.

"There should be," the teen insisted. "Mrs. Z. always makes extra for us."

"Well, don't go asking her for anything." My sister grabbed my hand and yanked me toward the door. "Come on. Before the Kelly kids give up on us and sell our spot to the highest bidder."

Lucky for us, the twins had stuck it out, and lucky for

them, I upped the payment to six bucks each. After the kids had happily run off to spend their easily earned dough, Nia and I sat together on the bench overlooking Fort Lake, the site of a Revolutionary War battle. A dozen homes around the water claimed George Washington had slept here, but no one knew for certain where he'd laid his general's head centuries ago. Couples strolled around the tree-lined lake. A jogger in blue nylon shorts and a sweat-soaked white tee paused at the monument stone to check his pulse.

"Here." I pushed a paper sack of sweet potato fries toward Nia, setting the cup of dipping sauce on the bench between us. "Eat, while it's still hot."

"Thanks." She pulled out a fry, dipped it in the sweet tan sauce, and bit in. Her face glowed nuclear. "God, that's soooo good! I don't know why, but it always tastes better when you pay." She took another fry, followed the same ritual. "How was the barbecue?"

Let the games begin. "Actually, it was an eyelash shy of a disaster. I tried to cancel and managed to reach all the other guests except Sam."

Her eyes narrowed as she studied me over the rim of her soda cup. "Sam? Sam *Dillon*? You invited Sam? Why?"

"To prove to you that I was giving him a chance. But then you bailed, I told everyone else not to come, and Sam showed up a half hour early. It wound up being the two of us. Talk about awkward." I edged the comment with lots of bite and rolled my eyes.

A flush crept into her cheeks. "I'm sorry, Paige. I feel awful about cancelling last night."

"Yeah, well, I definitely could have used a buffer," I grumbled.

Near the lake's edge, two toddlers chased each other and screeched. Meanwhile, their mom chatted with another woman nearby. Honestly, this place might seem idyllic, but why invite tragedy? I shook my head and returned to my conversation with Nia, but I stayed focused on the kids. "The only good thing about last night is I can honestly say Sam's still breathing and I'm not in jail, so we managed to muddle through."

"He didn't say anything to upset you, did he?"

My attention swerved from the toddlers to my sister. "Like what?"

"I don't know. Anything. You seem…" She paused, cocked her head. "…tense today."

I pointed toward the lake. "Look at those kids. You'd think their mother would keep a closer eye on them."

"No, it's more than that. You're so uptight, you're practically brittle."

"I guess being nice to Sam last night took its toll on me."

Her expression darkened. "I'm sorry. Had I known it would be you and Sam alone, and that you'd be so miserable afterward…"

Oh, boy. If I didn't rein myself in, the devil would be picking out a penthouse suite for my eternity. "The night really wasn't that bad. Sam made a few snarky comments that got my back up, but I bit my tongue and let his idiocy roll off me. By the end of the evening, we actually became kind of…pleasant toward one another."

I wondered if hell had air conditioning.

My eventual damnation would be worth it because Nia's dazzling smile reappeared. "That's wonderful. I'm proud of you. I can't imagine it was easy for you to keep your mouth in check around him."

Oh, if she only knew.

I sipped my soda to keep from saying something incriminating and stupid. God, my head hurt. I hated myself. I hated Sam. I hated the trust Nia placed in me. I wanted to go home and hide under the covers. Until the year 2040.

"You and Sam." She bit another dipped fry, chewed,

and swallowed. "What did you two do all night?"

Wow. If she ever gave up her gift shop, she'd make an excellent investigative journalist. "Nothing. Why?"

"What do you mean nothing?" She slapped her hands on her lap. "You threw him out after inviting him over?"

"No. Of course not. He stayed for dinner."

She leaned back, her elbows resting on the back of the bench and her head tilted toward the slant of sunlight coming in through the gap between the posts. "And…?"

Why? Why couldn't she let this go? Why did she have to make my sins so much worse by insisting on details I didn't want to share? "And nothing. He grilled the mako, which was delicious by the way, and the corn. We had iced tea and pasta salad on the side, and then he went home."

After he kissed me. And I kissed him back.

"You had a good time?"

Could the ground open up and swallow me now? Please? Time to change the subject. "I thought we could go to the Labor Day celebration tonight. Check out the fireworks."

And check out Sam, who would also be there. Maybe he and Nia could create fireworks of their own. Part of me hoped Nia would say no. Part of me didn't want them to spend time together, which was ridiculous.

Until last night, I'd wanted nothing more than to see these two as a couple. One night with Sam, a few kisses later, and a queasiness filled my belly at the thought of Nia sharing that kind of magic.

I told myself I didn't want to run the risk that Sam might tell her about last night, about what we'd really done. I was *not* jealous. I refused to be jealous. I didn't even like Sam Dillon. No matter how his kisses curled my toes.

Chapter 16

Nia

I barely arrived back at the store when Briana started in with her cross-examination. "Iggy says he didn't come into work at all yesterday and his mom was in the city with Irenka at a Broadway show. So there was no inventory and no pierogis."

Great. Briana Levinson, girl detective, was on my trail.

"That's right," I said as I breezed past her toward the counter.

"So why'd you lie to us?"

"Because I didn't want Paige to know where I was last night." I picked up my apron and pulled it over my head, glad for the opportunity to hide my face from scrutiny—even briefly.

"I don't like the sound of that," Iggy grumbled from behind the wall of greeting cards in the rear of the store.

Crap. He came in early today. *Quick, Nia. Think of something.*

"Oh, relax. I have a surprise planned for her, and I had details to take care of last night. That's all."

"Well, next time you plan to use me as your excuse, give me a heads-up." Iggy's eyes narrowed to dangerous slits. "You're lucky your sister didn't ask me about this so-called inventory before I heard about it from Briana."

I ducked my head. No one had chastised me like this since Daddy passed away. No one had needed to. "I know, and I'm sorry. Paige showed up without warning. I panicked." The phone on the counter rang, and I reached for it. *Saved by the bell.* "Nature's Bounty Gift Shop, how can I help you?"

"Hello, beautiful, how are you today?"

I knew his voice instantly, but still couldn't believe he called me. "Aidan?" I whispered, cupping the receiver close to my mouth.

"While I'm sure you have people greet you that way all the time," he said, "I have to admit it's a little disconcerting that you have to ask if it's me."

"Sorry, can you hold on a minute?" I quickly pushed the red button to silence my end of the conversation, then turned to Iggy and Briana who watched me with open curiosity. "Part of Paige's surprise," I explained hastily. "I'll take this in the storeroom."

"Uh-huh." Iggy's reply was flat, emotionless, but filled with questions nevertheless.

Two pairs of eyes bored into my shoulder blades as I strode away, but I didn't falter. Only after I'd closed the door and locked it did I pick up the wall phone located behind a stack of cardboard boxes.

"Sorry about that," I murmured. "I was just finishing up with a customer." Lie number five. Or six, for the day. I'd lost count. "Thanks again for last night. I had a great time."

"Me too. That's why I'm calling. I wanted to know if you plan on going to the Labor Day fireworks show tonight. I thought we might go together."

Together? In public? In my hometown?

"Oh, gee, umm..."

Why didn't I live in Manhattan where there were probably a thousand things to do tonight? How could I bow out without admitting I didn't want the nosy townspeople to see us together? I shivered. I could almost *feel* the whispered rumors on the back of my neck. *Did you see Nia with that Coffield fellow? What do you suppose he sees in her? The same thing that Greenwich stockbroker saw in her mother. Easy pickings.*

"Actually," I said at last, "I was planning to work in my hot spot tonight."

"Oh." He sounded disappointed. "I suppose you prefer to work alone, yes?"

Was he wrangling for an invitation? A thrill passed through me. "I thought you wanted to see the fireworks."

"I can see fireworks anytime. I don't know if I'll ever get another chance to see the work of such a talented artist."

I swear fireworks crept into my cheeks.

"How about it?" he pressed. "Would you like some company tonight?"

My first reaction to his question was absolutely not. The last thing I needed was for any of my neighbors to recognize him. How would I explain a Coffield at my house?

Then the saner part of my brain realized that virtually everyone would be down at the beach for the fireworks. If we timed this right, he could be at my house and gone with no one the wiser.

The crazier section of my mind knew that Aidan's interest in me would eventually wane, leaving me like some tragic Gothic heroine. Eventually, I'd become a modern-day Miss Havisham, roaming around my empty house, mourning the man who got away.

Both hemispheres in my head agreed that I should take full advantage of any time I could spend with him until the miserable day when we parted for good.

I waggled my eyebrows, a bad Groucho Marx impression, and laced my voice with sultry innuendo. "I suppose you want to check out what I have in my lehr."

"'What you have in your lair?' Is that like inviting me up to your apartment to see your etchings? Because I'm not that kind of guy."

"No, silly." I laughed. "A lehr, L-E-H-R, is an annealing furnace. It's a time- and temperature-controlled box where I store my sculptures while they cool. You have to remember that when completed, the glass is hotter than a few thousand degrees. At that heat level, if a piece is cooled too quickly, it will crystallize. Did you ever take a glass dish from the oven to the refrigerator and have it explode? Or place a hot liquid in a glass mug and watch a crack form down the length? That's what happens when the glass is cooled too quickly during the creation process. The lehr gradually drops the temperature over hours to cool and protect the glass's molecular structure."

"Okay, then." He dropped his voice. "I'd love to see what you have in your lehr, L-E-H-R. And if we have time, what's in your L-A-I-R." The husky promise skittered across my flesh, raising goose bumps.

"Come by at eight-thirty." I gave him the address. "I'll be in the carriage house at the back of the property. Just follow the driveway to the end. If the music's blaring, stay outside until I turn it down or off completely. That's a safety precaution. The louder the music, the more dangerous the conditions inside. If or when it's quiet, you can walk right in. Got it?"

"Wouldn't a 'caution' sign on the door have the same effect?"

"No," I said airily. "I can't hum along to a 'caution' sign."

"Point taken. Should I bring anything? Wine, maybe? I happen to know an excellent vintner."

"I bet, but no." I smiled. Occupational hazard for him, I supposed, to want to bring a bottle of wine to any event. "Especially no alcohol. I don't imbibe when I'm working. And you won't either. A few more rules. Dress comfortably, but cover exposed skin—pants and long sleeves. It gets extremely hot in there. Wear cotton, nothing made of rayon or nylon, which could melt."

"Melt? Really?"

I shook my head. "A thousand degrees, remember?"

"Is there any danger?"

Only to my heart. I swallowed my fear. "Not if you

follow my rules. Got it?"

"Yes, ma'am, I got it. I'll see you at eight-thirty."

"I'm looking forward to it," I replied.

And I was. Really. For the rest of the day, I might as well have walked on clouds. I'd never invited a man into my hot spot. Even Paige rarely ventured inside, although she avoided the place because she despised the extreme heat from the two furnaces.

Both times Aidan had come into my shop, he'd shown a true appreciation for my work. Now I wanted to hear his opinion on my lineup of fall items. The pieces in my *lehr*.

The worst part of the afternoon occurred when Briana went home at four-thirty, leaving me alone with Iggy. Over the next half hour, he glared at me and shook his head, saying nothing. At five o'clock, he flipped the sign to "Closed" and stalked toward me, his soldier's eyes intense.

"Okay." He pulled the stool away from the cash register with an ear-splitting screech and patted the top with a sharp *smack-smack-smack*. "Sit. Let's talk."

The hot seat? Thanks, but no thanks. I feigned interest in rearranging the painted seashell "floral" arrangements. "What do you want to talk about?"

"Don't go squirrely on me now, Nia."

I moved on to the mini Christmas tree and toyed with the shell ornaments hanging there. "I'm not."

"No? Oh, my mistake." He stepped forward and put a hand on my shoulder. "Are you in some kind of trouble?"

"What?" I blinked. "No. Of course not."

"Well, something's definitely up. The Nia I know doesn't lie, doesn't sneak around, and doesn't dive into the storeroom to take phone calls."

"I told you it's a surprise—"

He held up a hand. "I know what you told me. I also know that we're more than just employer and employee. We're friends. So I would hope that if you needed help of any kind, you'd turn to me."

My steely resolve softened. "Iggy, I—"

He turned around and walked away before I could form a coherent argument. "That's all, Nia. Don't compound the issue with lame excuses, okay? Just be careful, and remember I'm here if you need me."

I couldn't reply. Seriously, nothing in my head seemed appropriate. Finally, I followed him, kissed his cheek, whispered, "Thank you," and left the store.

~~~~

Paige

I'd made the mistake of telling Nia I'd meet her in front of the beach concession stand at eight o'clock— apparently so had every other resident in this town and the neighboring villages for twenty miles. The crowd surrounding the clapboard building rivaled Times Square on New Year's Eve.

Now officially closed until next year, the concession stand served hundreds of hot dogs, fries, ice cream, and mixed drinks every day from Memorial Day to Labor Day. The smell of the last snacks of the season clung to the air and had a way of permeating clothes and skin. Keeping a fair distance away, I walked around the entire stand, from the barren area where the picnic tables usually stood, to the rear where the rest rooms were located, to the edge of the parking lot.

Snippets of a hundred different conversations rang in my ears. Seagulls waddled the grounds, seeking anything edible a negligent person might drop. Of course, to a seagull, almost anything was edible. I'd once seen one of the scavengers lift a three-pound London broil off a flaming barbecue when the griller's back was turned. Quite a comical sight, actually. The bird flew off with the steak while some poor tourist shouted and waved a set of tongs at the aviary felon.

I weaved through gaggles of strangers, seeking Nia's auburn head at the top of the crowd. Sometimes, her height came in handy. Not tonight, though.

No Nia anywhere.

I did, however, run into Sam. Twice.

"Are you still looking for Nia?" he asked when I came upon him on my second go-round, this time near the outdoor showers.

"Yes." I glanced at my watch. Twenty after eight. "And I'm starting to get worried. She was supposed to meet me at eight."

Sam dismissed my anxiety with a wave of his hand. "She's probably still looking for a parking space. It's crazy out there. Main Street's already lined with cars on both sides for three miles. We're using the town trolley to transport people down here. Come on." He jerked his head. "Walk with me. She'll find us eventually."

I played lost puppy and followed along beside him. The night was soft, the air tinged with salty moisture from the incoming tide, with a clear sky perfect for the fireworks show.

Sam spoke to virtually everyone we ran into, shaking hands with tourists, offering more personal greetings to local residents. Strange how the uniform made the man. He stood tall, a beacon of safety and respect in the throng of families, teenagers, and senior citizens. I couldn't think of one snarky comment to toss his way.

Near the boardwalk stairs, Dominic Bautista stopped to say hello, arm draped possessively across the shoulders of Evan Rugerman. "Hey, Sam. Paige. Nice night, huh?"

"Dominic?" I feigned a heart attack by clutching my chest. "Is it really you? I haven't seen you since I was...like...twelve."

"Don't jinx it," Evan said with a grin. "This is Dom's first night off in over a month. Thank God he finally found another vet to partner with."

"You did?" Sam punched Dominic's shoulder. "Congrats. Who's the new guy?"

"The new *doctor*," Dom replied, one brow arched, "is Jayne Herrera. She's a transplant from Brooklyn."

"A woman?" Sam sounded stunned.

"Sexist pig." I punched him in the forearm, which was like punching a cement block. Pain sizzled across my knuckles. "Ow." I rubbed my hand against my cotton blouse to soothe the ache. "Brooklyn? Really? Talk about a change in venue. I bet she's in for some major adjustments to life in our small town." The pain hadn't ebbed, and I clasped the injured hand inside the uninjured hand to soothe the ache.

Before I knew it, Sam grabbed my hand and kissed my knuckles. His hooded eyes sparked as he smiled at me. "Better?"

"Oh ho!" Evan waved his index finger between Sam and me. "So that's how it is."

I swerved my attention from Bedroom Eyes to Bedroom Bod. "That's how what is?"

"Friday night at The Lookout, I thought I was your hero, your knight in shining armor. Remember? I got Gary off your case and even managed to finagle you a glass of ginger ale from Old Sauerkraut Face. Now I find you're two-timing me with Sam."

"Ahem!" Dom shot a dangerous look at Evan.

Evan ruffled his hair. "In a completely platonic way, of course," he amended. "Not that I blame you for hooking up with the police chief. A girl who gets into trouble as often as you should have connections in law enforcement. Makes skating away from punishment a lot easier, I bet."

I couldn't decide which misconception I wanted to address first and wound up sputtering, "I'm not...he and I aren't...who said I was...?"

Sam laughed and wrapped an arm around my waist.

"She definitely keeps me guessing. Thanks for coming to her aid the other night, Evan. Nia and I had our hands full with Terri in the ladies room."

"Yeah, I heard about that. God, she's a mess, that one."

"Terri's not a mess," I interjected. "She's in pain."

I'd raised my voice, and I think Sam thought I was about to become emotional because he pulled me closer and ran his hand up and down my bare arm in a comforting manner. "Come on, sweetheart. Let's go." He then turned to Evan and Dom. "Have a good night. Enjoy the show."

He started to lead me away, but I pulled out of his hold and folded my arms over my chest. "That's not funny."

Sam's face took on an expression of newborn innocence, an expression I wouldn't buy with other people's money. "What?"

"You know 'what.' Calling me 'sweetheart' and thanking Evan for taking care of me the other night. You let Dom and Evan think we're a couple."

"So?"

"*So?*" I practically screeched my frustration. Instead, I put that excess energy into putting plenty of distance between us. "I hafta go. I need to find Nia."

I strode into the crowd just as the first colorful burst lit up the sky.

Chapter 17

Nia

At eight o'clock, I turned off my music in the carriage house and waited the longest thirty minutes in history. While my furnaces stayed on, all of my tools sat untouched. I wouldn't run the risk of beginning a project only to have Aidan show up two minutes later. If I kept him waiting outside too long, someone might see him. Or worse, he might get tired of standing around my yard and leave.

While I sat alone in the quiet hot spot, my ears pricked at every noise outside. If a squirrel dropped an acorn, I probably heard it and flinched. I tried to stay occupied. I sat. I stood. I walked. I sat again. I got up and moved my chair. I spotted a few gold chips from one of my projects on the floor and picked them up. I rearranged the water bottles in my mini-fridge so that all the labels faced the same way. I sat some more. I organized my bags of colored glass in alphabetical order. Nothing I did sped up the clock.

Finally, I heard tires scraping the gravel outside. The gleam of headlights shone under the door. My heart skipped a beat. Or two. My mouth dried to sawdust, and the heat inside the studio nearly suffocated me. Outside, the car's engine shut off.

Diving into the refrigerator for water, I calculated how much time I had. Two minutes, tops.

The car door opened, then closed with a loud click. I twisted off the bottle cap. His footsteps crunched closer. I slugged down the icy water in less than a dozen gulps, but my throat still felt dry.

Rap, rap, rap! Although I'd told him he could walk right in if the music wasn't playing, he knocked anyway. Either he wanted to show me his good manners, or the man didn't follow directions. From what I'd seen of him so far, I opted to believe the former. Tossing my empty bottle into the recycling can, I tried for a sedate walk to the door and wound up speed-walking.

Slow down, I told myself. Play it cool.

My hands shook as I fumbled with the latch until I yanked the handle. The sudden opening of the door had me nearly tumbling into him. So much for cool. Or sedate.

He stood in my doorway, a white cardboard box in his hand.

"Umm...hi," I managed, then winced. Seriously, could I sound any dumber?

"Hi yourself. I know you said no wine." He hefted the box. "But how about pastry? I stopped at Pierre's Patisserie in town."

I had to grip the door to stay upright. Pierre's. Without trying, Aidan had zeroed in on my greatest weakness. This man was serious trouble to my cardiovascular system—in more ways than one.

"What'd you bring me?" Okay, I sounded like a five-year-old checking Daddy's pockets for surprises, but this was *Pierre's*, a treat normally reserved for special occasions: birthdays or million dollar lottery wins.

He grinned. "Can I come in first?"

God, I was a dolt. "Sure. I'm sorry."

"Don't apologize." His lips brushed my cheek, feather-light but swoon-worthy. Or maybe that was the scent of chocolate in the air. "I think you're adorable." He stepped past me over the threshold and stopped. "Whew!" He waved a hand in front of his face. "You weren't kidding about the heat."

I stifled a groan. Maybe Paige was right. Only another glassblower could possibly understand why I loved working in what was, literally, a sweatshop. Disappointment weighed down my words as I murmured, "We don't have to stay in here. We can go up to the house if you want."

"Are you *kidding*? After I dressed for the occasion and everything?" He spread his arms wide. "How'd I do?"

While he placed the box of sweets on my chair, I looked him over, pleased. Apparently, his knocking on the door was due to good manners, as I'd surmised, because he nailed the clothing rules without a misstep. He wore a long sleeve cotton shirt, buttoned to the neck, and khaki pants with heavy lace-up work boots. No belt, which was smart because I'd forgotten to mention how hot metal buckles could become.

"Perfect." The word came out before I could consider any other description.

Honestly, no other word would fit. I could stand here and stare at him while years passed by outside my studio. I couldn't tear my gaze from him, couldn't believe he was here. Butterflies took wing in my stomach. My heartbeat sped up, pounding heavy metal against my ribs.

My scrutiny must have unnerved him because he shuffled his feet, cleared his throat, and pointed to the bakery box sitting on the chair. "Don't you want to know what I brought? Think of the possibilities: Napoleons, Sacher tortes, tiramisu…so much chocolate, so little time."

He did *not* play fair. "You had me at Napoleons," I said with a decadent sigh.

"Too bad." He smirked. "I didn't bring any Napoleons."

Scoundrel. "So what *did* you bring?"

"Un-un-unh." He wagged a finger. "Show me around first."

"Un-un-unh." I imitated him perfectly. "Get those into the fridge first before they melt and I'm forced to lick the cardboard."

He chuckled. "Fair enough."

While he picked up the box, I strode to the mini-refrigerator and pulled open the door. I rearranged some of the water bottles and pulled out one for each of us. I definitely smelled chocolate when he set the box in the empty space on the shelf. So maybe he wasn't one hundred percent scoundrel after all.

"Okay," he said after I closed the door again. "Let the tour begin."

I started with the obvious large equipment—the first furnace in the row, a ginormous blue box with a square, open door. "My furnace. This is where I melt the products I use to make glass."

"Don't you just use sand?"

"No. And it's not the kind of sand you're thinking anyway. I don't exactly stroll down to the beach with a pail and shovel. The sand I use is silica, but I also work with color rods and dichroic glass, which adds images to the finished product." I pointed to the shelves mounted on the wall where I'd just alphabetized my bags according to color. "In their raw states, some of this stuff looks like ice cubes, some like powder, and some like wands. No matter what I use, though, the end result is glass. Depending on what I plan to make, I add different metals and chemicals to enhance color, shine, and durability." I pointed at the open furnace door. "This particular furnace goes up to twenty three hundred degrees, which keeps my ingredients, what we call a batch, in a molten state."

He whistled through his teeth as he looked around my work area. "Now you've managed to intrigue me even more."

"Why?"

"Forgive me if this sounds sexist, but this all looks so...masculine. Blow torches, steel poles, those heavy work gloves..."

I looked down at the heavy Kevlar gloves protecting my hands. Yeah, he had a point, I supposed. "Ah, but the completed pieces aren't quite as masculine as the equipment would have you believe. Wanna see?"

His eyes widened in surprise, and maybe, delight. "You're going to make something while I watch?"

"If you want, sure. Something basic and simple, but it'll give you the general idea. Only if you're interested, though. I don't want to bore you."

"Are you kidding? Yes." To lend credence to his enthusiasm, he nodded. "Definitely. What can I do to help?"

I pointed to the chair placed far enough away to keep him safe. "Have a seat and watch. If you have any questions as I go along, feel free to ask."

After a sip of water from my latest bottle, I preheated my steel blowpipe and dipped it into the open square of the furnace where the crucible full of molten glass sat. When I pulled it out again, a globule the size of a walnut glowed vivid red-orange on the end.

"Interesting color," Aidan remarked.

"Don't get attached to it," I advised him. "No matter what color glass I'm working with, it always comes out of the furnace this same shade. This particular batch has chromium, so when it cools, it'll be a beautiful shade of green."

I cooled the other end of my four-foot pipe in a nearby bucket of water before placing my lips around the end and blowing gently. Within no time, I had a bubble inside the red-hot glass globule. I capped my end of the pipe to keep the heat trapped inside. "See that bubble? That'll eventually be the piece I create tonight."

I rolled the glass on my marver, a large flat piece of wood that smoothed the exterior. Over the next several minutes, with the aid of a host of tools, I added layers and colors, even using the second furnace with the round opening—the glory hole—to keep my glass fluid while I worked with it. Throughout the process, I continually rolled and cut the hot glass with my shears and tweezers. At last, the color and true shape of my piece became apparent: a wine bottle.

"It'll be a Christmas ornament when I'm completely done with it," I said. After fine tuning the glass for a few more minutes and adding details, I brought the ornament to the one piece of equipment I hadn't yet discussed, the large sealed box nearest the door. I lifted the lid, and additional heat wafted out to bathe my face in a fresh cloud of steam. "Ta-da. The infamous lehr."

He got up from his chair, followed me, and leaned into the box. A dozen additional items—the colorful gourds I'd crafted for autumn—sat inside. "Wow." When he reached for one, I pulled him back.

"No. Don't touch." I carefully set the wine bottle next to the other settling glassware and closed the lid. "Most of those pieces are still too hot to handle."

"So are you." His hands wrapped my waist, and he pulled me closer. His mouth came within a whisper of mine...

Twisted Sister's *We're Not Gonna Take It* blared from my cell phone in the heat resistant box near the door. Paige. I knew she had some disco standard as my ring tone, so in retaliation, I'd chosen something obnoxious with the perfect band name to irk her.

"I'm sorry," I said, pulling away. "I have to take this."

"Of course." His face mirrored his disappointment as he took a step back.

I commiserated completely. Paige had the worst timing. After removing my Kevlar gloves, I took my phone out of the box and punched the connect button. "Hello?"

"Nia? Where *are* you?" The noise in the background made her voice barely audible. It sounded like she was calling me from a foxhole. "The fireworks already started."

Shoot. I'd *totally* forgotten I promised to meet her at the beach. "Oh, God, Paige, I'm soooo sorry. I forgot. I'm in my hot spot."

"Are you kidding me? I've been looking all over for

you for more than forty minutes, and you're not even here?"

"I'm really sorry," I repeated. "It totally slipped my mind."

"That's just great. Every time I try to set you up with—" She stopped there.

"Set me up? What are you talking about? Set me up with what? Or is it a who? Are you talking about a date?"

"No. It's nothing. Forget it. I'm going to stick around to watch the rest of the show. May as well, right? I'll talk to you tomorrow."

"I'm really sorry, Paige," I offered once more.

"Yeah," she bit off curtly. "Me too." The background noise switched to silence when she hung up.

"You were supposed to meet someone tonight?" Aidan asked, his head tilted upward, eyes alight.

"My sister. For the fireworks show. She's peeved, but she'll get over it."

"Is this the same sister whose barbecue you were supposed to attend yesterday?"

Was that only yesterday? It felt like eons ago. I grimaced. No wonder she sounded so upset with me. I'd ditched her twice in two days. "That's her. My twin, Paige."

"Twin? There are two of you?"

If I had a dime for every time I'd heard that line…

"Yes and no. We're fraternal twins, not identical. We don't look anything alike."

"Do you have any other siblings?"

"Nope. Just Paige and me."

A flush of color rose in his cheeks. "Now, *I'm* sorry."

"What on earth for?"

"I made you blow off your only sister twice this weekend. When we finally meet, she's going to hate me."

When they finally met? Oh, no. He and she would never meet. This was a weekend fling. Nothing more. My

Duet in September   178

throat tightened, and I took another swig of water.

Wait. We had another date for Friday. Okay, so maybe this was a few days more than a simple weekend fling. Still, this wasn't a permanent relationship.

An invisible fist punched me in the gut, and my knees buckled. Inside my chest, my heart cracked in half.

God, help me, I'd fallen for him. Hard and fast. From the minute he'd first strolled into my shop, he'd been too tempting to ignore. Not that I'd really struggled against the attraction. Now I couldn't imagine putting an end to our time together.

I am the world's biggest idiot.

I sure could pick 'em. Stupid me, I couldn't fall in love with Iggy. Solid, dependable, *local* Iggy knew my secrets and cared about me anyway. No, I had to reach for the unattainable. Major league unattainable. On so many levels.

Imagine Aidan introducing me, the daughter of the town floozy, to his mother, the *contessa*. Shivers danced over my flesh.

And his father? Mr. Image Conscious? I bet Ogden Coffield would be thrilled to see the heir to his huge fortune involved with a woman whose social stature rose slightly above that of "homeless mutt." No doubt even the Ogden family dog had a more prestigious lineage than mine.

Why on earth did I continue to pursue a relationship of any kind with this man?

"Is something wrong?"

Aidan's question, accompanied by a frown, shook me out of my self-analysis, but not the self-pity.

"This was a mistake. I'm sorry." I put my hands on his chest, intending to push him toward the door. "You should go. See the fireworks."

He stood his ground, bracing his feet apart, and I couldn't budge him no matter how hard I tried. "Why? What's wrong? What did I do?"

"Nothing. Honestly. It's me." He had to go. Now.

"What do you mean it's you? What's you?"

"I can't do this. Please just go." *Please. Before I break down into a puddle of tears.*

My persistence did not pay off. He folded his arms over his chest. "Nia, stop. If something's wrong, tell me. Maybe I can help."

He would say that. Because he was my Prince Charming. A Prince Charming I couldn't keep.

I took a shaky breath, brought my growing panic under control. "No," I said then forced a smile. "Really. It's okay. I guess my conversation with Paige reminded me you wanted to see the fireworks, too. Instead, I'm boring you silly with my dumb hobby."

His thumb traced a line from my lower lip to my chin. "I'm exactly where I want to be."

As his mouth touched mine, I made myself a promise. Just tonight. I'd find a way to cancel our date on Friday. We'd say goodbye tonight, and I would never see him again.

I could do this.

Chapter 18

Paige

The Tuesday after Labor Day was what we locals called "Reality Day." After the three-month stream of summer tourists, the crowds disappeared. Most of the kids went back to school, lifeguards no longer monitored the beaches, hotels reverted to off-peak rates, and life in Snug Harbor returned to some semblance of normal.

For my something different on Day Six of Dara's Thirty Day Challenge, I opted to skip coffee with Nia in favor of a morning workout at the gym. The bike ride with Sam on Saturday had shown me how out of shape I truly was. Since I paid a monthly fee to a place I'd yet to step foot inside, today I would put that money to good use and give my muscles a workout before going into the office.

Besides, I was still ticked at Nia for standing me up. Again.

I spent a good thirty minutes on the elliptical machine, all the while thinking about my sister. Two days in a row, she'd let me down, which was so atypical for her. Maybe the car accident had shaken up her brain.

And Sam! There was another conundrum. What kind of game did he play last night? Letting Dom and Evan think we were dating? I like a joke as well as the next person, but *that* episode didn't register so much as a snicker on my humor scale.

Not to mention Evan's comments about my troublemaking side. Me! I hadn't broken a rule since that M&Ms incident thirty years ago. What did he mean that I needed a connection to law enforcement? For what?

I certainly had a lot to think about while I burned up useless calories. With my mind buzzing, I pushed myself harder on the machine, hoping to sweat out my confusion. Eventually, I had to face the truth: my workout only made me more tired and frustrated. Where was that adrenaline high I'd felt on the bike the other day? Right now, I couldn't even muster up the energy to smile.

Maybe I was more an outdoor enthusiast than a gym rat. Maybe the artificial light didn't give me the same euphoria as natural sunlight. As long as the weather stayed mild, I promised myself I'd perform my workouts in the fresh air and sunshine. Once winter came, I'd take advantage of my gym membership.

Still, today's activity counted as another way I'd broken out of my routine, and I'd learned a lesson about myself at the same time. Win/win. Thank you, Dara.

The rest of the day passed without incident, which, to be honest, began to wear out my patience. Where was all the good fortune Dara's Disciples had boasted about? When would it be my turn to experience life-altering, positive changes from the universe?

On Wednesday morning, I called Nia and got her voicemail. I left a message that I was too busy to meet her and went to the Surf Deli on my side of town for my coffee before work.

"Muffin crumb!" A basso voice shouted from behind me when I stood next on line.

I barely turned around to identify the speaker before Lou Rugerman swept me into a bear hug. He picked me up high, leaving my feet dangling inches above the floor.

"Mr. Rugerman," I gasped.

"Call me Lou, Paige."

I squirmed. "Lou, please. Put me down. It's undignified to lift your accountant off her feet."

"Dignified, shmignified," he growled, but at least he put me back on the floor. "A girl as pretty and smart as you doesn't have to worry about looking bad." His gaze skimmed me from my royal blue blouse, down past my white and blue floral skirt, to my bright yellow sandals. "You make my old heart feel twenty-five again. I will never understand why my son never went after you."

"Sure you do," I replied with a saucy wink. "Because I'm not his type."

He shook his shaggy head. "Pathetic. If I were twenty years younger…" He sighed. "Oh, well. At least my son's loss is Sam Dillon's gain, huh?"

I was checking out the basket of fat, golden muffins when he spoke, but that last comment snapped my head up to him fast. "I'm sorry. What?"

"You and Sam. Evan told me he saw you two together at the fireworks show the other night."

"Oh, no." I waved my hand. "We're just friends."

Lou's grin resembled the sharks he hunted in the Atlantic. "Yeah, that's what Evan told me the first time he brought Dominic home for dinner."

"No, really," I insisted. "There's nothing romantic between Sam and me. You know how he likes to kid people. He just took it too far the other night."

"You don't have to hide your feelings for my sake, muffin. I've suspected Sam had a crush on you ever since I heard what happened before your senior prom years ago." He wagged a sausage finger in my face. "That boy never took a swipe at anyone until that moron, Glen Bergen, shot off his foul mouth about you and your mother."

"Me and…?" His foul mouth? I blinked. Twice. If Lou wanted my full attention, that comment gave him the ammunition. What did he mean?

Sure, Glen Bergen was supposed to be my prom date all those years ago. But a week before the big night, he called to cancel, saying something about having to go out of town to visit his grandparents. I'd always suspected he'd asked me to be his date on a dare or a bet or something equally as shaming, so my bruised pride hadn't bothered to verify Glen's story. In fact, I'd never told Nia—or my dad for that matter—but I was kinda relieved when he backed out. Still…Lou made it sound like Sam had somehow influenced Glen's decision.

I set my hands on my hips. "What exactly did Sam have to do with Glen and me?"

Beneath his bushy black beard, Lou's color rose pink in his weathered cheeks. "Nothing. What are you getting this morning?" He turned to the bulky bald man behind the counter. "Her order's on me today, Mike."

"Oh, thanks, Lou," I said, "but—"

"No buts. Place your order, muffin crumb."

I had been considering one of the giant orange cranberry muffins displayed in the wicker basket near the cash register, but Muffin Crumb was not about to order a muffin. It sounded almost cannibalistic. "Just a coffee, please," I told Mike. "Light and sweet."

"You gotta eat, Paige," Lou said, parental concern sharpening his tone. "Get a bagel, too. Mike, give her one of those French toast bagels with some hand-whipped cream cheese."

French toast bagel? My steely will power softened at the very idea. I knew there was a reason I missed living here. Good luck finding a decent bagel anywhere in Albany, much less a bagel flavored like French toast.

Minutes later, Mike handed over my coffee and the bag that held my bagel, a bag that distinctly smelled of maple syrup. My stomach growled in anticipation.

"Here you go," Mike said. "Have a good day."

"Thanks." I turned to Lou. "Thanks for breakfast."

"Someone's gotta look out for you. And if Sam isn't doing the job properly, you tell him *I* will."

I surrendered. Why argue? Soon enough, Sam and Nia would realize they were meant for each other—with a little help from *moi*. Then even Lou would have to admit the truth and lop off my part in the so-called love triangle.

Two more days. The village clambake was just two

days away now. This time, I wouldn't let my sister squirm away. Nothing would keep me from pushing her into the arms of the man who loved her. Not even me.

~~~~

Nia

Paige blew me off for coffee on both Tuesday and Wednesday. Not that I could blame her, but I really wanted to talk to her. That comment she'd made Monday night about setting me up haunted me. Had she meant setting me up with a guy? Why?

Had she found out about Aidan? I couldn't see how. The only people who'd come close to catching us together were the Bergens, and even if they'd seen me with him, the last person they'd gossip to was Paige. So why set me up? Unless she thought I needed someone in my life. Someone besides her. Why? Did she worry I couldn't handle life on my own? Why would it matter?

Unless she wanted to go back to Albany…

The thought had hovered in my head for weeks. When I heard her talk about Sam being at her barbecue, about how she'd had to put up with him because she wanted to prove something to *me*, a bomb went off that I couldn't ignore. Maybe I was wrong about my sister. Maybe she really didn't belong here. Somehow I had to find a way to talk to her about possibly returning to Albany, where she had room to grow, to *be* someone.

In Snug Harbor, she'd stagnate. Like me.

In addition to my concerns about Paige, my feelings for Aidan kept me twisted. I still hadn't backed out of tomorrow's vineyard trip. Oh, I'd tried. I'd picked up the phone at least ten times and dialed the first two digits of his phone number. Then my throat would close up, my palms would dampen with sweat, and I'd disconnect. To be honest, I really didn't want to cancel the date. I behaved like an addict, constantly craving my drug in secret while masking my need on a regular basis.

I needed to talk to someone, someone who'd understand and not judge—which, of course, left out my sister. Paige would berate me big time for getting taken in by Aidan's looks and charm. Honestly, though, he had a lot more to recommend him. I wasn't that shallow, and neither was he.

No, Aidan Coffield was handsome and charming, but he was also generous, compassionate, encouraging, and all the things I'd hoped to find in my soul mate one day. And I was crazy about him—which should be a good thing, right? But it wasn't a good thing at all. Because Aidan had that fancy last name, that pedigree that would make any kind of future between us impossible. God, how I wanted to curl up into a ball and hide until my heart healed itself.

I needed a friend, someone who could talk me through my feelings without making me feel like an idiot. With Paige a no-go, only one other person came to mind.

I decided to call Francesca and ask her to meet me at her convenience. With her emergency room schedule, there was a possibility I'd wind up meeting her at two in the morning, but desperation drove me to consider any time if she could help put my mind at ease.

I dialed her cell, expecting to connect to her voicemail, but I was pleasantly surprised when I actually got her on the second ring.

"Hello?"

"Francesca? It's Nia. Hi."

"Hey. What's up?"

Although Paige sometimes found her brusque, I understood her "all business" mien was a byproduct of the inordinate stress in her job. Today, I appreciated that attitude. I didn't want to be coddled. I needed cool logic. Emergency room doctor kind of cool logic.

"Can you and I get together at all today? I need to talk to you. Name the time and place. Whatever works for you."

"God, Nia, I'm sorry, but I'm swamped. I'm going on vacation tomorrow and I've got a thousand things to do before I leave. I haven't even packed yet. Is it crucial?"

My love life? Crucial? Hardly.

"No." I swallowed my sigh of disappointment. "I'm sorry to bother you. I should have remembered you were leaving tomorrow."

For her first vacation since she'd planned her aborted honeymoon, Francesca had decided on a wild and indulgent tour of Costa Rica. The first half of her week would include hiking the rainforest, horseback riding in the jungle, and climbing a volcano. Days four through eight would pamper her with spa treatments, soaks in natural springs, and a beachfront villa. A best of both worlds scenario. Then again, that pretty much described Francesca, who never did anything halfway.

"Have a great time, safe flight, and all that. We'll talk when you get back." I hung up and stared at the phone in consternation.

Now what? Maybe I should try talking to Paige. Maybe she wouldn't be so harsh if she understood how I truly felt about Aidan.

I should call her. Or better yet, show up at her office. Take her by surprise.

Yes. Much better. If she balked, I could tell her my visit was my "something different" for today. In fact, since she'd picked up lunch for me the other day, today was my turn. I made another quick call, this time to The Hearth, a homey luncheonette on the strip. I ordered two buffalo chicken wraps with extra bleu cheese dressing, and of course, diet soda for irony.

Purse and keys in hand, I called to Iggy. "I'm out to lunch for an hour or so. Think you can hold down the fort 'til I get back?"

He stepped into the doorway from the storeroom and indicated the lack of shoppers with one broad arm sweep. "I'll try to keep the crowds from rioting. Meanwhile, Lassie, you get help."

"Arf, arf," I retorted.

He mimed tossing a ball toward the exit, and I took the hint to get out.

Chapter 19

Paige

I was on the phone when a shadow crossed my desk. Someone had entered my office.

"Yes, of course," I told the caller, Georgia Chambliss, a widow in Florida. "The rate of return is *a lot* higher, but so are the risks."

Anytime an investor wanted to move large sums from safe annuities to the personal bank account of a starving artist, my antennae went into overdrive. I rolled my eyes, and I caught sight of Nia, who stood near my desk, a large brown bag in hand.

"Lunch time," she mouthed.

On the other end of the phone, Mrs. Chambliss continued squawking about *her* money. "You can't stop me from diversifying, Paige."

I flashed Nia two fingers, the amount of minutes I hoped I'd need to get the widow Chambliss calm and conservative again. "No, but your late husband set up the trust to protect your financial security."

"Felix set up the trust with *Donald* Wainwright, not you. What makes you think you know what my late husband wanted for me?"

Oh, I don't know. Maybe...my degree and CPA license?

"You never even met him," she insisted.

I didn't have to meet him. I hadn't met Georgia Chambliss either, but I had a pretty good idea what kind of woman she was. "I didn't meet your late husband personally, but he left us very detailed instructions for the dispensation of his estate." Daddy had even scrawled in pencil in the margin, *crazy clown car clause*, which told me plenty as well. I didn't need a cryptographer to figure out what he meant. At the circus, the clowns always piled into or out of one teeny car. It was an image my father always used when referring to a client whose problems snowballed due to poor judgment.

One phone conversation, and I knew what both Felix Chambliss and Daddy had feared. Given enough matches, Felix's widow would blaze through all the money, particularly on bad investments. Investments like this modern artist she wanted to sponsor, who just happened to be thirty years her junior and her latest escort around Palm Beach. The woman was self-indulgent, self-important, and self-absorbed. Too bad she wasn't self-reliant. A little online digging gave me a clear idea about this lothario's true nature. Clearly, Mrs. Chambliss didn't do her homework. But at least I could prevent her from destroying her financial future over a few honeyed words from a handsome, young conman.

"I'm going to call my lawyer, Ms. Wainwright." The threat in the widow's tone was obvious.

I wasn't the least bit intimidated. In fact, I knew her attorney would back me one hundred percent. "That would be advisable, Mrs. Chambliss. If he has any questions for me, he can reach me here until five tonight or during the day tomorrow. I'm sorry I couldn't be of more help to you in this matter. Have a good day."

"Yes, well...goodbye," the woman replied and hung up.

Placing the receiver back on the box, I sighed and looked up at Nia. "Shoot me. Please."

She snapped her fingers in an "aw, shucks" manner. "Sorry. I left my sniper rifle in my other purse."

"What good are ya?" I harrumphed.

Waving the bag over my desk, Nia proclaimed, "Behold. I bring you tidings of chicken in the sauce of Buffalo, enveloped in flaky flat bread."

I pointed a finger at her. "*You're* flaky flat bread."

"Let's leave my chest out of this, shall we?"

"Ha ha." I relaxed into my chair and offered a cool smile. "So, how *are* you? Long time, no see."

"Yeah, about that…" She shuffled from one foot to the other, obviously contrite. Good. I wasn't ready to let her off the hook just yet. If guilt was the only way to guarantee she'd be at Friday's clambake, I'd call in every favor she owed me since we were five.

"I really am sorry," she said at last, then reached into the bag. "I brought a peace offering. Buffalo chicken wraps from The Hearth."

I moaned with delight as I removed the wax paper. The spicy smell made my taste buds pop. "Extra bleu cheese dressing?"

She grabbed the chair from behind Irenka's desk and while rolling it over, shot back, "Would you let me in the door without it?"

"Probably not." I bit into one end of the wrap and chewed. Ohmigod, this was sooo yummy. If Nia gave up glassblowing, she could have a future as a diplomat for the United Nations. No one would ever consider war while eating one of these delicacies.

"Good?" she asked.

"The goddess is appeased and ready to forgive," I replied airily.

"Then my work here is done." She settled into her chair and bit into her own wrap.

"This is my lucky day," I told her. "Lou Rugerman bought me breakfast this morning—a French toast bagel with cream cheese. Ever have one?"

Nia's eyes widened as she swallowed. "French toast? Seriously?"

"Seriously. Amazing. You gotta try one." I took a sip of soda, pleased that it was diet. I make no apologies for that quirk. If I could order a low-calorie hot fudge sundae, I would. Until modern science caught up with my desires, I cut back wherever I could. "Hey, that reminds me. I have a question for you."

"Shoot."

"This is gonna sound totally bizarro, but do you remember Glen Bergen?"

Color drained from Nia's face. "Who?"

"Glen Bergen," I repeated. "From high school."

"Wow, there's a name I haven't heard in a decade or two."

"Yeah, I know. But think back to our senior prom. You remember he asked me to go with him, right?"

"Uh-huh." She fussed with the waxed paper from her wrap. "I was supposed to go with Evan Rugerman. But that was a long time ago. What difference does it make now?"

I'd made her uneasy. I could tell from the way she focused on the napkins, the paper bag, and at last, her straw, which she'd chewed flat. Nevertheless, I pressed on.

"Lou made a comment earlier. About Sam. Something about him 'taking a swipe at Glen' for talking about Mom and me. Did you ever hear anything about that?"

Her lips tightened, and she shook her head. "Mmm-mmm."

I didn't buy the denial for a second. "Lou heard about it from Evan. *Your* date."

"*His* son." She shrugged. "So?"

She knew something. Something she tried to hide from me. Shaking my head at her, I sighed. "Still trying to protect me, Nia?"

"What do you mean?"

"You know exactly what I mean. I might be the older twin, but ever since Mom left, you always took on the job of keeping me safe, keeping me from getting hurt, keeping all the secrets. For God's sake, you didn't even tell me Daddy was sick until he was on his deathbed."

She flitted her fingers at me. "Oh, please. It's not like

you could've done anything for him."

I had to tighten my hand on my wrap to keep from slapping her silly and almost squeezed the saucy chicken onto my desk blotter. "I could have been here sooner. I could have helped you take care of him. But, no. You had to play the Wainwright martyr. Again. Poor Nia, the good twin. The one who stayed behind." I edged my tone with biting sarcasm. "Daddy's princess."

She gasped. "That's not true. Yes, I stayed behind. But not because of Daddy."

"Why then?"

"For you. So you could get away from here. You were so smart, Paige. I mean, scary smart. You deserved a better life than you could ever have here. I didn't want you to throw away your future."

I studied her carefully. "Like *you* did?"

"No," she replied too quickly. High color rose in her cheeks. "Not really. I was never going to set the world on fire. Face it. I was a B student with a flair for art. Not like you. You got the exceptional grades, earned the full scholarship. And look where it took you. I mean, my God. You got all the way to the state capitol! That's why I didn't tell you about Daddy right away. I knew you'd come home out of some kind guilt-induced sense of responsibility."

Tears choked my throat when I thought about seeing Daddy in the hospital after I'd first returned home: bone-thin and too weak to lift a hand in greeting. "He was my father, too, Nia."

"Yes, I know. But you hate this town. You always have. You had a real life in Albany. You could still have that life. You shouldn't be here, you should be there. The sooner you go back, the happier you'll be."

"Are you for real?" I leaned forward over the desk until we were nose to nose. "What brought this on?"

She shrugged, took another sip of soda before answering. "The challenge, believe it or not. I realize you insisted we participate in this thirty day thing because you're bored. Don't deny it. Be honest. If you were still in Albany, you would've watched that Dara episode, thought, 'Hmm…interesting. Maybe Nia should try something like that,' and then you would have gone on with your day-to-day life. You tossed this challenge at us both to 'shake things up.'" She pointed an index finger at me. "Your *exact* words. But I think you really wanted to shake *me* up. So, okay, you did. More than you know. Now it's time for you to go home. To *your* home. Which isn't here anymore."

Anger coursed through me, too hot and sudden to stifle. I slammed my hands on the desk and shot to my feet. "You don't know squat, Nia. Who put you in charge of my life? And when? When Mom left, you didn't automatically become my mother. You're not even older than me. Since when is Snug Harbor not my home? I grew up here. I know most of the same people you do. I came back of my own accord, took over Daddy's business of my own accord, and I'm staying of my own accord. Because I *want* to be here. *This* is home. Not Albany. Snug Harbor. You wanna do something different tomorrow? Schedule a CAT scan. Because you've got some serious brain damage if you believe that crap you just spewed. Now get out of my office. I've got work to do. Go back to your little shop and your martyred life."

Hitching her purse onto her shoulder, she skulked away. "I'm sorry, Paige. Everything I ever did, I did because I love you."

Of all the stupid…

I watched her walk out, then tossed the rest of my lunch into the garbage can. What kind of drugs had The Hearth put into the wraps to get Nia all wack-a-doodle on me? One minute she was smiling and exuberant, the next she became downtrodden Nia, Snug Harbor's sacrificial lamb.

No wonder she and Sam had never hooked up. She

probably threw the same mixed signals his way. *Well, sorry, sister mine, but whatever game you're playing, I'm not rolling those dice.*

I took a deep cleansing breath. Then another. I was one wrong move away from my head exploding.

Back to work. Back to the peace and logic of numbers and projections, dollars and cents. I logged onto my computer and checked the status of a few mutual funds, then for the heck of it, I punched in the web address for the Comptroller's Office for the State of New York. Not much had changed since I'd left my job there. The same boring news cluttered the home page, the same photo of the Comptroller sat in the right hand corner welcoming visitors.

No, I didn't miss my old job. I missed the ability to become invisible, a characteristic I couldn't pull off in this tiny town.

Sure, I was bored here. If I thought about it, though, my ennui was due to my own inactivity. I hadn't tried to connect with any of the newer businesses in town. I'd allowed myself to rest on Dad's laurels, taking over his client list without attempting to create my own stable. I needed new customers, those who didn't stay because of some misplaced loyalty to my late father, clients who needed and would accept my educated guidance. Unlike Georgia Chambliss.

I leaned back in my leather desk chair, thoughtful. I should probably go to that clambake on Friday to network with other professionals in the area. Sam would be a huge help. He could introduce me to people I'd never met. My conscience sent a sharp needle reminder, but I ignored it. The fact that Sam would be there had nothing to do with my decision to go.

A movement caught my eye, and I looked up as a woman stepped into my lobby. For a long minute, she stood near the corn plant in the Chinese pot. I watched her look over the two desks, the framed photos of Daddy with various local dignitaries, and the silk flowers a feng shui expert had recommended for luck. She wore her dyed blond hair in a short, spiky style that flattered her sharp cheekbones and long neck. There were deep crinkles at the corners of her blue-green eyes and around her lips. Her gray tailored blouse with cap sleeves and the black jersey skirt hung too loose on her thin frame.

Decades had changed us both. Still, our gazes locked, and I knew.

"Hello, sweetheart," the woman whispered hoarsely.

"Mommy," I heard myself say in reply.

Chapter 20

Paige

On shaking legs, I stumbled toward my mother's open arms. Time melted, and I was eight years old again.

"My baby girl," Mom crooned as she enveloped me in a tight hug. "My sweet beautiful Paige, all grown up."

Tears filled my eyes, and I thought my heart would burst from pure joy.

My mother.

Here.

As a kid, I'd dreamed of seeing her again, of finding out the answers to the questions that had plagued me since the day we'd come home from Grandma's and discovered Mom was gone. Now I had my chance, and I wouldn't let it pass me by, no matter how gobsmacked her sudden appearance made me.

"Mom," I whispered into her embrace. "What are you doing here? Where have you been all these years?"

She never hesitated. "I heard about your father. I came to pay my respects. After I left his grave, I thought I'd come here to his office. I didn't know why, but now it seems obvious. The universe sent me here to find you."

Either she'd rehearsed what she'd say on the off-chance she ran into one of her long-lost daughters, or she spoke from her heart. Too soon to tell which, so I neither accepted nor rejected her little speech out of hand. Though, I admit, the universe comment threw me. I didn't remember my mother as a New Age guru. Still, twenty-five years had passed and my memories of her tended to revolve around the smell of warm chocolate chip cookies and lavender perfume.

She kissed the top of my head. "My beautiful girl."

"I missed you, Mom," I told her.

"I missed you, too."

I pulled away to look up at her. I needed to see the truth in her eyes. Now. "But you left us. You never called, you never tried to contact us. In twenty-five years."

"I know."

She knew. Not exactly the response I'd hoped for. "Why?"

"I made a mistake."

"A mistake?" I jerked back as if she'd burst into flames. Fury surged through me. "Let's get something straight, Mom. Crashing your shopping cart into your car is a 'mistake.' Forgetting to give your kid lunch money before school is a 'mistake.' But walking out on your husband and children because you were bored? Leaving nothing but a note? And then having no contact for twenty-five years? That's abandonment."

Her sudden arrival had twisted the tap on emotions dammed for decades. All the disappointment, the anger, the loneliness poured from my mouth in a deluge. "I don't care that you'd fallen out of love with Daddy. That was between the two of you and happens to lots of couples. But what did *I* do wrong? And Nia? We were *kids*. How could you so totally forget about us? Birthdays, Christmas, graduations, we never got a phone call, a card, nothing. Did you ever think about us? Because we thought about you a lot. Like, 'Where were you when Nia fell off the roof and broke her arm? Where were you when I won the State Math-o-Lympics?' Mrs. Seifert across the street took us prom dress shopping. Not *you*. You weren't there for any of the important moments of our lives. Jeez, even for Daddy, you showed up *six months* too late. Now you pop up out of nowhere and tell me you made a 'mistake'? I'm not sure, Mom, whether you made the mistake when you left or when you came back."

Spots of color rose in her high cheekbones. "You're

right. But I do want a chance to explain. To you and Nia, if I can." Mom looked around the office. "Is she here?"

If I had any doubt that Mom had completely forgotten us over the years, looking for Nia in this office confirmed her total lack of interest. Counting today's visit with lunch, Nia had been in this place exactly four times in her life. Numbers bored her, desks made her feel penned in, and if I remembered correctly, she'd only mastered the finer points of email in the last few years. She could list twenty different shades of red and describe the nuances of hues in each, but still couldn't text messages on her cell phone. That was Nia: poster child for the technology challenged.

"Nia's not here." A blessing, really. Because my sister wouldn't exactly give Mom a warm reception anyway. She'd never forgotten that horrible day, still lived under the shadow of the *Wainwright Family Scandal*. Wasn't that why I'd pushed for her participation in the thirty day challenge—to break her out of her safe, unassuming, don't-make-waves-and-no-one-will-notice-you box?

"Oh. That's too bad," Mom said. "Where does your sister live these days? Far away?"

God, how I hoped she wasn't sitting in my parking lot, pouting, right now. If she should see Mom walking out of here and recognize the woman who'd deserted us and launched the family scandal...? I shivered. "She lives in Grandma's old house. Here in town. She just doesn't come to Daddy's office."

"Maybe you could call her." Mom's eyes lit up. "Have her make an exception today."

The more I considered that option, the more I realized I had the formula for a major league family Armageddon on my hands. In Nia's currently overemotional state, this latest powder keg would probably have the same effect as a mini H-bomb in her hair. *Kaboom.*

Un-unh. No way. I wouldn't bushwhack my sister that way. I folded my arms over my chest, becoming a solid wall, impenetrable and inscrutable. "Maybe you should start with me and we'll take it from there."

Mom cocked her head, and her spiky blond hair reminded me of Tweety Bird. "What do you mean?"

"Remember? The universe sent you to find me?" I reminded her. "Maybe you're supposed to tell your story to me first. Then I can decide if you need to share the details with Nia."

Her lips twisted in a disapproving moue. "You two always protected each other. Even from me."

"Good thing, huh?" I retorted.

Of course, she had a point—not an accurate point, but she was close. Generally, Nia protected me. Sometimes, like a few minutes ago, her interference enraged me. Deep down, though, I understood Nia felt responsible for me. She'd been shielding me from hurt since the day she found Mom's note.

"You're really going to 'vet' me before you'll let me see my other daughter?" Mom asked, incredulous.

I said nothing. I didn't even mention the fact that, in my opinion, she'd surrendered all rights to both her daughters when she walked out the door twenty-five years ago.

"Can we at least sit down?"

At that moment I realized we still stood near the front entrance—where anyone on the street could see us. "Sure." I softened my stance enough to sweep an arm toward the chair Nia had recently vacated. "Have a seat. Would you like some coffee? Or water?" I treated her the way I would a potential new client.

"No, thank you." She breezed past me to take the seat in front of my desk. Once there, she settled her big pink purse in her lap. "Where would you like me to start?"

"How about the day you skipped town with your lover?" Part of me inwardly winced. After all, she was my mother, not a murder suspect about to be grilled under a bare bulb in an empty room. At the same time, though, she was the woman who'd abandoned us without a backward glance, without a second thought. For Nia's sake, as well as my own, I had to tread carefully. I practically tiptoed to my chair and perched on the edge, prepared to flee or leap across the desk, if necessary.

Mom merely shook her head. "No. I'll have to go farther back than that. To when I first met your father. Did he…ever tell you about that?"

"No. After you left, Daddy never mentioned you again."

She flinched, which I guess, was the reaction I'd wanted. But I felt no gratification. Cracks began to form in my impenetrable wall. Nia and I had lost our dad, and who knew? Maybe the universe *had* seen fit to send our mother back to us in some sort of cosmic penance.

What kind of ingrate tossed away such an amazing gift?

A cautious one, my conscience suggested. Face it, what kind of woman turned her back on her children? A cold, selfish, unfit one.

For now, I'd have to straddle the fence.

"I came to Snug Harbor with my family," Mom said. "We were camping at The Dunes."

The Dunes, on the south shore of town, had been a popular spot for RV enthusiasts for decades. Slots with the shortest walk to the beach were booked years in advance. Oftentimes, by the same family for generations.

"Not because we were on vacation, mind you." Mom's tone took on a sharp edge. "We came to live there. Full time. In a tent. Hidden in the dunes, where we didn't have to pay for reserving an actual campsite." Shaking her head, she sighed. "You don't know how lucky you were to have a father like Don. *My* father had trouble paying bills. Or keeping a steady job, for that matter. There was never enough money in our house. Forget about prom dresses.

We didn't always have a roof over our heads. This time, we did, but it was a canvas roof. At night, I'd sit out on the beach." Her eyes glossed over as she spoke, and I assumed she lost herself in the memories. "There was this house set back in the bluffs I longed to visit. A big old Victorian with turrets and lots of scroll work on the gables, and a glow from a circular window beneath the highest peak."

I knew that house well. "Grandma's house."

She nodded. "I would look at that house every night and swear one day, I'd live in a place just like it. In the meantime, however, I had more pressing problems. Like finding something to eat. Mom and Dad spent whatever cash they had on whiskey and cigarettes. Food was not a priority in my household. So I'd leave the beach and walk to the drive-thru on Main Street. Do you know the place? Is it still there?"

"Parson's." I supplied the name of that formidable institution of burgerdom. "And yes, it's still there."

"That's the one." She pointed an index finger at me. "The minute someone tossed their bag into the trash and drove off, I'd pull it out and rummage through for anything edible inside for me and my brother."

Talk about crazy clown car. The surprises kept on coming. "I didn't know you had a brother."

"Mmm-hmm. Charlie was three years younger than me. Some nights, I did pretty well in the Parson's garbage. Other nights, we were reduced to eating discarded pickles and licking the onions off the paper wrappings."

She dropped her gaze from me to her skirt and plucked at the folds. "Anyway, this went on for a couple of weeks until one Friday night after Parson's closed for the evening, a young man came out the back door with a takeout bag. He asked me if I knew anyone who could use some of the evening's leftovers. Said he hated to throw it away, but since the food had already been cooked, he couldn't save it for tomorrow. Of course, I took it, with the lame excuse about a poor family I knew camping at The Dunes. We both knew the truth, but he just nodded and told me to come back the next night and he'd give me another bag. I did, and he did. And when I came back the night after that, he gave me another bag. The next night, another. The whole summer passed with him providing me with burgers, fried chicken, hot dogs. Some nights, he'd meet me with the bag of food and an ice cream. No one had ever taken such good care of me."

A dreamy expression softened her face. "Every night, Don and I talked and got to know each other. He was different from the boys I'd met before. I mean, he had to know my circumstances, but he never let on. He didn't tease me or look down on me. Then I found out he lived in that house. My dream house. I really believed it was a sign. He and I were meant to be together."

"Because of Grandma's house?" Of all the dopey…

Then again, I supposed it made as much sense as the thought the universe had brought us together, which in my book, was still debatable.

"I was young. And very naïve." She shrugged. "Anyway, my parents managed to hold onto the camping spot until November. That's when someone found us. Silver-tongued Dad had made some kind of deal with the park rangers, which bought us a little time. If they let us stay, he'd help them patrol the area, to keep away any miscreants who intended to destroy property. Like I said, my dad wasn't very good about jobs. A week before Thanksgiving, he got drunk one night, and a group of teens set fire to the men's room. We were booted out the next morning. My time in Snug Harbor had come to an end. I don't know why I did it, but when my parents told me we were leaving, I ran off. I wound up in the woods behind Don's house. As soon as he heard I had to leave, he asked me to marry him. I said yes."

"How long did you know him?"

"About five months."

"No way." My sensible, never impulsive father? The creator of the "crazy clown car clause" proposed to a woman he knew a few months? Talk about wacky.

She smiled as if she knew what I was thinking. "Yes, he did. Not only that, but he immediately took me into the house and announced our engagement to his parents. Told them he and I had been dating for more than a year and that I was pregnant so we had to get married fast."

The bottom fell out of my stomach. Crap on a cracker, that idea had never occurred to me.

"I wasn't pregnant, mind you. Your father and I had never even kissed at this point."

Relief poured through me. I don't know why, but I guess the whole parents having sex thing gave me a bad case of the icks.

"He wanted his parents on our side, you see. So he offered up a fictional pregnancy and the added bonus that my parents had disowned me when they found out. I don't think either one of us thought the deception through. We were young, impulsive, and afraid. After we were married, we realized we'd have to produce a child within six or seven months to continue the lie through to fruition. When time passed without a blessed event to fall back on, we opted to tell everyone I'd miscarried." Frowning, she sighed, and her grip on the purse strap tightened. "I lived in your grandmother's house for three years while your father got his degree and CPA license. My 'dream house.' Ha. A nightmare was more like it. Your father worked at Parson's and went to school full-time so I barely saw him. And while your grandparents never wavered in their support of him, they weren't quite so open toward me. I couldn't blame them. They saw me as an interloper, someone who'd 'trapped' their son into marriage. Which, I had. But he'd trapped me too. No one knew that. I was totally alone. Even my brother was gone."

I didn't know how to respond. I mean, I'm not a stone. I understood the pain and confusion she probably felt as a young woman in a strange house with people who didn't particularly like her. Still, that didn't explain the last twenty-five years.

"I kept hoping we'd leave Snug Harbor when your father received his license, but no. He wanted to establish a practice here. With some help from his parents, we bought a house on the north side of town, and here we stayed. Then you and your sister came along. Suddenly, I had roots. The girl who had never lived in the same place for more than six months now had a twenty-year mortgage and twin infants to care for. Your father worked long hours to get the business off the ground, and I knew so few people here. As lonely as I'd been at your grandparents' house, I was even more desolate when we moved." Shrugging, she splayed her hands on the desktop. "You know what it's like living in Snug Harbor. Everyone had heard the alleged pregnancy story that forced our marriage, and in this tiny, closed-minded town, I was the immoral woman no one wanted to associate with. As you and Nia grew older, I tried. Really. I joined playgroups, took you both to the local park to meet other mothers, and volunteered at your preschool. No matter what I did, I never seemed to fit in. Then you two went to school full time, and I was all alone again. The older you two got, the more isolated I grew. That's when I met Raymond."

"Raymond?" The question escaped my mouth mere seconds before I knew who she meant. *Him.* The guy she'd left us for. I waved off any explanation she might attempt. "Never mind. I got it."

"No, I don't think you do get it. Your father and I were never a couple. Oh, we put on a front for the neighbors and for you girls. Neither of us was truly happy. Raymond came along when I was probably at the lowest point in my life. I know now that he sensed that weakness in me, but

Gina Ardito

205

back then, I thought he was going to rescue me from a lifetime of boredom and loneliness."

"So what happened? Did you marry him?" I hoped not because as far as I knew, my parents never divorced.

"Raymond's affection for me lasted as long as it took for us to reach the Connecticut border. Four hours after I ran off with him, he left me in a rest area. He even took all my belongings, which were in his trunk. All I had was twenty bucks tucked into my purse."

Tears filled my eyes, and I sniffed them back. "Why…why didn't you call home? Daddy would have come to get you and we would've gone back to normal."

"We were never normal, Paige. I knew that. Deep down, your dad knew it too. At the time, though, I was too ashamed to call him. I felt like the world's biggest idiot. I'd always prided myself on my street smarts, but I fell for the first good looking guy who tossed meaningless compliments at me."

"So what *did* you do?"

She shrugged. "I got lucky. The fast food place in the rest area had posted a help wanted sign. I got the job. All those years with my parents ducking security guards and rent collectors managed to pay off because I lived at the rest area until I saved enough money to get an apartment."

"You *lived* at the rest area?"

"Sure. It was open twenty-four hours, well lit, with lots of security and fairly clean bathrooms. I even found a private ladies shower area that I guess was set up for truckers. I wore a uniform to work so clothes weren't much of an issue. I survived. Once I had my own place, I worked and attended school, got my high school diploma, then went into paralegal studies. I work for a law firm in Hartford now."

"But, I don't understand." My head spun with details swirling through a maze of questions. "Why didn't you contact us when you got back on your feet? At least to let us know you were okay."

"That wouldn't have been fair to any of us. I had hoped your father would have moved on, found love with someone who truly loved him back."

"Did you? Find love with someone?"

A smile touched her lips, but with no happiness behind the expression. "You have to truly love yourself before you can love someone else. That's part of my reason for coming here. I needed to face my past, to come to terms with all the wrongs I'd done, especially to you and Nia. You're right. I did abandon you. But I also knew you would be so much better off with your father than with me. Don was generous and loving and patient and all the things I believed I wasn't. Plus, you had family here. In the end, I was right. All of our lives would have been so much harder if I'd taken you with me."

Had she lost her mind? I slapped my palms on the table. "You should have come home. *That* day. Or even the next day."

"I couldn't. Honestly, I didn't belong in this place. I still don't. I only came now to say goodbye to the man who showed me more kindness than I deserved."

Realization crept into my brain and, I swear, I gaped at her. "In other words, you never intended to see me or Nia."

"To be honest, I wasn't sure. I didn't know how you'd react, if you'd be happy to see me or despise me."

That comment stung, and I lashed out to return the pain. "I'm still trying to make up my mind."

She didn't even blink. "And Nia?"

Nia. I knew what she meant. Did I plan to tell Nia about her? The truth was, I had no idea.

Chapter 21

Nia

On Friday morning, I offered special thanks to the cosmetics experts who'd created my dark circle remover pen. Since my brain had spent the last twelve hours jumping between my anxiety over today's visit with Aidan and yesterday's argument with Paige, I hadn't slept much. The rings under my eyes looked as if the Indy 500 had taken place above my cheeks during the night. After a shower complete with my most expensive body wash and a deep conditioning treatment for my hair, with my makeup carefully applied, I stood in front of my closet, seeking the perfect outfit from the creative chaos within. I wanted to wear something that made me look totally put-together, but as if I'd dressed with careless aplomb.

Where was Tim Gunn when I needed him?

I finally opted for a silk tee in an emerald tone, a pair of tan cotton capris, and flat closed-toe shoes. For extra oomph, I used a sunny yellow and green paisley-patterned scarf as a headband.

When I studied my reflection in the full-length mirrored closet door, I grimaced. Why couldn't I be a petite beauty like Paige? All I needed was a brown pageboy wig and a pillbox hat, and I could be a drag queen impersonating Jackie O.

Disgusted, I turned away from the mirror. No amount of wishing could change the facts. Even Tim Gunn couldn't make a red-headed stork look feminine and classy. Besides, no matter how good I looked on the outside, my insides were a mess. My stomach somersaulted, my heart pounded, and I could water the lawn with the amount of sweat in my palms.

To regain some semblance of control, I touched the charm bracelet at my wrist. My talisman had been a gift from Grandma, a good luck charm that always soothed my frazzled nerves. Inhaling and exhaling several times, I forced a smile onto my face, and vowed to put yesterday's disagreement with Paige on the back burner for now. I'd have to tackle one problem at a time.

Not that Aidan was a problem, per se. My feelings for him were the main issue. No one else had ever made me as giddy and as happy as he did. I found him wandering through my mind at all hours. Yesterday, after my run-in with Paige, I'd been so tempted to call him, just to hear his voice. Crazy, I know.

Crazier still, I gave in to the temptation, but I hung up the minute he answered. At least I'd had the forethought to block my number so he wouldn't know I was the culprit.

Pathetic, party of one, your table's ready.

Yeah, I know. I'd only known him a few days. Still, I really, really *liked* him. I mean, genuine this-could-be-the-start-of-something-big kinda like. While my thoughts once again zipped to Aidan, I started out of the room at too quick a pace and stubbed my toe on the bedframe. Pain speared through my foot, and I sucked in a breath. Great. My legendary lack of grace under pressure had arrived right on time. Today was going to bite, I just knew it. Some inner sense told me I stood poised on the precipice of disaster.

Why did he have to be Aidan Coffield? Why couldn't he be some schlub from a nearby town with a family of similar financial means to mine? Someone who didn't have a countess for a mother and a tycoon for a father? Someone who wouldn't care I was a small town girl?

If not for those differences, you might seriously pursue him, my heart explained. *At least his social stature ensures you'll consider this what it is: an end-of-summer fling.*

Yeah, right. Because spending the day with him at his vineyard today had absolutely nothing to do with seriously pursuing him. Because the amount of time he ruled my thoughts *every* day didn't indicate the depth of my ever-growing attraction.

I left my bedroom, grabbed my purse, locked up the house, and climbed into my rental car for the twenty-minute drive to Caleb's Point, home of Piping Plover Vineyards. The day had turned out perfectly, warm and bright with the merest hint of a sea breeze and low humidity. I tried to take the weather as a sign that I had nothing to worry about, but I could almost see the black cloud of doom looming on the horizon.

The car's GPS directed me up an expanse of driveway lined on each side with leafy grape plants tied to tiers of wire fencing. At the end of this long road stood a magnificent three-level Italian villa-style building designed in hues of cream and copper with arched windows and a terracotta roof. The views of lush greenery set against the backdrop of the blue-gray Long Island Sound beneath a chambray sky took my breath away.

Aidan had recreated the beauty of Tuscany in Caleb's Point. I fell even harder for him. I'm not as mercenary as that statement probably makes me seem. I meant that a man who could design something so incredibly beautiful had an artist's soul. That facet of Aidan, which I had seen whenever he studied my sculptures, curled into the corner of my heart and settled there. God, how I wished things could be different between us.

As I climbed out of the car, he appeared on the front portico—all gentleman of the manor-like. My pulse kicked up at least two notches.

Down, girl, I told myself.

He wore a pale blue polo shirt over faded jeans. Embroidered on the right breast of the shirt was the yellow-threaded outline of a tiny bird on stick legs, the vineyard's logo, a piping plover. I walked toward him, and he scaled the marble steps at a trot, without ever touching the gorgeous stone bannister. We each came to a stop at the edge of the curved walkway, a breath apart.

"Hey." He leaned forward, kissed me, and cupped my hand in his.

My body surged with electricity. Every nerve ending tingled. I managed a shaky, "Hi," in return.

"I'm so glad you're here." He led me forward toward the stairs. "Would you like to start your tour with the vineyard itself or the house?"

I held back, my gaze sweeping up the creamy stone walls. A house. This magnificent building was a real house? I had assumed the villa to be a façade to lure in tourists. "Someone actually *lives* here?"

His smile warmed my insides. "I live here."

He lived here. Why was I surprised? The classical beauty of the house and the land suited him like…well, like a hand-tailored suit. "Just for now, though, right?" I surmised. "Until the vineyard's grand opening?" Maybe I'm a dunce, but I couldn't wrap my head around the idea that he actually lived in this fantasy palace.

"No. More like permanently." He shrugged. "Well, at least until my mansion in the Hamptons is finished."

Disappointment sent storm clouds into my happy valley. "Oh."

He chuckled. "I'm kidding, Nia."

Was he? I studied him with a critical eye, ignoring the optical illusion of a halo the late morning sun lit around his head. "About the Hamptons or here?"

"About the Hamptons. I really do live here. Creating a vineyard from the ground up—literally—is a twenty-four/seven endeavor. Especially in the early years. I moved in before we planted the first row of grapes. I live here now, and I'll probably still be living here when I'm seventy."

I don't know why, but tension left my bones in one huge rush. "Oh, thank God."

He cocked his head, and the sun's rays glinted off his hair in fiery lights. "You are the most…confusing woman."

I started to defend myself, but he continued before I could form a coherent argument.

Taking my hand again, he squeezed my fingers and murmured, "I think that's one of the things I love most about you."

Love? Had he just used the L word? Without prompting? Okay, now I slid from pathetic to downright needy. In all honesty, the man had an unfair advantage over me. Every time he paid me a compliment, I got gooey. If he kept it up, I'd be the consistency of melted caramel in no time. At this stage, imaginary birds circled my head and the lyrics from that old Carpenters' song, *Close to You*, played in the background.

To hide my pleasure, I gave him a dismissive wave of my hand. "You don't know anything about me."

"I don't know *everything* about you, but I'm learning. Either way, you definitely keep me intrigued. I've enjoyed what I've discovered so far and I can't wait to find out all your secrets."

Why do birds suddenly appear, every time you are near…

I didn't know what to say. I mean, I could hardly admit that I hid secrets because then he might pester me for revelations. Yet, I didn't want to lie either.

"To make a really good wine, you have to learn patience," he crooned in a tone far more suited for seduction than for casual banter. "The first buds need a lot of nurturing. Then, as they break and grow, they need something strong to cling to." He drew a line down my cheek with a fingertip. "Warmth and tender care bring out the ideal balance of color and juice. With the right attention, in loving hands, you'll grow an abundance of sweet grapes that yield perfection."

The words, so innocuous on the surface, wreaked

havoc with my senses. No matter what he said, the intensity in his gaze as he touched me conveyed he discussed something much more personal than grapes and winemaking. I shivered.

On the day that you were born, the angels got together…

He leaned closer and brushed his lips against my cheek. "God, you smell great." Pulling away, he added in a much more conversational fashion, "So…how about we tour the actual vineyard while the sun's not too strong? After that, we'll have lunch on the back terrace. Sound good?"

How on earth could he switch gears so suddenly? Particularly when I could barely draw breath without shuddering. Lost in the cyclone of emotions his winemaking analogy had left behind, I could only nod.

"Terrific. Let's get started." His hand took mine again as he led me past the double-sided staircase, then around the building. "I have a favor to ask."

"You do? What?" I groaned as I considered what that favor might be. "Oh, no. Not the grape lamps again."

"No." His laughter rippled down my spine like water in a Jacuzzi, but stopped as he grew serious again. "You know I'll be having my grand opening here on the first of October. There are a lot of people who'd like to see me fail."

I couldn't hide my amazement. "Who on earth would want that? Do you mean the other vineyard owners?"

He shrugged. "Mostly. Including my father."

"But why?" I couldn't fathom the idea that a father would see his child as competition. Daddy couldn't have been prouder than when Paige got her CPA license. I remember feeling a little bit hurt by my father's boasting about his "chip off the old block" daughter, but at least he'd never wanted Paige to fail.

"My father and I don't always see eye to eye. He

disagrees with a lot of my choices."

I don't know if Aidan directed that particular statement toward me or not, but I certainly felt the sting. How would his father react to Aidan dating a nobody from Snug Harbor? Unease slipped into my muscles, and I squirmed. "I'm not sure I understand…"

He waved me off. "It's not important. The truth is, Nia, I value your opinion. You have an artist's eye and little experience with vineyards. That makes you an asset to me. I'd like to run some of my plans for the opening by you. Get your take on them. What do you say?"

What could I say? "I'm flattered, but I really don't know anything about the grand opening of a vineyard."

"Like I said, that's what makes you an asset. You come into this unbiased. You won't tell me how so-and-so did it. If you genuinely don't understand or like something I've planned, it's a pretty good guess that my standard visitor will see things your way. As we go through the vineyard today, I'll point out my plans and you feel free to give me your honest opinion, okay?"

I replied with a hesitant, "Okay."

A few workers strode past, each greeting Aidan by his first name. Clearly, they didn't stand on ceremony here. Just another reason for me to melt around him. He might have been born with a silver place setting in his mouth, but he didn't lord it over anyone.

He stopped in front of a tremendous open storage area that resembled a dairy barn or stable for Clydesdales—at least three floors high. Gigantic stainless steel towers, reaching nearly to the top of the vaulted ceiling, stood in rows like silver sentries from another planet.

"Most of our wines are stored in these vats while they age. We've got a barrel room, too, for the oak-aged wines."

I glanced up at the sheer size of the vats and strained my neck in the process. "You mean all of these are filled with wine?"

His gaze followed mine upward when he replied, "They *will* be by next week. At least until bottling."

"How many bottles do you make?"

"In a year? Right now, we do about ten thousand, total. I'm hoping to increase production exponentially over time. My father's first year at Coffield's Bluff, he did five thousand. Now, he's the 'wine king of Long Island.'" Once again, bitterness sharpened his tone. "Which is bizarre when you consider very few bottles of Long Island wine ever make it *off* the Island. I want to change that."

I couldn't help but wonder if doubling his father's first year production spoke of that same rivalry he'd mentioned between them. Still, I didn't utter my thoughts aloud. How could I?

I glanced past him and studied the landscape, intent on finding a way to change the subject. The colors of nature bloomed and delighted me with their artistic palette. I pointed to several long rows of gnarled trees laden with red and yellow fruit. "Are those apple trees?"

"Yup. Pear, too." He turned briefly to look at the orchard, then back to me. "I'm also growing peaches, raspberries, and blueberries back there."

Now, there was a contradiction I hadn't anticipated: smooth, suave Aidan Coffield as Farmer Brown. "That's pretty ambitious. Are you planning to corner the fruit market or something?"

He laughed. "No, it's more about cross-pollinating. Grapes pick up the flavors in the soil and air around them, which carries over into the wine. That's why a French cabernet won't taste the same as a cabernet from Chile or Australia. Long Island has a nice salt tang in the air, thanks to the Atlantic Ocean on the south and the Sound to our north. That tang flavors all the local wines. I'm hoping the fruit orchards will create a rich, sweet flavor the neighboring vineyards can't copy."

"Very clever." I studied the empty vines in the

foreground. "So where are all the grapes?"

"We just finished the picking yesterday. Most of the grapes are already going through the destemmer."

"Oh." I stifled a sigh. "Too bad. I would have liked to try my hand at picking them."

His forehead puckered, and a frown marred his features as he looked me up and down. "Most women I know wouldn't want to get dirty or sweaty doing such manual labor."

I arched an eyebrow. "After watching me create glass in thousand degree heat, you honestly believe a little dirt and sweat is an issue for me?"

Stroking a hand over his chin, he waited a beat before the smile returned to his face. "No. That's why I saved a small row for us to pick together."

Excitement leaped up inside me. I felt like a child who'd just received a pony for Christmas. "I get to pick the grapes?"

"Only if you really want to. If not, I'll have Raoul bring out the picker."

"Fat chance." *I* was the picker today. "Do I get to stomp them with my feet, too?"

"Not unless I want the Board of Health to close me down before I even open." He bobbed his index finger like a chastising parent. "If you're a good girl, I'll let you use the pressing machine."

An embarrassed laugh escaped my lips. "I know it's stupid, but whenever I think of pressing grapes for wine, I always remember that old *I Love Lucy* episode. You know that one? Where Lucy goes to a vineyard to learn about winemaking? She climbs into the vat to crush the grapes with her feet and winds up in a catfight with the other woman in the vat? Or would that be considered a *grape*fight?"

He shook his head slowly. "Actually, I'd call that 'farce.' Trust me, a 1950's sitcom is not indicative of winemaking, not in that era and definitely *not* today. In the modern age, we use machines. We've got harvesters, destemmers, pressers, even a label maker."

I pouted my disapproval. "The modern age hardly seems fun."

"Maybe not, but it's cleaner and a lot faster. And less expensive in the long run. Do you have any idea how long it takes to pick a season's grapes? A harvesting machine can clear an acre in about an hour and a half. By hand, that same acre takes six hours."

"Six hours?!" Panicked regret set in, and I gasped. "Oh my God. You didn't save a whole acre for us, did you?"

"No." His laughter rang out inside the cavernous room, easy and without sarcasm. "Just a row. An hour's work, tops." He pointed that index finger at me again. "I have to warn you. It's dirty work. In fact, come on into the office back here. You can lock up your things in my desk. You'll want to stow your purse and remove your jewelry. I'll also give you a work shirt so you don't ruin what you're wearing."

I looked down at my silk tee and fought back another sigh, this one of disgust. *Way to go, Nia. You totally overdressed for the occasion.* Okay, but no way I planned to admit my mistake. I waved him off with a careless air. "You don't have to lend me a shirt. It's really not necessary."

"Yeah, it is." He turned toward the door marked Employees Only, then looked back over his shoulder, a quirk of humor riding high on his lips. "Besides, I love the idea of you wearing something of mine."

There was that L word again. My caramel center liquefied to a puddle of mush.

Just like me, they long to be, close to you...

My heart and I were doomed.

~~~~

Paige

Talk about mind-blowing. Mom was back in town. After twenty-five years.

Somehow, I had to break the news to Nia before someone else found out and blabbed. I'd tried to explain to Mom that Nia had never forgiven her for her disappearing act and probably wouldn't stick around long enough to hear the other side of the story. She was Daddy's ally, one hundred percent.

Our mother, however, seemed to have pinned her hopes on some kind of sappy reunion. She planned to stay in town—at the ritzy Hermitage, *the* playground for moneyed elite in Snug Harbor. Apparently, Mom had cash to burn these days.

Not that she'd buy my affections. Or Nia's for that matter. No amount of money could ever atone for the years of anger, hardship, gossip, and heartbreak Mom had caused us.

All day Friday, I tried calling Nia, but got no answer. By two o'clock, when I still connected to her voicemail, annoyance took hold of me. "Oh, for God's sake," I snapped at the recording. "Childish much? Listen, Nia, when you're over your snit, call me. It's important." I slammed the phone onto the cradle.

"Now there's some sisterly love for you."

I looked up from my desk phone and into Sam's crinkled eyes. He stood a few feet away, that familiar smile warming my tummy like a shot of rum. His uniform only enhanced his he-man attitude, and my heart pitter-patted.

"Sam?" I managed to say through my quickly drying throat. "What are you doing here?"

"I had a disturbance call a block from here. Thought I'd pop in to make sure you were okay."

A chill of fright rippled across my bare arms. "Oh, my

God. What happened? Should I be worried?"

"Not unless you groomed Mrs. Pomerantz's poodle. The old bat just tried to demolish a row of sinks at Petopia Groomers because Tara gave the dog the wrong cut."

"Well, in all fairness to Tara at Petopia, Mrs. P. and her fleabag dog, Fury, are evil incarnate. Tara deserves a medal for attempting to take a pair of scissors to that fat ball of fur. Have you seen how low to the ground Fury walks? Take a good look. With his golden fur and sausage shape, I'd swear he's part gerbil."

"Fury's a gerboodle?"

I laughed so hard, tears came to my eyes. "Gerboodle. Oh, God, Sam, that's too funny."

He took a bow. "Thanks. I'm here all week." Sobering, he pointed to the phone. "So what's with you and Nia?"

I shrugged. "She's miffed at me. We had an argument yesterday, and now she's giving me the 'silent treatment.' Normally, I'd give her time and room to stew, but something's come up, and I can't play her game this time."

Without waiting for an invitation, he sat in the chair opposite my desk. "What's come up?"

I opened my mouth, then clamped my lips shut. It felt disloyal to discuss my mother's sudden return with Sam before Nia knew. Then again, this kind of news could be the catalyst to getting these two together. To blab, or not to blab…that was the question.

"Are you going to tell me, or do you plan to stare at me until moss grows on our northern sides?"

I took a huge breath to buy time and consider the consequences. "Before I tell you, you have to promise not to tell anyone—not even Nia. Especially not Nia."

Leaning forward, he rested his arm on the edge of my desk. "What is this, a slumber party? What's next? Truth or Dare?"

"I'm serious. I need to be the one to tell Nia. I just hope I get the chance before someone sees her and spews the news."

"What news? What exactly is going on?"

"Promise me first."

"Oh, for cripes…okay." He raised his right hand. "I solemnly swear not to divulge anything Paige says to me right now, or may I wake to find I've become a gerboodle." Lowering his hand, he widened his eyes at me. "Satisfied?"

Satisfied? I was downright tickled, but I steeled my emotions into a flat, "It'll do." A thought popped into my head, and I added, "You want some coffee?" I jumped to my feet, but his hand came down on my wrist.

"No time."

"Since when does a cop turn down coffee?"

He rolled his eyes as if we were still in high school. "Will you stop stalling and talk to me?"

"Okay, I'm sorry." I lowered myself into my chair again. "It's just hard. I never thought I'd actually say—"

"Paige!" He snapped his fingers near my nose. "Focus!"

At his bark, the words flew from my mouth. "Mom's come back to town."

The big bad cop suddenly looked stunned. "Wait. What? Mom? Whose mom? *Your* mom?"

"Imagine that," I said with a mirthless grin. "I've managed to leave you without a clever retort."

"Yeah, well, this is big." He leaned closer, his voice taking on a tender tone. "Are *you* okay?"

His concern touched a chord and left me flustered. "Yeah, I mean, no. That is…" I sighed. "I'm a mess. I've been a mess since she strolled in here yesterday to pay her respects to Dad. I still haven't told Nia that she's back. And if *I'm* a wreck, this is going to *destroy* Nia. I don't know what to do, how to tell her."

"What exactly did your mom say? How'd she explain herself to you?"

"It was weird," I admitted. "I don't think she expected

to see me here." I thought back to yesterday's reunion. "No, wait. I *know* she didn't expect to see me here. She came right out and said so."

I proceeded to give Sam the gory details. I was an accident victim, describing the truck that had run me down. When my voice started to shake with my words, he took my hand in his. Warmth and strength flowed into my veins. How did he do that? Did all policemen have the ability to offer comfort with a simple touch? Or was this one of the multitude of innate gifts Sam had in his arsenal to devastate the fairer sex? Either way, the contact seemed to ease some of my tension.

"I actually felt sorry for my mother when I heard her side of things," I concluded. "But you know Nia. She may be an artist, but she sees life in black and white. No gray ever. Of course, Mom is insisting on seeing her now that she's seen me. She seems to think Nia's going to fall weeping into her open arms."

"Because that's what you did?" Sam asked. No condemnation tinged the question and only compassion shone in his eyes.

I nodded. "It was automatic. The minute I saw her, I became eight years old again."

"That's understandable. When your mother left, you and Nia dealt with her loss the only way you knew how. Neither of you ever fully grew up. Part of you both stayed eight years old."

"Sez you," I retorted and stuck out my tongue.

"There's the proof right there," he said, pointing a finger at my face.

"Oh, please, Dr. Freud. Who died and made you my analyst?"

"I have a degree in psychology, Paige. It helps to understand people in my line of work."

"Yeah, well, let's hope that psych degree works better at solving crime than it does on me. You couldn't be more wrong about my grown up tendencies."

"Ya think?"

"I *know*, pal. Think about this. I mean, you may be onto something with Nia. Look at what she does for a living. She runs a gift shop. In her spare time, she makes little glass knick-knacks. I'm the one with the CPA license. I've got a very grown up job, thankyouverymuch. I handle other people's money." Guilt washed over me, hot and itchy, at the way I belittled my sister's career choice, but I wanted to prove my point.

"Tell me something, Paige. What was Nia's favorite subject in third grade?"

"Art," I replied without hesitation. "That was always her favorite subject."

"And you won the Math-a-lympics that year, didn't you?"

"Yes, but…" I let my argument trail off. Honestly, I couldn't deny his theory. He'd pegged us both. I considered my options. I still had to do my something different today, and suddenly, I knew what it was. I leaned toward him, a plea creasing my face. "Will you help me tell Nia about Mom?"

His hand on mine squeezed my fingers, reassured me. "If you need me, I'm here for you. *Whenever* you need me." He rose then, releasing my hand. "I should go. Are you going to the clambake tonight?"

Warm and fuzzy from this interlude and his promise, I murmured dreamily, "Most definitely."

"Good. I'll see you there." He leaned forward across my desk, brushed his lips against mine, soft and sweet.

Long after he strolled out of my office, I stared at the empty chair, my mouth tingling and my imagination creating fantasies of Sam and me.

Wait. Sam and *Nia*. I was just the future sister-in-law. That realization jolted me back to earth, exploding my dream bubble with the sharp stab of reality.

Chapter 22

Nia

The day passed in a blur of laughter and hard work. Most women probably would have preferred a short walking tour, maybe a sample tasting of different wines, and then a lunch of lobster thermidor or chilled shrimp salad at some open-air restaurant. Very classy and dignified: two things we've already established I'm not. Nor did I expect that kind of afternoon.

Instead, I dug in the dirt, checked out the root stock, picked scads of grapes, and learned how to use the destemmer and crusher. I even climbed into the driver's seat of the monstrous harvester, a tractor-style machine that rode over the rows of grapes and picked the vines clean without a casualty. I didn't actually use the machine, but Aidan did turn it on so I could get the full effect. Between the noise of the engine and the violent vibrations of the blades beneath me, I felt like I was riding a dragon. Back in the storage area, I designed and printed a personalized label, the way a couple might for wedding favors. Not that I made a wedding label. I chose to stencil my first name in a pink curlicue script. I resisted the urge to add Aidan's name and a big, goofy heart. Not easy, trust me. Instead, I opted for my birthdate, month and day only. Through it all, I offered my honest opinions and made some recommendations to enhance the guests' enjoyment at next month's grand opening.

Time flew by. I couldn't remember when I'd had so much fun—definitely not since childhood.

Afterwards, for lunch, Aidan grilled two marinated salmon steaks and roasted vegetables on a barbecue. We sat on the back terrace, an outdoor courtyard, which was only accessible from the house's interior. Vineyard visitors would never see the slate patio with colorful beds of impatiens, begonias, and early mums. This, he told me, was his private domain, a place for him to relax after a long day of toiling in the sun. I was flattered he'd share his utopia with me. The moment I stepped outside, the artistry of the site called to me. Sunlight dappled the area through the canopy of leafy trees. A miniature waterfall babbled over a rock formation.

Halfway through the meal, I glanced at the solar clock on the marble wall. After two o'clock already! I'd soon have to say goodbye and head home. My good mood dissipated. I didn't want to go. The more time I spent with Aidan, the more time I wanted to spend with him.

"Did you enjoy yourself today?" His question jolted me out of my doldrums.

Joy returned. "Are you kidding? I had a blast. I can't thank you enough."

He smiled and leaned back in his chair. "I'm glad to hear you say that because I'd like to see you for dinner later, maybe review some of your ideas then. Are you free?"

"Tonight?" I'd promised Paige I'd attend that dopey clambake tonight. "Oh, gee, umm…I can't. I have plans with my sister."

"Again with your sister?" On a dramatic sigh, he ducked his head. "Okay. This time, I guess I should back down. I've rearranged your plans with her three times already this week. I just hope she appreciates my sacrifice. Where are you two going anyway?"

I answered before I thought of the consequences. "The village clambake. It's totally stupid, I know, but—"

"You're going to that?" He sat up, his face aglow in the late afternoon sun. "Perfect. I can meet you there. This'll be great. You can introduce me to your twin."

Introduce him? As what?

Panic gripped my brain and cut off all routes to logic. Introduce him? To not only Paige, but the entire town? So they could all whisper behind my back, compare me to my mother, renew the gossip that had weakened my family? *The biggest problem with being Ogden Coffield's son is that nothing in my private life is very private.*

Including, I'd imagine, intimate details about his girlfriend. What if someone dug into my personal life now because I was seen with Aidan? What if they discovered the truth about my father? I could hear the jeers now. Mocking laughter rang in my ears. Good God, what was I doing? I no more belonged in this paradise than a mosquito. Did I have to face public ridicule before I'd accept the truth? A cold sweat broke out on my nape and down my back.

I looked at the clock again as if noticing the hour for the first time. I didn't have to fake a horrified expression. My panic had reached a fever pitch. "Ohmigod, I hadn't realized how late it is. I have to go." I shot to my feet. "Could you grab my purse from your office? I really have to fly. I'm so sorry. Everything was wonderful. Really."

Confusion etched lines in his brow, but he rose gracefully. "Of course. Come on."

I followed him back into the house, the gorgeous house where the walls now seemed to pen me in. Ninety minutes ago, I'd gawked at the clean lines of the beamed ceiling and marveled at the dream kitchen. Now all I wanted was to flee. Fast. My heart pounded against my rib cage, echoing thunder in my ears.

He led me into the office outside the storage room. Keys in hand, he unlocked the lowest drawer of the metal desk and pulled out my white leather satchel purse. "Here you go."

"Thanks." I didn't kiss him, barely waved as I pulled my bag against my chest and took off at a run.

When I neared the rental car, I fumbled inside my

purse for the key ring lying in the bottom. After yanking the keys out of the dark interior, I pushed the unlock button on the fob. The resounding click reassured me, and I dove into the safety of the driver's seat and slammed the door. My breath came out ragged, uneven, and my hands shook violently, but I managed to start the engine. As I gripped the steering wheel, I reached for my talisman, only to touch bare skin. Aidan hadn't returned my charm bracelet from the bottom of the desk drawer. No help for it. I'd have to write off the loss. I couldn't go back. Not now. I slid the gear into drive. My tires probably spat gravel when I hit the gas. I didn't care. All I knew was I had to get out of there.

I reached my street in record time. Thank God, no cop had clocked my speed. The roof of my house drew closer as I turned into the driveway. I yearned for the comfort of home, and I planned to fall apart the minute I locked the front door behind me. Already, tears filled my eyes, waiting to spill. Once I parked, I unclipped my seatbelt and stumbled out of the car. House key at the ready, I clambered up the stairs, my gaze focused on the doorknob that, with one simple twist, would bring me peace. There, I could come unglued, shatter into pieces, and then reassemble myself. Tomorrow, I'd find a way to go back to my normal life—the life I'd known before the day Aidan Coffield had strolled into my store and taken up residence in my heart.

On the top step, I stopped short. A woman sat in the rocking chair on my porch. She rose slowly, her arms outstretched toward me. Her blond hair was cut in a different style than I remembered, but the face had changed very little. She'd haunted my dreams for decades. I blinked, but she still stood there, a memory come back to life.

No. It couldn't be.

"Hello, Nia," my mother said. "It's so good to see you again."

The world spun, and I jerked my head past the railing

in time to vomit my lunch all over my rock garden.

~~~~

Paige

I still hadn't heard from Nia when the time came to attend the town clambake. I dialed both her house and her cell and connected to voicemail yet again.

I even called the store, but Iggy insisted he hadn't seen her since yesterday. "She was pretty upset when she came back from lunch," he told me. "But she wouldn't tell me what happened."

Yeah, well, no need for me to fill him in on that sorry episode. "Did she mention if she had plans today?" I asked.

"No, but that's not unusual. I mean, this is Nia we're talking about. Her days off are usually spent in that studio of hers. Tomorrow afternoon, I'll show up here and there'll be half a dozen new glass pieces on the sale shelf."

"Yeah, probably. Thanks, Iggy." I hung up.

Where on earth could she be? Even if she'd locked herself in her studio, she would have answered one of the two phones. Okay. Enough. I'd have to drive over and drag her out of the house by her hair.

I climbed into my Jeep, prepared for the ride to the south side of town.

Honestly, what did Sam see in my sister? Lately, she'd been acting so weird: forgetting meetings we'd set up, blowing me off, and that whole episode in my office yesterday. None of which made my matchmaking task easy, let me tell you.

After all the trouble I'd gone to in bringing her and Sam together, Nia had better have me as maid of honor at their wedding. And godmother of their first kid.

Yeah, I know. I'd spun one-eighty on my opinion of Sam Dillon. I admit, I'd allowed my teenage angst to color my adult opinion. He definitely wasn't the same jerk I'd known in high school. I can't say with any certainty that I owed my change of heart to Dara's thirty-day challenge, but I couldn't deny that if not for some things I'd done differently over the last week or so, I wouldn't have spent time with Sam and drawn this new conclusion. I mean, I honestly liked the guy now. I could see a future with him at Christmases and birthdays, quiet dinners on cold, winter nights.

If you need me, I'm here for you...

He really was a prince.

Nia sure was a lucky girl. I gripped the steering wheel tight enough to whiten my knuckles as an unfamiliar feeling crept into my psyche. Once again, I realized I envied my sister. How could I have never seen the wonderful man who lurked beneath the surface?

Finders keepers. Nia had seen the real Sam, and I wasn't about to stand in the way of true love because I'd finally woken up.

Thanks to the road block for tonight's clambake, I had to detour off Surf Lane. Guess who stood at the corner, directing traffic? Sam, of course. I slowed to a stop beside him and rolled down my window.

"Can't talk, sweetheart," he said. "Park on the grass, and I'll catch up with you later."

I wanted to tell him I was on my way to Nia's, but my mouth came out with something entirely different. "Thanks, Sam. I'll keep a cold beer waiting for you."

"Make it a cold water. I'll be off duty in a half hour, but still in uniform. Now, go."

As if to punctuate his order, the car behind me blared its horn. On a screech, I hit the gas, lurching my Jeep forward and onto the grass. Decision made. My sister was on her own.

When did I become Nia's babysitter anyway? She was a big girl. If she wanted to show up, she knew how to get

Duet in September

here. A car pulled up beside me, blocking me into my spot. No changing my mind now—even if I wanted to.

Maybe she wouldn't come. Okay with me. In fact, I kinda hoped she'd stay home. I didn't plan to discuss Mom's arrival in the midst of a crowd. And after all my frantic messages today, she'd demand answers. If she didn't show up tonight, I could meet her at the store before she opened for the day tomorrow, talk to her then. I'd even bring coffee. Yes, that would be so much better. I still didn't know what I'd say, and I really hoped I could get Sam to stop by to help me find the right words, but somehow, I'd muddle through, with or without him.

I climbed out of my car, joined the cluster of people heading toward the path that led down to the shore. The night was clear with a soft breeze and starlit plum skies.

On the beach, a large white tent hung over three rows of wooden picnic tables. Running in an L shape around the perimeter, a line-up of banquet tables draped in white cloths held Sterno racks with covered foil trays nestled inside. Angelo Rosado, the local deejay, had set up his booth against the dunes, his multi-colored van parked on the sand for the power to keep the music pumping. While people arrived, he played soft, instrumental jazz, perfect to allow greetings and conversation.

Another table, draped in red, held flyers and business cards for all the various area businesses. As I dropped a pile of my own promotional paperwork there, I perused some of the other services for possible new clients. I found a brochure for a local aerial advertiser, the cover photo showing a small plane flying over a crowded beach with a banner trailing behind it that read *Picture Your Ad Here!* Hmm…that might be an interesting way to drum up some business. I took one and stuffed it into my purse.

"Paige!"

I turned when I heard someone call my name, then stifled a groan. Terri strolled toward me, a large red plastic cup in her hand. Oh, boy. I was so not in the mood to deal with a drunken scene tonight.

My expression must have given away my disappointment, because she offered a self-deprecating smile and hoisted the cup higher. "No worries. It's diet soda." She leaned close to whisper. "I'm checking into rehab tomorrow."

"You are? Really?" At her enthusiastic nod, I threw my arm around her shoulders and hugged her tighter than a vise. "Oh, God, Terri, I'm so proud of you!"

She hugged me back, albeit with less fervor, thanks to the soft drink in her hand. "Yeah, well, this has been a long time coming. You and I both know that. Dr. Florentino hooked me up with a place in the Adirondacks, a mountain retreat sort of thing. She says they have the best results of any place in the area. I'm terrified, but excited at the same time."

"Can I do anything for you? Water your plants or something?"

"No. Everything's good. Is Nia here? I wanted to tell her, too."

I scanned the throngs of people milling in small groups around the tents. "I don't think so." A flush of guilt crept up my throat, but I quickly gulped it down. "Not yet. She's supposed to meet me here, but I didn't see her car when I parked. I've been calling her cell, but..." I shrugged and let Terri draw her own conclusion.

"Oh." Frowning, she sipped her drink, swallowed. "Well, if I don't get a chance to tell her, would you let her know I'm sorry and that I'll talk to her again in ten weeks? Totally sober for the first time since I was fourteen." She crossed her fingers. "I hope."

"Will do," I told her and hugged her once more. "We're all pulling for you, Terri. Go get well, and we'll have a great big party when you come back. We'll celebrate with chocolate and cheesecake and mani-pedis."

Duet in September

"Perfect!" Her laughter tickled my ear. "Thanks, Paige."

We broke apart and Terri strolled away, flagging down another person. This time, she'd stopped Gary, the scary bartender from The Lookout. I guessed she felt she had to make amends to some of us before she left Snug Harbor. I shuddered, thinking of how that overgrown ogre might react to Terri's approach. Not that I was much in the line of muscle, but I hovered nearby in case she needed back-up. She must have offered him the prettiest apology ever. Wonder of wonders, he not only hugged her, but then he kissed her cheek!

Imagine. Terri sober, Gary sweet, and Nia irresponsible. I stared up at the moon, expecting to see it change from white to blue, or a flock of pigs flying by. Nope. Totally normal night. Maybe something in the sea air brought out new personality facets in people I'd known for decades. Now, if Sam came up to me and told me he'd secretly loved me for years, the night would be perfect. Totally backwards, but perfect, nonetheless.

Was it wrong to wish Sam had fallen for me instead of my sister? No need to answer that. I still had a fully functioning conscience. I also had the hots for Sam. In a big way. The weight of my guilt turned my legs to buckets of wet cement, and I sank down onto the bench of the nearest picnic table. With my elbow propped, I rested my overtaxed head in my hand.

I must have sat that way for a while, my eyes staring out at the crowd, seeing no one, registering nothing. I came aware when I spotted Evan Rugerman talking to some tall, good-looking guy and pointing in my direction. At me?

No. Maybe someone near me. I looked around and when I turned back, Mr. Tall, Dark and Dreamy was heading toward me. Who *was* this guy? I kept my gaze pinned on him, waiting for the moment he'd veer off-course and approach someone else. As he drew nearer, the only thing that changed was his smile, which grew wider and warmer.

He seemed to know me, but honest to God, I'd never seen him before in my life. Trust me, I'd remember someone this gorgeous. He might have looked yummy far away, but up close, this man was downright decadent with dark chocolate eyes, cocoa hair, and a face meant for statues of gods in some faraway Greek isle.

"Paige?" He stopped in front of me, hand outstretched.

Confused but polite, I offered my hand and managed a curious, "Uh-huh."

He clasped my hand in his much larger one. "I'm Aidan. It's so nice to finally meet you."

"Uh-huh," I repeated. Apparently my usual gift of gab had deserted me.

My blank brain probably registered in my blank expression because he clarified, "I'm dating your sister...?"

"No, you're not," I blurted.

"Yes, I am." He cocked his head. "Aidan Coffield? Hasn't she mentioned me?"

I shook my head while my gray matter tried to absorb what he said, one sentence at a time. "You're dating Nia? Since when?"

"About two weeks now," he replied. "I'm sorry to disturb you."

He turned to walk away, but I had no intention of allowing him to drop a bombshell and escape unscathed. I needed answers.

"Hey, wait a sec! Don't go. Please?" When he looked back at me, I pointed to the opposite bench. "Sit, though, because looking up at you is giving me whiplash."

He smiled again, and I swear, fireworks lit up the darkness. "Now I see the resemblance," he said. "You two have the same sense of humor."

"Slow down, okay?" I told him as he joined me at the table. "I'm trying to catch up. You've been dating Nia for two weeks. What'd you say your name was?"

"Aidan Coffield?"

I blinked. "As in Coffield's Bluff and Coffield's Wharf? Those Coffields?"

"I prefer to think of myself as the owner of Piping Plover Vineyards, but yes, Ogden Coffield is my father."

"Wow." I couldn't form a coherent response. Was this a joke? Nia? Dating Ogden Coffield's son? How did these two even cross paths?

"Nia didn't tell you?"

"Nope." A shadow darkened his features, and I actually felt sorry for the guy. For his sake, I added, "Don't read anything into that. She and I haven't spent a lot of time together lately. And when we have…well…let's just say our communication has suffered from outside forces." Terri's drunken binge, our disagreement, and Mom's sudden reappearance, to name a few.

"It's my fault you haven't seen much of her," he replied. "That's one of the reasons I wanted to come here tonight and introduce myself. I know she's cancelled plans on you a few times recently. To spend time with me."

And not tell me. Exactly how often had my sister lied to me? "When did you last see her?"

"This afternoon." He frowned.

"She was with you today?" What kind of game was Nia playing now? Why hadn't she told me about Aidan Coffield? What other secrets did she keep?

"I was supposed to meet her here tonight," he said. "Do you know where she is?"

Now I frowned. "No. I've been trying to reach her all day. Obviously, she was with you earlier, which explains to some degree why she didn't answer her cell. I'm guessing she changed her mind about coming, though. She's probably in her studio."

"The hot spot in the carriage house?"

"You know about her hot spot?"

"Sure. I was there with her last week."

Holy moly. He really had spent time with my sister. A lot of time from the sound of it. So how come she hadn't shown up here tonight?

I think I knew. Because she didn't want me to know about this guy. No. Not me. Sam. She must have given up on Sam.

Poor Sam. How on earth could he possibly compete against Aidan Coffield? On paper, the two men had a lot in common. Both good-looking, both seemed to care about Nia. Aidan had money, but Sam had waited years to win Nia. That kind of loyalty deserved the reward, in my opinion. Now, though, Sam would have to move fast, before this guy completely stole Nia's heart.

I shot to my feet, which totally took Aidan Coffield by surprise. "You know what? I hafta go see somebody right now. Are you sticking around?"

He shrugged. "I told you, I'm meeting Nia here."

Not if I could help it. "Okay, I'll see you in a bit then. If I run into my wayward sister in the meantime, I'll send her over here." *Yeah, right.* "Nice meeting you."

Chapter 23

Paige

I took off like a bullet, past the clusters of people coming down to the beach while I climbed up toward the parking lot. A hundred mentions of "excuse me" later, I ran face-first into Sam. Even if his uniform buttons hadn't cut into my cheek, I still knew him from the familiar sensation of his arms around me.

"Slow down before you hurt yourself," he admonished gently. "Where are you off to? And where's my water?"

I pulled away from him and waved off his questions. "Forget that. There's something I have to tell you. Right now."

"Oh?"

"Yes." I yanked on his hand, dragging him toward the closed snack shack. We'd need privacy for what was about to happen. The lights around the building illuminated most of the area, except for a small patch of shadow near the stairs leading down to the outdoor shower. Naturally, I led Sam to that darkened place. When I was sure we were out of earshot and sight of any nosy townspeople, I told him, "I just ran into Aidan Coffield on the beach. Do you know him?"

Sam appeared pensive for a moment. "Sort of. I've spoken to him once or twice. On the phone. Why?"

There was no easy way to say this without hurting him. Better to say it quickly—get him moving to Nia asap. "Did you know he's dating Nia?"

"He is? Whoa. That was fast."

Fast? Whoa? Was that all he could say? On a shriek of frustration, I stamped my foot. No time for delicacy. I had to go straight for his jugular. "Idiot! Don't you realize what this means? If you don't tell her how you feel now, you're going to lose the woman you've loved for years to some guy who won't waste time sweeping her off her feet."

He had the nerve to smirk. "You think so? I mean, I'm not one hundred percent sure she feels the same way about me…"

"Trust me," I snapped. "She's crazy about you. Why wouldn't she be? You're amazing. And sexy. And everything any woman could possibly want. Besides that, you love her. So stop waiting for Cupid to hit her with an arrow already."

"Maybe you're right," he replied. "Maybe I should let her know how I feel."

"Yes!"

Before I could say anything more, he wrapped an arm around my waist, pulled me against him, and planted his mouth on mine.

I lost myself. This man's kiss not only curled my toes, I swear he curled my hair. He definitely managed to curl around my heart and squeeze. I clung to him for a very enjoyable minute until sanity returned.

I finally jerked away and when I could speak again, I voiced my outrage. "Okay, clearly, you don't need the practice, Sam. So stop fooling around with me and get out of here. Tell Nia how you feel."

Grinning, he pulled me up against him again. "Nia knows how I feel, Paige. I love her."

Even though I knew it, a piece of me died when he said it. My heart slowed, and breathing became a Herculean labor. In the game of love, lucky Nia won the grandest prize.

"I love Nia like a sister," he clarified. While his index finger traced my cheek, he murmured against my ear, his hot breath sending shivers down my spine. "It's you I want. It's you I've always wanted."

My knees buckled. "Me?" I stared up at him, shock

muffling my voice to a whisper. "You love *me*?"

He nodded once, a slow, certain motion that sped up my heart rate and lightened my lungs. "Is that so hard to believe? I've loved you since the day you took a swan dive at the senior picnic. I'd always admired you, but when I carried you out of the bushes, I realized I loved you. I still love you. I want to take care of you when you're sick, make you laugh when you're crying, and hold you when you're scared."

I looked up at the moon. No blue tinge. No pigs. A perfect night. Not backwards at all. But, still. Since high school? "Why didn't you ever say anything?"

That eyebrow of disbelief arched in my direction. "On the off-chance you'd take me seriously? Or to make you stay in this hick town?" He shook his head. "No way, sweetheart. You needed to get away from here. When you were living in Albany, I told Nia that if you ever came back of your own free will, I wouldn't let you leave again without a fight. But I didn't want to fight *you*. You had to decide you want to be here for good, that this is home. Once you did, I planned to go after your heart full throttle."

The words from my argument with Nia roared through my ears. *I came back of my own accord, took over Daddy's business of my own accord, and I'm staying of my own accord. Because I want to be here.* This *is home. Not Albany. Snug Harbor.*

"Nia told you what I said the other day," I realized aloud. "There was no disturbance at Petopia, was there?"

"Of course there was." His dark chuckle rumbled through me. "But…Paige, sweetheart, did I really need to check on you because Mrs. Pomerantz—all ninety pounds of her—got angry at the groomer a block away?"

Sucking helium couldn't make me float higher. I had to smile at how blind I'd been, and for how long. Even Lou Rugerman had tried to tell me how Sam felt. Seems everyone knew but me. "You really love *me*?"

His thumb brushed my chin. "I really love *you*. More importantly, how do you feel about me?"

I pursed my lips at him. "Kiss me again and find out for yourself."

So he did.

~~~~

Nia

I didn't want to let my mother into my house. Honestly, I couldn't. Grandma would haunt me for a lifetime if I let this woman cross her threshold. I know how harsh that sounds, but seeing my mother again after all these years was not going to be one of those sappy, Hallmark Channel reunions. I had my reasons for wanting nothing to do with her, reasons I'd never shared with Paige, or even my father. Some wounds cut too deeply.

Once I stopped ruining my azalea bushes with my lunch, I raced past her and into my house. I bolted straight for the bathroom where I quickly brushed my teeth and gargled, although a quart of mouthwash wouldn't remove the sour bile taste.

When I stepped out again, my mother loitered in my foyer, a half-smile on her face. "Not exactly the greeting I anticipated."

I fisted my hands at my sides. "No? Try this one on for size. Get out."

Sighing, she shook her head. "Paige warned me you'd be difficult."

My stomach plummeted, and I gripped my abdomen. "Paige? You've seen Paige already?" An occurrence I would have prevented, given the opportunity. This woman was poison, and I would never let her hurt my sister again. "When?"

"Yesterday."

Oh, God. Poor Paige. She must be a mess of confused emotions right now. And where was I when she needed my support? I hadn't checked my phone—either of them—all day.

"You should have heeded her warning," I told the woman in my hall.

She was *not* my mother. Not in the myriad ways a woman mothered a child. I didn't recall any warm, fuzzy memories of bandaging skinned knees, baking cupcakes for birthdays, help with homework, or makeup tips. All I remembered was a note and, years later, a doctor's puzzled statement.

"Nia, please." She held out her hands as if to reach for me.

For what? A hug? Too late. By about twenty-five years.

"I have nothing to say to you." My head pounded. Anger heated my skin from the inside out. A red mist obscured my vision. On trembling limbs, I managed to reach the staircase and my hand clutched the bannister. "You wanna see how 'difficult' I can be? Watch this. Get out. Now. You found your way here, find your way out. Don't make me call the police."

If she attempted an argument, I never heard a word over the high-pitched buzzing in my brain. I had already deleted her from my presence. I climbed the stairs, then strode down the short hall into my bedroom where I collapsed onto my bed. As I'd promised myself on the drive home, I shattered. While tears flooded my pillowcase, I pounded my fists on the mattress.

Today had officially become the worst day of my life—worse than the day my mother left, worse than when Daddy died. The ringing telephone on my bedside table blared, and I glanced up to see the Caller ID illuminate. Paige's cell.

I had a pretty good idea why she was calling, and I let

her go to voicemail. No great urge to hear her message now. Curling into a ball, I clutched a bedroll to my abdomen. I only regretted throwing up in front of that woman. I would have preferred to retain my dignity. Let her know that her sudden appearance meant nothing. Less than nothing.

Images of my mother's hurt expression melded into the same look on Aidan's face when I sped away from him at the vineyard. I squeezed my eyes shut to seal out the memories. More pain I could lay at Mom's feet.

When I opened my eyes again, the room was black, except for the greenish glow from my alarm clock, which read 2:13 a.m. I'd fallen asleep for nearly ten hours. No use in trying to climb under the covers. I might as well go down to my hot spot, work on my new autumn pieces.

I changed into more appropriate work attire and grabbed my cell out of my purse. When I powered on, the phone buzzed. The screen lit up. *22 Missed Calls* and *7 Voicemail Messages* blared at me. I dialed the number to retrieve my messages as I headed downstairs. I knew what I'd hear.

Sure enough, message after message came from Paige, each one growing more impatient. She started with, "Hey, we need to talk. It's important. Call me back as soon as you can. Bye." Two calls later, she segued into, "Childish much? Listen, Nia, when you're over your snit, call me. It's important."

Snit? What snit? I nearly slapped my forehead when I suddenly remembered. I hadn't spoken to her since our disagreement in her office. Did she now know I'd been testing her? That I'd given Sam the green light? Had he said anything yet? Maybe one of her other messages would give me a clue.

By the time I reached message number six, I heard, "Forget it. I'm stopping by the store first thing tomorrow morning. I'll bring the coffee. Extra larges because we've got *lots* to talk about."

That Paige sounded happy, excited, in love. God, I hoped so.

The voice on the last message had me fumbling the phone. Aidan. "Hey. I don't know what happened tonight, or this afternoon for that matter, but you can rest easy. I won't bother you anymore." There was a long pause before he added in a ragged tone, "I really thought better of you, Nia."

Yeah. Me, too.

Despite the sting to my heart and conscience, I had to let him go without a follow-up call or explanation. Better he dislike me now than despise me later.

The biggest problem with being Ogden Coffield's son is that nothing in my private life is very private.

Understandable. And the problem with being a Wainwright was that we had too many skeletons in our closet. Each one more gruesome than its predecessor. If Aidan ever learned the truth, he'd count his blessings we kept our interludes a secret. Especially with his vineyard set to open next month. The last thing he needed was a scandal attached to his name—even through his casual associates.

Stuffing my phone into the pocket of my work pants, I opened the front door and stepped out onto the porch. From the corner of my eye, I caught movement to my right. A shadowy figure rose. What the—?

I quickly reopened the door and jetted back inside. After securing both the lock and the deadbolt, I flipped on the porch light.

The woman moved into the illuminated beam, and her blond hair registered on my frantic brain. My heart took longer to calm down.

"Are you out of your mind?" I demanded. "What kind of lunatic sits on a porch all day and all night?"

"Someone who has a lot to say and is willing to wait for the opportunity," the woman replied. "Nia, please. Talk to me."

Apparently, my mother hadn't left when I told her to. She'd remained here, waiting to pounce on me. The woman must have a death wish, or more likely, she had a yen for men in uniform and *wanted* to be arrested. May as well grant her last wish and have her tossed in the county jail.

"I'm calling the police," I shouted through the door and pulled my cell from my pocket.

"Fine. Go ahead. Be sure they use their sirens and flashing lights when they show up here in the dark of night. They can arrest me, carry me screaming off your porch, and I'll be back the minute I make bail. Then we can start the process all over again. And again and again."

I shivered at the idea of my neighbors watching this drama unfold, which was, no doubt, her intention. The woman wasn't just insane; she was diabolical.

"Or," she added, "you can open the door now, give me fifteen minutes of your time, and be done with me, once and for all. Which would you rather do, shortcake?"

Shortcake. No one had called me shortcake in decades. Not only because my height made the nickname ludicrous, but also because my mother was the only person in my life who knew the secret behind that particular moniker. As a child, I'd hated my red hair—how it set me apart from my blond twin and mother and my dark-haired father. Mom told me I was a strawberry blonde, like the doll, Strawberry Shortcake.

"Shortcake?" she repeated.

I lifted my gaze to the ceiling and begged Grandma's forgiveness. On a sigh of defeat, I opened the door. My mother's smile seemed superior. To keep from attempting violence, I focused my attention on the gingerbread scroll beyond her head while I muttered, "Come in. Let's get this over with."

"Thank you."

As she stepped inside, I swept an arm past the

staircase. "I'm sure you remember where the kitchen is in this house."

I had no intention of offering her any hospitality. This was war. Despite the years that had passed since her death, I still felt Grandma's comforting presence in the kitchen. I'd take any allies I could find—even the dead ones.

I followed behind my mother, pausing only to turn on the lights when we reached the curved archway near the kitchen. Instantly the room sprang to life and with it, my Grandma. Warm, golden cabinetry, gleaming appliances, the soft, homey touches she and I had both added over the decades put me at ease. I could practically feel my grandmother's arms around me, an invisible afghan of comfort and support.

I stood tall, a force of steely outrage, as I looked down on my diminutive mother. She might be tiny, with a designer suit that gave the appearance of a middle-aged professional woman, but I knew better. I knew a shark in Donna Karan when I saw one.

"Okay." I folded my arms over my chest. "You've got ten minutes." I'd reserve the additional five minutes for my own questions.

She didn't argue. Instead, she stared at me, an insipid grin pasted on her traitorous face.

"Time is ticking," I reminded her.

"I'm sorry. I'm just…drinking you in. You're beautiful, Nia. Stunning, really."

"Uh-huh." I was soooo not buying her butter. I rolled my hands. "Would you mind speeding this up? I have work to do."

She leaned a hip against the butcher block counter, the action so like Paige, I sucked in a sharp breath. "Where would you like me to start?"

"Oh, I don't know. Maybe why you left. Or how about why you suddenly felt the need to come back after twenty-five years?"

"I came back to say goodbye to your father."

"Really?" I retorted. "The note you left all those years ago wasn't sufficient?"

"That'll do, Nia," she snapped. "I understand you have some animosity toward me, and I will even admit you don't have to love me, but you will grant me respect. I *am* your mother."

"You lost that title, and the respect it garners, the day you chose some guy with a fat wallet over your family." My words shook, emotion rattling me. Hurt, anger, and confusion spewed from my lips. "Do you know Daddy died calling *your* name? He never forgot you, never gave up on the idea that you might come back. Up until he died, your clothes were still in his closet—just in case. In all those years, you never called, never wrote, never took a moment to think about him—or your daughters, for that matter."

She dropped her gaze to my terracotta floor, the first attack of conscience I'd seen in her since she appeared on my porch hours ago. "You're right, and I'm sorry."

"Sorry?" I repeated, my tone growing shrill. "You think I let you in here for an apology?"

Her head snapped up, and her hands flew to her hips. "Then what *do* you want from me?"

"One thing." I held up my index finger and waited two beats of my heart. "I want the name of our real father."

My mother gasped, and her eyes rounded to perfect azure marbles in her pale complexion. "H-how did you f-find out?"

At least she had the sense to refrain from lying to me. Score one for her. Which made the current tally a thousand to one, in my favor. "Doesn't matter how I found out. I want the truth. Not some fairy tale like you probably told my sister."

"Paige." She said the name as if it had just come to her. "Does Paige know?"

I remained ramrod straight, the power of right keeping

me stern and implacable. "That Daddy wasn't our real father? No. At least, *I* never told her."

"Who told *you*?"

"Daddy's oncologist. They worried he'd need a blood transfusion and tested me as a candidate. Imagine my surprise to learn that he's not my biological father. That he couldn't possibly be my father." I relaxed my posture and leaned on the counter, feigning a conversational stance far from the turmoil raging through me. "So who is?"

Her gaze dropped to the floor again, and she shook her head. "Not now. Don't ask me now."

I quirked a brow. "Excuse me?"

Her shout nearly shook the copper pans off my overhead rack. "I said not now! I won't tell you now. Not when you're so full of hatred you couldn't possibly understand."

The confession hit me like a slap across the face. "Oh, well, that's ducky, isn't it? What's to understand, *Mother*? Exactly how many men were you sleeping with nine months before our birth?"

Ruddy color spotted her cheeks. "My marriage is none of your business."

"My parentage is."

She seemed to collapse into herself, shrinking before my eyes, and she sighed. "You're right. We have nothing to discuss. I made a mistake coming here. I can see that now."

"At last, we agree on something."

As she skirted past me, I fired the last volley. "I'll be seeing the police for a restraining order tomorrow on behalf of Paige and me. Go back to whatever hole you crawled out of. You're not welcome here."

The minute the front door slammed, I sank to the cool kitchen floor and rested my head on my bent knees. I didn't know who I hated more: my mother or myself.

Chapter 24

Paige

By eight o'clock the next morning, I sat in my Jeep outside the rear entrance to Nia's store. Sam had promised to meet me in the parking lot. I have to admit, just thinking about him gave me the warm and fuzzies. Knowing he'd loved me for years turned those warm and fuzzies into hot and gooeys. I still couldn't believe how wrong I'd been, how I'd misconstrued his feelings and Nia's.

I had to hand it to Dara Fitzsimmons. Thanks in part to her thirty day challenge, I'd found love. And in a weird way, I'd also been reunited with my mother. Which brought me full-circle to Nia and the reason I was sitting here when I'd normally be snuggled under my comforter in my air-conditioned bedroom at this time of morning.

Sam's cruiser pulled up next to my Jeep, and my heart thump-thumped. *Nia*, I reminded myself. *Think of Nia.* I was about to ruin her day.

As he unfolded his sexy bod from the driver's seat, I quipped, "Did you bring your Taser?"

After closing his car door, he leaned an arm on my roof and smirked. "Oh, come on, sweetheart. It won't be that bad. Nia's an adult. I know she'll be surprised by the news, maybe a little shocked, but I seriously doubt she'll become violent."

I cocked my head and twisted my lips. "Have you ever talked to Nia about our mother? Trust me. This is *not* going to go well."

"I think you underestimate your sister."

"I think *you* underestimate my sister." I shuddered at imagined destruction: locusts, famine, boiling seas. Okay, maybe not. Still, Nia's rage wasn't pretty. Thank God I

Duet in September 246

brought a sacrifice to appease her wrath.

Reaching into the passenger seat, I scooped up the cardboard carryout tray that held three coffees. Yes, three. I was an attached woman now and made a conscious effort to think about my guy's likes and dislikes. In the coffee catalog, Sam preferred black with two sugars. Real coffee, he'd told me. None of that girlie sludge with foamed milk and chocolate syrup.

He swung open my door and took the coffees from me, allowing me to step out unburdened. Nice. Having a boyfriend sure came in handy.

One deep inhale for courage, and I strode forward, prepared to battle the Nia Monster. I pulled open the back door and stepped inside to silence. An ominous silence. I'm not exaggerating. Nia loved noise and chaos. She claimed her brain couldn't focus in a quiet room. To enter the store twenty minutes before opening and hear nothing put me on edge. I stared back at Sam in confusion. He jerked his head forward. Into the Valley of Death...

"Nia?" I called. Uncertainty raised my voice an octave. "Are you here?"

"One sec," came her muffled reply. "I'm in the storeroom."

I stiffened. The words were perfectly normal, but the tone not so much. Something was off. *Very* off. I leaned backward and, through clenched teeth, murmured, "I don't like this, Sam."

He nudged me forward with the corner of the cardboard tray. "Don't be silly. Go on."

I inched into the store. Fine hairs danced on my arms. My stomach kinked. I reached the customer area and stood, waiting, as if for the firing squad to appear. No firing squad, just my sister came into view. My heart cracked. She looked more brittle than burnt paper.

"Well, well," she said with a grim smile. "I wasn't expecting Sam with you. Does this mean you two are officially an item?"

Concern overshadowed my earlier happiness. "Nia, you look awful," I blurted. "What's wrong?"

"Bad night." She waved off my concern. "But you two obviously had a great one. I want details." She reached for one of the covered cups in the cardboard tray. "And coffee."

"What do you mean, a bad night?" I demanded. "What happened?"

"Coffee first."

I fiddled with the cups Sam held until I found the one labeled with a black x in the skim milk box. "Here. Sip. Then talk."

Taking the offered cup from me, she shook her head. "I have a better idea. *You* talk while I sip."

I hesitated and glanced at Sam, who gave me a curt nod—the mute equivalent of his vocalized, "Go on, sweetheart."

"Umm…okay. Something's come up that you should know about," I began. No, that wasn't right. "Well, actually it's not really a some*thing*. It's more a some*one*."

Again, Nia waved me off. "No, no. I'm not interested in who's come up. I probably already know. I want to know what happened between the two of you." She used her coffee cup like a conductor's baton to point at Sam and me.

Wait. What? I actually did a double take. "You 'probably already know'? What does that mean?"

"Never mind. Come on. Tell me what's up with you two."

"No." Impatience spiked my temper. "What's going on with *you*, Nia? You've been acting weird for weeks now."

The smile she offered looked grim. "Don't be ridiculous. Nothing's going on."

"No? Two words. Aidan Coffield."

Her complexion paled, and her eyes widened, but she recovered quickly. "Who?"

"Don't play games, Nia. I met him last night at the clambake. He said you were supposed to meet him there, but apparently you stood up both of us. He also said you'd been dating him for weeks. Weeks. You never even mentioned him."

"There was nothing to mention. His stepbrother hit my car. He felt guilty about it and took me to dinner to make up for all my inconveniences."

"And the visit to your hot spot?"

"Oh, for God's sake. He owns a vineyard. When he was in the shop, he saw my grape lamps and wanted to order them for his grand opening."

A memory tingled my brain cells. "The flowers! He's the guy who sent you flowers."

Pink color flooded her cheeks, and she toyed with the lid on her coffee cup. "Yes."

"The *old* guy," I reminded her.

Her head shot up, defiance shooting like neon from her eyes. "Okay, so I lied. What's the big deal?"

"The big deal is why." I propped my hands on my hips. "Why didn't you say anything about him? He seems like a super nice guy who's genuinely interested in you. Why keep him a secret?"

"Because there was nothing to say. You really think someone like Aidan Coffield would be interested in a relationship with me?"

"Why wouldn't someone like Aidan Coffield be interested in you?" Sam asked before I could. "You're attractive, bright, fun. What's not to be interested in?"

I would have hugged him right there if Nia hadn't snapped.

"Yeah, right." Her bitter laughter stung the air. "Especially when he finds out my tramp of a mother has come back to town. Isn't that the most charming news?"

I gasped. "You *do* know."

"She came to see me yesterday." Her voice grew

sharper than icy steel. "Looking for a touching reunion. I threw her out. Which reminds me, Sam, I'm going to want a restraining order. You can help us with that, right?"

"Us?" I asked.

She didn't elaborate or wait for Sam to provide details. "That's why I didn't show up at the clambake last night. Not because I was avoiding you or Aidan. Mom showed up, and we had words. Very hurtful, angry words."

"Well, I'm both sad and relieved to hear that." A new voice intruded into the conversation.

And there he stood, the subject of our conversation, in the aperture between the hall and the store's main area.

"Aidan." My sister lit up like nighttime on Broadway, all aglow in flushes of pink and red. "What are you doing here?"

He held up her charm bracelet, a gift from Grandma years ago that Nia wore constantly. "You left this at my house yesterday. I planned to return it to you at the clambake last night, but you didn't show. At first, I thought you stood me up, especially after I met your sister and she knew nothing about me." He turned toward me and smiled. "Hi again."

"Nice to see you, Aidan."

"Same here." He handed the bracelet to Nia, placing it into her palm. "This morning, I found this on my dining room table and realized I might have judged you too harshly in my message last night. I thought I'd take a chance and stop by. I was going to wait until you opened the store, but your back door was unlocked, and I heard voices in here. So I just came in. I hope that's all right."

Nia's gaze stayed locked on him. "Yes, of course. Thank you."

The minute her fingers made contact with his, her whole face took on a nuclear glow. I stole a glance at Sam who shrugged. This was serious. No matter what she might say in denial, my sister was head-over-heels, stars-in-her-eyes, rainbows-and-unicorns in love.

I didn't need to be reminded that a week ago, I was convinced she was in love with Sam. But the electricity zinging between Nia and Aidan Coffield made my hair crackle. A blind, anti-social hermit could feel the heat. While I might be a little dense about matters of the heart at times, I was not a blind, anti-social hermit. What I saw between my sister and Aidan was love. Real love.

A sharp elbow nudged my shoulder blade, and I turned to face Sam. "Let's go," he murmured. "You and Nia will have to catch up later."

We slipped out the way we came in, and I doubt either one of them ever noticed. The minute I stepped into daylight, I exploded with excitement. "Holy Valentine, Batman! Did you see those two? They are seriously hot for each other." I shook my hand as if to cool down my flaming fingers. "Whew! Do you think we look like that?"

He pulled me up against him. "I don't know. Let's find out."

His lips touched mine, and I forgot all about my sister, Aidan Coffield, my mother, and everything else but love. Sweet, gooey, warm, fuzzy love. Mine.

~~~~~

Nia

My mouth dried to dust. While my heart danced in my chest that Aidan had come back, my brain groaned in defeat for the very same reason.

"What happened last night?"

His question jolted me back to reality.

"Nothing." I opened the cash register to check the small change situation. Fives. I was low on fives. I'd have to take a trip to the bank at lunchtime. Pick up some extra singles to tide us over during the long day.

"Nia."

Why did he always have the ability to make my name sound like a caress? My knees wobbled, but I bolstered myself against the stool behind the counter. I couldn't look at him. One glimpse of his dark eyes, if I even sensed caring in his expression, I'd fold.

"You should go," I said through my dry throat and touched the heart-shaped charm dangling from the silver chain on my wrist. "Thanks for bringing back my bracelet."

"Nia, look at me."

On a deep breath, I looked up. I couldn't stop the tears from shining in my eyes. And of course, he noticed. A sympathetic sigh escaped his lips.

His thumb traced my chin. "What's wrong, Nia? Talk to me."

I shook my head. "Go, Aidan. Please."

"No." This time, iron laced his tone. His posture stiffened, and he folded his arms over his chest. "You owe me an explanation, and I'm not leaving until I get it."

Too much upheaval and too little sleep brewed a noxious cocktail in me. I spewed with the force of an active volcano. "I *owe* you? For what? For a few weeks spent in your company? Tell me, Mr. Coffield, exactly how much do you charge your dates? Is that where your family's wealth originated?" I threw my hands in the air. "That must be what we've been doing wrong all these years. Wainwright women are known to give it away for free while Coffield men apparently charge by the hour."

His lips twisted downward. "Found out about the family coffers, huh? Well, you can't say I didn't warn you."

I punched a button on the register and when the drawer popped open, I grabbed a fistful of twenties. "Here. Is that enough to pay for your time these last few weeks?" I slapped the money on the counter. "Now we're even. Go."

"I should have known you were too good to be true."

He didn't touch the cash, but he leaned closer over the counter, all pretense of civility erased from his face. He smoldered, each word hard and hot as buckshot. "But I had no idea you were so seriously deranged. You hide it well. Keep the money. You need it more than I do. Spend it on analysis."

"Get out," I growled.

For a long minute, neither of us moved. We simply glared at each other. Furious energy flowed in the breath of space between us.

"Goodbye, Nia." He turned toward the rear of the store, and I gripped the counter's edge to keep from running after him.

This was for the best. I couldn't continue falling for him.

I watched him walk away, each stride another crack in my heart. The rear door opened, then closed again. I felt the air change, become heavy and cold. Shivering, I went about opening the store for another business-as-usual day.

I managed to get through the work day, zombie-like, but functioning. Afterwards, I drove home and climbed the stairs to the front door. No one sat on my porch tonight. Good, I told myself. The only person I'd welcome right now was an axe murderer.

I let myself in and tried to breathe in the comforts of home, but came away chilled and empty. Food held no appeal, nor did sleep. Only one place could soothe my frazzled nerves. I changed my clothes and headed for my hot spot.

While my speakers blasted an assortment of raucous classic rock, I focused on creating new works in glass. I had no particular designs in mind. My brain couldn't seem to land on any particular idea so I just lost myself in the routine of heating, swirling, blowing, and shaping. Both my cell and house phone rang at least a dozen times. I ignored them. I didn't want to talk to anyone, didn't want to relive memories of the last few weeks. I only wanted peace. Impossible, I know, but hey. I could wish, right?

Funny thing about glass: turn the heat up high enough, and it adapts to any shape with the right amount of cutting and scraping. People, on the other hand, more fragile than glass, tended to disintegrate under fire. I hated myself for what I'd said to Aidan today. Poisonous words meant to kill any tenderness he might harbor. I shook off the image of his stricken expression and chugged from my water bottle to remove the bitter taste from my mouth.

Hours later, David Lee Roth wailed at me to *Jump* when I assessed the night's work. I placed the finished pieces in the lehr and stared in chagrin. I'd created half a dozen robin's egg blue wine goblets, etched with stick figure piping plovers in the center of each bowl. Not hard to see where my mind had taken up residence. The cracks in my heart splintered, and I sank to the floor, a weepy mess.

A mere day had passed, and I missed him already. After my mother left, Paige, Dad, and I had struggled to find a new normal. Now I'd struggle again to find a life without Aidan. I'd known him less than a month, yet in that brief time he'd tied my world—and my heart—into knots that kept him wrapped up inside me.

If I were a different person, living a totally different life, I would have clung to him, maybe even married him eventually. *If* I could have been worthy of a prince like him. I didn't care about his family money, although I would have preferred he had a lot less zeros attached to his bank balance. His pedigree, on the other hand, I didn't deserve.

The Coffields were Long Island royalty, and I was the daughter of the town tramp. I didn't even know the man who fathered me. He could've been a criminal, for all I knew. I bet the contessa would be *thrilled* to see her son linked to a woman with a mottled past. Didn't every woman in high society want a bastard for a daughter- in-law?

I was getting ahead of myself, of course. Aidan and I had barely started dating, and here I was anticipating marriage trouble. Not that we'd ever have reached that stage. Eventually, I would have had to tell him the truth. Once he knew about my unknown father, my mother's abandonment, he'd realize I was shoddy goods and move on to some Hamptons princess. I had hoped the pain would be less brutal now rather than later, but tonight, my heart felt shredded.

My cell phone rang again, rattling against the insulated box on the wall. In the break between songs blaring from my speakers, I caught the familiar vocals of Twisted Sister. Paige. Well, even talking to my sister beat sitting on a dirty floor, mourning what could never be. I eased myself to a standing position and carefully removed the phone from its safe haven. Hitting the connect button, I placed the phone to my right ear, and plugged a finger in my left ear.

"What?" I shouted over the music.

"I'm in your yard," Paige shouted back. "Drop what you're doing and come out with your hands up."

Cute. Apparently, my sister, happy in love with the town sheriff, assumed law and order humor would amuse me. She was dead wrong.

"Give me five minutes." I could have said no, but what would be the point? She'd only hang around outside until I finally made an appearance. Mom might wait ten hours, but Paige could stay for weeks. I finished cleaning up, turned off the equipment, and silenced the music before stepping out into the late summer night.

The light sea breeze chilled my overheated skin. Crickets chirped. A rogue firefly blinked yellow-green in search of a mate. I knew exactly how desperate that bug felt.

"It's about time." My sister stood outside in the copse of maple trees that separated my yard from my neighbor's.

She wasn't alone.

At first, I thought Sam had come with her. As I tread closer, I realized the shadow behind Paige was much too small to be big, burly Sam. I sucked in a sharp breath when her companion's identity crystallized in my head.

"Why'd you bring her here?" I demanded of Paige.

My mother stepped out of the tree line. "Because I want to clear up a few misconceptions with both of you."

I turned toward my house. "I have nothing to say to you."

"You made the accusation, Nia Elise Wainwright," my mother snapped. "And now you'll give me an opportunity to defend myself. You owe me that much."

I whirled on her, my hands fisted to keep my claws sheathed. "You're the second person today to tell me I owe them something. And since I had to give him up, thanks to *you*, I think my debts are pretty much paid."

"Nia?" Paige took a hesitant step forward. "What do you mean you 'had to give him up'? Who? Aidan?"

Tears blocked my throat and, on a quick nod, I raced toward the sanctuary of my house.

"Why?" My sister's question came from too close behind me, and I turned to see her jogging nearer.

"Ask *her*." I stabbed a finger at Mom before opening my front door to slip inside.

Paige slapped a hand on the door and stuck her foot in the jamb, in a successful bid to keep me from avoiding her. "Talk to her," she said in a low voice. "Give her a chance."

"To what? To lie to me the way she so obviously lied to you?"

My mother reached the porch in time to hear my comments. "I've never lied to Paige. Or to you, for that matter."

"You said Donald Wainwright was our father," I reminded her, ignoring my sister's gasp while I turned my resentment on the woman I believed responsible for my pain. "But we both know that's not true, don't we?"

"Wrong, Nia. *Legally*, Donald Wainwright was your father, and I'm your mother."

"That hardly gels with Daddy's doctor's report that showed we couldn't possibly be related. 'Legally.'" I framed the word with curved fingers and an emphasis toward sarcasm. "What exactly does that mean anyway?"

My mother waved a large manila envelope under the yellow glow of the porch light. "It means, young lady, that you and your sister were adopted."

Chapter 25

Nia

"Adopted?" I stared at my mother, aghast. Adopted. The idea had never occurred to me. Why would it?

My mother must have smelled my blood in the air because she stepped forward and shoved my front door open with one quick punch. "Can we come in now or do you want your neighbors to hear all the gory details of your private life?"

I allowed them into the foyer, too shell-shocked to do more than shake my head. I kept hoping I'd wake and find today hadn't even happened yet. "Wait, hold up. What do you mean, we're adopted? That's impossible. I mean..." I pointed between the two of them. "...Paige looks just like you. She always has."

My mother spared a smile in my sister's direction. "Paige looks just like her father." Without waiting for any additional direction, she strode into the dining room and slapped her golden envelope on the gleaming top at the head of the cherry wood table. She pulled out the chair there and sat before turning to the two of us. "Care to join me?"

We could only follow, struggling to catch up physically and mentally.

"You know our real father?" my sister asked as she took the seat on our mother's left. "Who is he?"

"My brother, Charlie."

Her brother? So, wait. Our uncle, who we'd never met, was actually our father? My brain spun in a vortex of questions. My knees couldn't take anymore, and I sank into the chair on Mom's right.

"Did you know our mother, too?" I prodded.

"Not really," Mom said. "I never technically met her. At least, not in the way you would expect to meet your sister-in-law. She was already comatose by the time your father—I mean *Don*—and I reached the hospital."

"Comatose?"

"Mmm-hmm. Your mother suffered major complications during her pregnancy: high blood pressure, dizzy spells, blurry vision, all sorts of weird stuff. Within hours of the delivery, her kidneys shut down. She passed away three days later." She shook her head slowly. "At least she got to hold you both and tell you she loved you before she died."

"And our dad?" I said. "Your brother? What happened to him?"

Again, Mom shook her head. "Charlie was a mess even before his wife died. Afterwards, he was…lost. He wasn't prepared to take on the responsibility of newborn twins. He begged Don and me to take you both, to adopt you and raise you as our own, and we did." She scooped up the envelope and unwound the string clasp. "It's all in here. The adoption records, your birth certificates, there's even some photos of Charlie and Patty."

She flipped open the top and rifled through the contents. When she pulled out a photograph and slapped it on the table next to me, I drew closer. A bride and groom, beaming with love and joy, smiled up at me. The bride was tall with long red hair skimming her bare shoulders and hazel eyes that crinkled at the corners. I had the groom's chin and nose, but otherwise, the bride and I could have passed for…well…for twins.

"She looks a little like me," I said and gently traced the slope of the woman's face. My real mother's face.

As for Paige, put her in a tux and glue a pencil-thin blond moustache above her lip and bam! She was Charlie.

"Look," I told her and held up the photo.

Paige leaned over the table to get closer to the image of

our parents. "Wow," she murmured.

I stared into my sister's eyes. The same thoughts must have run through both our heads. In the course of the day, we'd lost our mother and father, found two new parents, and lost one yet again.

A sad smile creased Paige's face, and I turned back to Mom. "So where's our father now? Why didn't we ever meet him?"

Mom sighed, and her blue eyes watered. "Eight years after you were born, Charlie was killed when his motorcycle slid on a wet patch of asphalt and collided with a truck."

"Eight years later? Around the time you…" Paige didn't finish the sentence. She didn't have to.

Mom nodded. "The lowest point in my life." Her voice was rough, sandpaper on an open wound.

"Why didn't anyone ever tell us the truth?" I asked. "I mean, in this town? Surely everyone knew we were adopted. That's an awfully big secret for this town to keep."

"No one knew. Well, no. That's not true exactly. Don and I knew. Your grandparents knew. No one else."

"But how could that be? I mean, you couldn't exactly be your slim, petite self around the gossips in this town one day, and then present your new twin girls the next without pricking some old bat's sonar."

"Sure I could."

My mother then proceeded to explain her history to us, how she met our father—*Don*—the made-up pregnancy scare to get married, her loneliness and isolation, first in this house and later in the house on Wavecrest. Paige seemed to take most of this information in stride, which meant she already knew a lot of the details. I, on the other hand, drank it all in with varying degrees of bafflement, empathy, and outright wonder.

"What about school records?" Paige asked. "Didn't the

school require copies of our birth certificates to enroll us?"

I knew how they'd meandered around that issue. "Grandma," I told Paige. "Grandma was the secretary for the Snug Harbor superintendents for twenty years."

Mom nodded.

One question ran uppermost in my mind, and I had no ready answer. "Why didn't Daddy tell us when we were older?"

"I would imagine because he didn't want you to feel abandoned by the last remaining parent you had." She offered me a sad smile. "It's why I left you in his care. He and I were never right for each other, but he was, by far, the very best father for you girls. I never doubted he'd take care of you and love you until the day he died."

"He did. He was the best dad there ever was." Tears stung my eyes.

I would have thought after all the crying I'd done in the last twenty-four hours, the inner well would be dry by now. But no. That familiar lump rose in my throat, and I sniffed loudly. Paige and my mother joined in and soon, all three of us were a weepy mess. We cried for what we'd lost: people and time, as well as for what we'd gained: knowledge and truth. My heart and conscience bled as I thought of all the horrible thoughts I'd ever conceived about this woman. She wasn't a saint; she'd made mistakes. Who hadn't? She was, after all, like the rest of us, *human*.

For the first time in twenty five years, I placed my hand inside this woman's. "I am so sorry, Mom."

She squeezed my fingers. "I'm sorry, too, baby."

Love surged between us.

Mom pushed her chair back and rose, arms open wide. "Can I hug both my girls now? Please?"

We practically tripped over ourselves to embrace. Arms encircled, more tears flowed, and joy infused us from head to toe. Nothing in the world had ever felt as warm and wonderful as this moment.

"Now that that's all settled," Paige interjected from her place on Mom's right side. "What's for dinner? I'm starving."

I laughed and so did Mom. Mom. Weird, huh? I couldn't wait to tell Aidan about—

Aidan.

I loosened my embrace around Mom and Paige to turn away. No way did I want them to see me cry about Aidan. I was pretty sure they'd discern the difference between tears of misery and tears of joyful reunion. "I can probably whip up something quick," I murmured and aimed for the fridge to hide my face from their scrutiny.

"Nia?" Paige, of course, saw right through my subterfuge. "What's wrong?"

"How hungry are you really?" I said. "I can stir fry a quick orange chicken with broccoli, if that's good enough. Or I can pull a tray of eggplant parmigiana out of the freezer if you're looking for something more substantial." My voice cracked on the last word.

Substantial. I could have had something substantial in my life. Maybe. Instead, I'd taken a man's heart, more fragile than glass, and shattered it.

I yanked open the refrigerator door only to have a hand reach out and slam it shut again.

"Hey." Paige said low in my ear. "Talk to me."

I clamped my lips closed and shook my head.

"What happened with Aidan?" she prodded.

Broken at the mention of his name, I sank to my knees on the floor and covered my face with my hands. "I screwed up big time."

Paige knelt beside me. "Tell me."

"Nia?" Now Mom joined the circle around the refrigerator. "What's wrong, baby girl?"

I couldn't spill my guts in front of her. Especially since her alleged past was the reason I'd decimated my relationship with Aidan.

Duet in September

My sister must have sensed my reasoning because she answered for me. "Love problems."

Dismissive, but accurate I guess.

Mom took my hand and pulled me up and into her arms once again. "Now you listen to me, Nia," she murmured. "Misunderstandings can be fixed. We're proof of that, right? Whatever the problem is, don't let it simmer. Talk it out." She stepped back to include Paige in the rest of her conversation. "As for dinner, I'll pass. I'm going back to my hotel."

"Wait, Mom," Paige said. "I'll drive you."

"Nonsense. It's a beautiful night for a walk. I've given you two a lot to discuss. I'm leaving that envelope for you to go through. There are documents in there you should review. I'll be at The Hermitage until the thirtieth, if you want to contact me. No pressure, mind you. Just in case you have any questions. And I'm registered under my maiden name. Harris." She winked. "I still know how to fly under the radar."

She hugged and kissed us both, and on the click-clack of heels across the parquet floor, disappeared into the night.

"She's different than I remember," Paige remarked, staring after her. "More...I don't know. Just 'more.'"

"Mom 2.0," I replied.

She laughed. "Yeah, maybe." Cocking her head, she ran a gentle hand up my sleeve. "Are you okay?"

"No," I admitted. "I can't believe I screwed up my life so totally. If I hadn't said anything stupid this morning..." I shook off the memory of the bitter words. "And on top of that, I reek." I turned my head to sniff my shoulders. "God, how can you stand to be so close to me?"

Rather than stepping away, she edged closer and wrapped an arm around me. "We're twins. We stick together through good and bad. If you stink, I kick your butt upstairs to shower while I fix something for dinner. When you hurt, I find a way to bandage the boo-boo."

I sighed. "Not this time."

She waved a hand. "Defeatist attitude due to delirium caused by body odor," she rattled off. "Go shower. Then we'll figure something out."

"Why can't you mind your own business?"

"A., because I'm crazy in love, thanks in part to you, and I want to return the favor."

"And b.?"

"B., because anyone who looks at you and Aidan can see you're falling for each other. One thing I learned lately is that love isn't conditional. If he really loved you yesterday, and I could tell he did, he still loves you today. He's just hurt right now. But we'll fix that."

I arched a brow at her. "Yeah? How?"

She shoved me away. "Shower first. Your fumes are killing my brain cells. I hope you've got that eggplant in a microwaveable dish for defrosting. Because I don't relish taking an icepick to my dinner, and I need a substantial meal to play Cupid. Now, scoot!"

~~~~

I had to admit my sister had a point. In the privacy of my shower stall with the hot water beating away the day's grime, I allowed myself a glimmer of hope. Maybe Aidan and I could rebound from today's disaster. He didn't seem the type to hold a grudge. Could he possibly forgive me? Give us a chance to start again?

After a dinner of eggplant parmigiana and hot French bread dripping with seasoned olive oil, I told Paige about Aidan Coffield. I told her *everything*: from our first meeting to the verbal warfare we'd exchanged this morning.

"I don't understand," she said when I finished. "You like him, don't you?"

"Of course I like him. I might even be in love with

him."

"So then why did you want to break up?"

I slapped my hands on the table, causing the silverware to clink against the dishes. "Because he's *Aidan Coffield*."

"And you're *Nia Wainwright*." She bugged out her eyes and formed a wide o with her mouth, clapping her hands on her cheeks. "So what?"

"Oh, come on, Paige, it's not the same thing and you know it. His mother is an Italian countess, for God's sake."

"I repeat. So what?"

"Can you imagine how she'd react to me? To her son's interest in me?"

"I don't see how it would be any of her business. He's a grown man. And Nia, he *seriously* likes you." Elbow on the table, she rested her head on her hand. "Now shut up and call him. It's getting late."

I looked at the phone beside me. "What if—"

"No what ifs. Call him. Now."

On a defeated sigh, I picked up the phone and dialed his number. I already knew it by heart. After the third ring, his recorded message clicked on. Great. Voicemail. I used the time during his "I'm unavailable to take your call" spiel to get my breathing under control.

At the end of the beep, I sped through my semi-rehearsed speech. "Aidan? It's Nia. I just wanted to say I'm sorry. Would you call me when you get this? Please? I'd really like to talk to you. Explain."

A fumbling sound filled the earpiece and then he came on the line. "I'm here."

Icy.

"Umm, hi," I said. Okay, now what? I glanced down at my notes. Yes, Paige had made me take notes. Thank God. "Aidan, I'm so sorry."

"You said that already."

"I know. I'm sorry."

Across the table, Paige rolled her eyes in exasperation.

I turned slightly away so I couldn't see her. This conversation beat up my pride enough without my sister's line by line reaction.

"Is there a point to this, Nia?" he barked. "It's late."

"Yes, there is." I swallowed, took another glance at the words printed in Paige's block handwriting. "You see, I've been struggling with what I feel for you since we met. At first, I thought I was just some late summer fling for you. I mean, I couldn't understand what someone like you could possibly see in someone like me."

"Someone like me…"

"You know what I mean. You're a *Coffield*, for God's sake. I'm a nobody. The more time we spent together, the more I worried about why you could be interested in me. I mean, I'm not some beautiful, rich girl with a summer place in the Hamptons and a penthouse in Manhattan. My parents aren't on any social register. My father never had millions of dollars in the bank."

"You think that matters to me?"

"At first, yes, I did. After a while, though, I worried more about what you'd find out about my parents." I took a deep breath before confessing my darkest sin. "I have skeletons in my closet, Aidan."

"And the Coffields don't?" he scoffed. "Every family has secrets."

"Please. Let me finish before you say anything else." I practically tripped over my tongue to get the explanation out before I gave in to my shame. "Maybe your family has secrets, but they're not like mine. That's why I purposely kept our relationship a secret. So that you wouldn't hear any gossip linked to my parents. I was afraid if you knew me, really knew me, if you found out the truth about my family, you'd want nothing to do with me. That was unfair of me, I know. You deserve better. I should have trusted you, should have confided in you. All I can say is that I'm sorry. I said some ugly stupid things today, but I didn't

Duet in September

mean a word. It was all my fear and shame that kept me from realizing how much you mean to me. I hope you can forgive me. I hope you feel for me a little of what I feel for you." I took a huge breath. "That's it, I guess."

"That's it? My turn to speak now?"

Did I sense a warm spot in the ice? God, I hoped so. "Yes. Go ahead."

"I never cared about your family or some stupid gossip. I, of all people know that gossip is never reliable. I truly enjoyed spending time with you. I found you witty and charming and beautiful."

"Oh." The heat of a blush warmed my cheeks, and my heartbeat raced. Hope lifted its sleepy head. He still cared. We could work this out.

"And for the record, I may be a Coffield, but that doesn't mean I have a summer place in the Hamptons or a townhouse in Manhattan. All I have is Piping Plover. My father disinherited me years ago."

"He did?"

"Yes, he did. You probably have more money in your bank account than I do. So you can bet the old man's opinion means nothing to me. *I* liked you, Nia. That should have been enough." His sigh came out like a hiss on my end of the phone. "But, in all your misconceptions, you did get one thing right."

"I did?"

"Yes. I deserve better. I deserve better than someone ashamed to be seen with me. You may claim you have feelings for me, but obviously, they're not as strong as I would have liked. I'm not some monster that needs to be hidden from your family and friends, Nia. Any woman who claims to love me had better be ready to announce it in the Sunday *New York Times*. She should know how I feel about her without needing reassurance. She'll want the world to know we're together because that's exactly what she'll get from me. I deserve that, too."

Hope dropped back into a coma. My skin chilled. "I'm sorry," I said again.

"So am I. Goodbye, Nia."

The phone went dead, and so did my heart.

Chapter 26

Paige

I would have expected Nia to crumble after her conversation with Aidan. In fact, she looked like death on toast when she hung up the phone. Bitterness tinged her tone as she shared the blow-by-blow details with me.

"He told me I should have known how he felt about me without needing reassurance," she summed up. Sinking her head onto her folded arms, she sighed. "He's right, though. I should have been more honest with him." Her hands scrubbed her face, pushing her hair into wild, shaggy disarray. "I can't believe how badly I screwed this up."

Disappointment pulled me into its inky depths, drowning my hopes for my sister's love life in a pool of sympathy. "So that's it then?" I asked. "It's over?"

"Oh, no." Lifting her head, she offered me a diabolical smile. "Not by a long shot. Mom was right."

"Huh?" I blinked.

An unholy light gleamed in her eyes that had nothing to do with the Tiffany lamp hanging over the dining room table. "We're living proof that misunderstandings shouldn't be allowed to fester. Imagine how our lives might have turned out if we'd known where Mom was and why she left. I still can't believe we were adopted and Daddy never told us. All those years I thought..." She shook her head. "I made a mistake, letting Aidan go. Now, I'm going to fix it."

"How?"

Her lips twisted in a grimace. "*He* prefers an announcement in the Sunday *New York Times*."

Beginning to understand how the wheels were turning in Nia's head, I couldn't help but laugh at her distaste. "Oh, ye of little imagination."

"Exactly." The diabolical grin returned, along with some evil plot hand-rubbing. "I plan to do sooo much better. If you'll help me."

"Are you kidding?" I bounced in my chair. "I'm in. I'm in. What do you need?"

"A game plan and an army."

"You're going to kidnap him and hold him hostage until he admits he still loves you?" I suggested.

"Not exactly. Someone else is going to have to distract him so I can give him what he thinks he wants."

"Well, I know I can count on Sam to help us. He'd do anything for me." Those warm and fuzzies embraced me every time I thought of my man. "And I bet Mom would be willing to get involved. Who else do you want?"

"I'll definitely need Iggy." Nia drummed her fingers against her cheek. "I wonder if Brice Howell could rig a breathalyzer. And I'm going to want to call Karen Brennan at the crafts store first thing tomorrow. She can get me the ribbons."

"Ribbons? What kind of ribbons?" What on earth was Nia planning? Did she think she could tie up Aidan and make him her love slave?

"You'll see."

Much as I wanted to knock my sister down and shake the truth out of her the way I might have when we were little, I knew I'd have to wait until she'd covered all her angles. Nia was a methodical planner, rarely impulsive. I slapped my hands on the table and stood. "Okay, then. You wash the dishes while I make coffee. Then, we'll start making some lists. I figure it's going to be a long night."

A long *night* proved an understatement. For the next two weeks, I organized everyone else's activities and made phone calls. Meanwhile, Nia spent every waking moment in her hot spot. If I'd have allowed her to sleep in that glass-forging oven, she would have jumped at the chance.

Duet in September

As it was, she rarely saw the sun over those fourteen days.

Amid all of the plans and schemes, I *did* finagle one surprise Nia hadn't considered. The *coup de grace*, in my humble opinion. Sometimes, cleaning out my purse reaped an unexpected reward, and this was one of those times. But I'm jumping ahead of the story right now.

On the thirtieth of September, I completed my last "something new" task: I called Aidan Coffield and asked him to meet me at The Gull and Oar restaurant. Convincing him to leave his precious vineyard the night before its grand opening for the public and press took some major league conniving.

"Please," I begged. "It's about Nia."

"Nia and I are no longer seeing each other."

Every word came out bitten, which told me he still cared way too much about my sister. Goody.

"I know that," I told him. "And if she knew I called you, she'd disown me." God, I hoped my nose didn't start growing from the lies I told. I didn't want to become Paigenocchio.

"Maybe you should heed your sister's wishes."

Time to turn up the heat. "Please, Aidan? It's urgent."

"Fine. I'll meet you on Sunday morning."

His sigh of surrender unleashed a chorus of *We Are the Champions* in my head. I had him on the string. Now to lure him into the trap with a little hustle and panic.

"No, Sunday will be too late! I'm really worried about her."

"Too late for what? What exactly is going on? Where's Nia?" The earlier iciness in his tone melted under the heat of frantic concern.

I had to stifle my smile. *Oh, yes. Come to Mama.* "It's too complicated to discuss on the phone. I promise I won't keep you long. Please say you'll come tonight."

"Eight o'clock," he said. "I'll give you an hour, but not a minute more. I have a lot to do to get ready for tomorrow."

"An hour will be perfect." I practically purred my satisfaction and had to commence a quick series of coughs to keep my happiness at bay.

"Are you all right?"

"Uh-huh," I croaked. "I'll see you at eight. Thanks, Aidan." The second I disconnected with him, I dialed Nia, then Sam, and gave each of them the same message. "We're a go. Eight o'clock. The Gull and Oar."

Poor Aidan. He was about to have the worst night of his life. With luck, though, the end result would be well worth his inconvenience.

~~~~

At precisely eight o'clock, Aidan strolled into the main entrance of The Gull and Oar. He wore a white, button-down shirt that emphasized his height and broad shoulders with a pair of well-cut jeans. I had no confusion regarding what Nia saw in this Adonis. The two were perfect for each other. Now, I just had to play my part to perfection.

In a pre-approved signal, I placed my purse on the table where I sat in the lounge. Hovering in the corner of the bar, Mom, garbed in a waitress's uniform, eyed Aidan carefully and requested a very specific drink order from the bartender.

Let the games begin.

"Aidan." I rose from my seat and waved him over. When he stood near my table, I looked up at him with a relieved smile pasted on my face. I kissed his cheek. "I really appreciate you coming here. I know how important tomorrow is for you."

He waited for me to return to my seat before settling in the chair across from me. "Then let's make this fast, shall we? What's going on?"

I frowned. "Don't you want to order a drink or

anything?"

"No. I have a long night's work ahead of me."

"At least get a soda. Or a coffee. Don't let me drink alone." I signaled to Mom, the waitress, hired by Chef Colin for one hour's work. Actually, she only needed a minute or two.

Aidan didn't even glance in Mom's direction. All his resentment simmered at me. "What's going on, Paige? Where's Nia?"

"She's home, I think." I took a sip of my club soda and lime.

"You think?" His forehead puckered with his obvious confusion. "So what's the big emergency?"

"Do you love my sister, Aidan?"

His face tightened. "That's none of your business."

"Well, see, I look at it this way." I took another sip and eased back in my chair, totally relaxed. "I'm pretty certain Nia loves you. And she's my sister. That makes your feelings toward her my business."

He glanced around the bar area, as if seeking Nia. Or an ambulance. "There is no emergency, is there?"

I said nothing, allowing him to simmer in his own juices. Behind him, in a perfectly choreographed dance, Mom maneuvered herself, laden down with a tray full of drinks, directly into Aidan's path.

"That does it. I'm outta here." He shot to his feet.

As he rose, his shoulder collided with Mom's tray, tilting it at a ridiculous angle. Three very large whiskey sours slid down, splashing all over him.

"Oh, my God, sir, I'm so sorry!" Mom gave the performance of a lifetime, feigning distress as she set down the empty tray and grabbed a fistful of napkins to blot the mess. She patted his sodden hair, then worked her way down his ruined white shirt, until he shook her off.

"Stop. Enough. Stop."

"But, sir, I—"

The smell of whiskey surrounded Aidan like an alcoholic cloud, and his fury boiled over. "Stop. Leave it. Just leave me alone."

"I'm sorry," Mom repeated. "Let me get the manager. We have to make this right, sir. I'm sure he'll want us to cover your cleaning bills and, of course, dinner tonight is on us."

"Do I look like I want to stay for dinner?" Sighing, he brushed a hand down the front of his shirt. "Get out of here." Then he turned his ire on me. "I don't know what game you and Nia are playing, but I really don't appreciate it. Especially not tonight. I'm done wasting my time." He turned to leave, whiskey droplets creating a trail behind him.

I made a half-hearted attempt at convincing him to stay with a weak, "Aidan, please, wait," but he continued out the door without ever looking back. I counted to ten, then picked up the phone and dialed Sam. "He's all yours."

Once I hung up, Mom bent to kiss my head. "Looks like my work here is done. Don't forget to call me and tell me how this all works out."

I grinned up at her. "I will. You're coming back for Thanksgiving, right?"

"Definitely. I love you, baby. Say goodbye to Nia for me."

"Love you too, Mom."

Once again, my mother left Nia and me. This time, though, I knew she'd remain close, not only in our hearts, but in reality.

Chapter 27

Nia

I'd thought of everything that night. And it all went off without a hitch. After Aidan left Paige at The Gull and Oar, he was allowed to get about half a mile up the road before Sam pulled him over with his cruiser lights flashing. One whiff of the whiskey soaking his clothes convinced Sam to insist that Aidan take a breathalyzer test. Too bad the breathing apparatus had been doctored by Brice Howell to report a false positive. At least, too bad for Aidan.

Good for me.

Sam had no choice but to take Aidan to the drunk tank, where he spent the night "sobering up." Very early the next morning, I made my way to Piping Plover Vineyards. Since Aidan had introduced me to most of the workmen the day I'd visited, no one questioned my appearance there before the grand opening to help with the last minute details. In fact, two of the guys unloaded the heavy boxes from my car. After they schlepped my very special surprise into the tasting room, I shooed them away so I could set up.

Paige and Sam met me at the vineyard for the grand unveiling. At approximately nine-thirty, Sam called the precinct to have Aidan released "until his hearing could be set." I bet the deputy who opened the cell heard quite a few invectives, but Sam assured me they were all accustomed to the angry hangover that was a routine part of the morning after in the drunk tank.

Aidan's car pulled into the driveway shortly before ten o'clock. I stood alone on that glorious marble portico as he stepped out. His eyes narrowed to slits when he saw me.

"What are you doing here?" he demanded.

"You invited me," I said, then pretended to get my first

appraisal of his stained clothing and rumpled appearance. I gasped and reached a hand toward the brown stains splotching his white shirt. "What happened to you?"

"Ask your sister," he muttered through clenched teeth as he strode up the steps.

"Paige? Paige did this to you?"

"In a roundabout way. But I'm guessing you know that."

"Oh, gee, Aidan, I'm sorry. I had no idea." I pushed him forward, giving him no chance to think. "Go. Hurry. The press will be showing up in mere minutes. Shower, change, get yourself presentable. I'll stall until you're ready."

He might have wanted to argue with me. In fact, at one point, as I prodded him into the owner's quarters of his villa-style building, he turned toward me, a dozen questions brewing in his coffee-colored eyes. All he said, though, was, "Thanks, Nia. Let's talk when this is all over."

I nodded. "You bet. Now, go."

The press and invited guests began arriving at ten a.m. I welcomed them warmly and had them make themselves comfortable in the villa's lobby while we waited for Aidan. Behind us, a wall of glass French doors waited to reveal my heart to Aidan. And the world. I took a deep breath as I envisioned what would happen when he finally saw what I'd done. He wanted the *New York Times*. I planned to give him a whole lot more.

Meanwhile, I ushered in the waiters and waitresses from the catering company, helped the guests to mingle, and made small talk as if I were the villa's mistress.

Everyone seemed to accept me in that role until one bulldog of a man voiced the question, "Who exactly are you?"

I looked up into the dark fathomless eyes of Ogden Coffield. He had one arm wrapped around the waist of a familiar woman.

"Nia the glassmaker, isn't it?" Camille said, her head tilted cobra-like, poised to spit venom. "From Snug Harbor?"

I stood taller, Aidan's requirements thundering in my head. *She should know how I feel about her without needing reassurance.* "Yes, that's right," I confirmed and held out my hand to Aidan's father. "Mr. Coffield, I'm very pleased to meet you."

"Who are you exactly?"

"You can just call me Nia for now," I replied with a sedate smile.

"She's the one who turned me down, Ogden," Camille announced icily. "For the wine stoppers. Looks like Aidan managed to wheedle what *he* wanted out of her though."

"Ladies and gentlemen…" Aidan's voice boomed across the crowded room just in time to keep me from replying with a zinger.

He looked a thousand times better, or maybe I only thought so because I looked at him through the eyes of a woman in love.

"Thank you so much for coming today. Welcome to Piping Plover, the newest vineyard on Long Island. I hope you'll enjoy the festivities I have planned for you. Shall we head into the tasting room where my sommelier will treat you to some of our first year's vintages?"

As if on cue, the series of glass doors swung open, and the crowd spilled forward. The room was decorated in warm golden oak and glistening brass. A gleaming bar against the far wall, approximately sixty feet in length, ran from one end to the other. Dozens of square tables, each set with four chairs, allowed guests a place to sit and chat while they sipped. Behind the bar stood shelves of wine glasses, ready to be filled with the various wines for tasting.

Standing beside Aidan as he entered, I knew the exact moment he noticed the glasses. He stiffened, stared open mouthed at the rows of delicate blue glass, then looked at me. "You?" he asked.

I nodded. "A peace offering."

He strode forward and nodded at his sommelier. The man lifted up the first bottle, and Aidan addressed the crowd. "We'll begin with my Pinot Blanc, a full-bodied dry white with undertones of apple and citrus."

The sommelier opened several bottles, and his assistants passed out glasses to the men and women in attendance. As each glass moved from pourer to taster, the pale blue ribbons tied to the stem caught the guests' eyes. Aidan finally took a glass and traced the etched piping plover in the bowl before he pulled the ribbon taut to read the bright yellow lettering framed by the same tiny stick-figure birds:

Nia Wainwright loves Aidan Coffield.

He turned toward me, a question in his eyes, and I nodded. Without saying a word, he surveyed the rest of the room and found the ribbons tied to the light fixtures, the chair legs, and bottles of wine for sale behind the cash register. Again, he turned to me and I shrugged.

"I overshot. Ordered a thousand ribbons but only had enough time to make three hundred glasses."

At last, he smiled. "So you still owe me seven hundred glasses."

"I probably would have been better off doing your grape lamps, huh?"

"Oh, I don't know." He pulled me into his arms, and I knew all was forgiven. "I'm guessing you'll have a lifetime to get the rest of them completed."

He kissed me, long and lingering. My knees turned to jelly, and my toes curled into the floorboards.

Paige chose that inopportune moment to tap my shoulder. "Umm, you might want to join your guests on the outdoor patio for a minute or two."

Separated from the bliss of Aidan's lips on mine, I glared at her. "Now?! Are you for real?"

She smiled. "Trust me. This will only take a minute."

On a sigh, I allowed her to lead us outside where I noticed all the guests milled, the wine glasses in their hands, their gazes focused on the blue sky above. A bi-plane drifted by, a huge banner trailing from its tail. In unison, the crowd read the words now so familiar to all of them.

Nia Wainwright loves Aidan Coffield.

This was something I hadn't planned. I stared aghast at Paige, who grinned like the Cheshire Cat. "A brochure I picked up at the town clambake," she said.

Aidan's voice whispered low in my ear. "Aidan Coffield loves Nia Wainwright."

Happiness infused me from head to toe, and I snuggled closer. "I know."

~~~~

Paige

So there you have it. One change every day for thirty days brought Nia and me a bounty of gifts we hadn't expected. We found our mom, who remained in constant contact—well, at least as much as her home and job in Connecticut would allow. Since Sam had pined for me for fifteen years, I let him out of his misery and accepted his marriage proposal that Christmas. Next June, ours will be the first wedding hosted at the Piping Plover Vineyards.

The grand opening was a smashing success with a write-up about the whole *Nia Wainwright loves Aidan Coffield* angle in the *New York Times* weekend section. Apparently, the reporter who covered the opening is a hopeless romantic. Since then, the vineyard has quickly become a favorite tourist spot on the East End, particularly for couples looking for the right venue to pop the question or share a special occasion. Of course, Nia's suggestions for events like ladies day and art weekends where they showcase the works of local artists helped create a constant buzz. Lucky for both of them, she managed to make good on the additional seven hundred glasses.

Tonight, Aidan plans to ask Nia to marry him. Mom and I chipped in to buy a full page ad, congratulating the happy couple. You can read it in tomorrow's edition of the *New York Times*.

Turn the page for a sneak peek at another Calendar Girls story...

Available Now!
Reunion in October
Book II of the Calendar Girls Series by Gina Ardito

Chapter 1

Emily

No one should have to face a morning with decaf.

As I stared at the ineffectual coffee in my mug, Roy bent closer and gave me the same perfunctory kiss as always. "See ya later, Em," he said, his focus already on the back door. "Have a good day."

A second later, he disappeared. From upstairs came the inevitable shouting match between Melissa and Corey about the bathroom. At sixteen, Melissa required hours in front of the mirror to agonize over her hair, her skin, her makeup, and her clothes. Corey, two years younger, had no patience for any girl, much less his older sister. Normally, I understood Melissa's insecurities. I remembered those days all too well. This morning, I had even less patience than Corey.

I sank into the nearest chair, and moisture seeped into the seat of my pants, straight through to my underwear. The sticky residue on the table revealed all. Someone had spilled orange juice and not bothered to wipe it up. Terrific. Some days, I went through more wardrobe changes than an awards show host. And the hits kept on coming…

For the moment, I couldn't move. Every muscle in my body weighed me down. My skull pounded with the pending doom of another headache—my second this week. Seven-thirty in the morning, and I was already exhausted. I still had to get my six-year-old, Gabriella, up and ready for school, then Lucas and I would go to the pediatrician for his eighteen-month

Gina Ardito   281

checkup. Above me, feet stomped, a door slammed, and Lucas's
inevitable wails pierced my foggy brain. Wonderful. What else
could go wrong?

"Moooooommm!" Corey's frantic shout echoed down the
staircase. "Something's the matter with Freckles."

Oh, no. Not now. Freckles, our fifteen-year-old beagle,
had seemed lethargic and off-kilter for about a week now. I kept
reminding myself to call the vet, but there just weren't enough
hours in the day. I pushed my sorry, wet butt out of the chair.

"Moooooommm!" Corey called again. "Hurry up. He
won't move. I think he's sick."

Meanwhile, Lucas had resorted to screaming to get out of
his crib.

"Coming." I trudged upstairs. First stop: the nursery for
Lucas, who stood at the rail, face almost purple as he screeched
his outrage. "Okay, sweetie," I crooned and scooped him up.
"Mommy's here. It's okay." I doubt he heard me over his own
bellows. Hoping to soothe him, I bounced him gently in one
arm as I carried him to the dressing table. The other arm snaked
into the nearby stack of clean diapers.

"Moooooommm!"

"Corey," I shouted back, "get ready for school. I'll check
on Freckles as soon as I'm done with your brother."

A rumpled Gabriella appeared in the doorway. Still in her
Care Bears nightgown, a hand-me-down from her older sister,
she rubbed her eyes. "Mommy?" she asked through a wide
yawn. "What's going on?"

I pulled off the baby's pajama bottoms and ripped the tabs
off his diaper. On a deep inhale that sent pain knifing into my
chest, I forced a calm tone. "Nothing, sweetie. Why don't you
get dressed? As soon as I'm done with Luke, I'll start your
breakfast. Waffles okay today?"

"Apple cimmanim?"

I smiled at her awkward pronunciation. "I think that can
be arranged."

"K." She toddled away, and I finished changing Luke in
record time.

"Mooooommm!" Corey again.

"I'm coming." I hefted Luke on my hip. "Come on, little

man. Let's see what's going on with Freckles." I strode to the end of the hall where my oldest son, barefoot and shirtless, crouched in the corner. Our beagle curled up on his right side against the closet door, with only the occasional flick of his ear to confirm he was still alive.

"He won't get up," Corey whined. "I think he's really sick."

I knelt beside the dog. "Okay, Corey. I've got it. Go finish getting ready for school. Your bus will be here in five minutes."

Melissa, wearing a pink t-shirt with "Juicy" in glitter across her chest and jeans with shredded knees, traipsed out of the bathroom. "What's going on?"

"Freckles is sick," Corey said.

"I'm not surprised." She shrugged. "He's old and he smells. We should just put him down already."

I gasped. "Melissa!"

"Well, it's true."

"You're a witch, Mellie," Corey said. "No wonder no one likes you."

"No one likes me because they know I have a loser for a brother."

"E-nough!" I said, exasperation cutting between each syllable. "Both of you. Bus. Downstairs. Go. Now."

The teens split into opposite directions in search of backpacks and shoes while I returned my attention to Freckles. The poor dog hadn't moved except for that one twitchy ear. With Luke still straddling my hip, I reached down to touch his muzzle. He felt unusually warm to me. Did dogs get fevers?

"Come on, boy." I nudged him behind the shoulder. "Get up."

The dog never stirred. I watched his chest rise and fall to make sure he was breathing. Yes, thank God.

"I told you," Corey said from the other side of the hall. "Something's wrong with him."

I jabbed my arm at him, index finger pointed at his chest. "Bus. Now. I'll call the vet. You go to school."

"Will you text me and let me know if he's okay?"

"Not during school hours. You can wait until you get home to find out how he is."

"But—"

"No buts. Go." *So I can panic without you watching me.* With one last sad look, he turned and headed downstairs.

Luke wrapped a fist in my hair and yanked. Hard. My scalp stinging, I rose, one hand braced on the wall to bolster my shaky haunches. God, I was seriously out of shape. When was the last time I'd done any exercise? At least two kids ago. Which might explain the distance growing between Roy and me.

Oh, I felt it. Hard to miss really. We rarely talked, and when we did, our conversations centered on the kids or the bills. At night, we both fell onto the king-sized mattress in our room, too numb and drained to do more than sleep. Somewhere—and I didn't know where—Roy and I had lost the spark we'd kindled in high school. Finding lost homework, money for school trips, and shoes the kids didn't outgrow a month after their purchase took time and energy away from spark-hunting.

Luke's fretting increased to crying, and I put thoughts of my crumbling marriage on the back burner, as I'd been doing for years now. "Okay, little man. Hang in there. Breakfast is coming."

In the kitchen, my feet stuck to the sheet vinyl floor with every step I took. Ah, yes. The orange juice. Something else I'd have to take care of. *One thing at a time.* I strapped Luke into his highchair and prepared banana oatmeal for him, apple cinnamon waffles for Gabriella. The oven clock glowed with the time, 8:03. I had twenty minutes to feed the baby, pack Gabriella's lunch, and drop her off at school before I took him to the pediatrician. Then it was daycare for Luke while I worked the twelve-to-eight shift as a 911 operator at the Snug Harbor Police station. Roy, home by five, would pick Luke up after his day as a janitor at Morrison General Hospital.

Now I also had to find a way to squeeze in a visit to Dr. Bautista for Freckles. How much would that cost me? In time and dollars? Only one way to find out. The vet's office wouldn't open 'til nine, a good news/bad news scenario. Good, because Gabriella would already be at school so she wouldn't hear the conversation. Bad, considering I had a full morning already and wouldn't get a chance to call until at least ten,

Duet in September   284

which pretty much guaranteed I'd be late for work. I could opt
for the twenty-four hour vet clinic, but that would require an
additional thirty-minute drive. And God knew what they'd
charge me. With Dr. Bautista, I could work out some kind of
payment plan if I had to.

A familiar tightness settled around my chest. I rubbed my
cleavage with two fingers until the tension eased. By then, both
kids had finished breakfast, and I raced them out the door to my
minivan for the next leg of my marathon day. For once, the
pediatrician ran on time, and Luke fell asleep the minute I
strapped him into his car seat after the visit. No better time than
now to call the vet.

I pulled out my cell, found his number in my digital
address book, and hit dial. When the receptionist answered, I
identified myself and gave her a sketch of my poor beagle's
condition.

"Dr. Bautista isn't in today, but Dr. Herrera is free at ten
forty-five," she said. "Can you be here by then?"

I'd never met the new vet, but I trusted Dr. Bautista
enough to hire someone competent and compassionate. "I'll
take it," I said.

If my luck held out, Freckles would only have a cold that
could be treated with an antibiotic, and I'd get to work on time.
If not, well, I didn't want to think about that right now.

****

Francesca

"What do we have here?" I strode into Examination
Room Five and stared at the blood seeping from a familiar
man's forehead. Oh, no. Not again.

"Hey, Doc." Joshua Candolero grinned up at me from the
hospital bed. His clasped hands wrapped a battered white
hardhat that sat on his washboard stomach. "Long time, no see.
How are you doing today?"

"Josh." My heart flipped in my chest as I eyed the
damage.

Yes, head injuries tend to bleed a lot, but for some reason, the blood level seemed excessive on such a gorgeous face. Josh, a carpenter in his father's construction business, had spent so much time in the E.R. at Morrison General Hospital in the last few months, I knew most of his vital statistics by heart. Twenty-eight, single, with no remarkable medical history aside from a wrist surgery, ten-plus years back, after a lacrosse injury. No known allergies.

On paper, Josh was a nearly perfect specimen of manhood, *except* for his penchant to be in the wrong place at the wrong time, resulting in frequent visits to my emergency room for treatment of superficial injuries.

I brushed away a lock of dark hair stuck to his brow and nearly lost myself in the unusual hue of his eyes, their almond shape a gift from his Korean mother. Not quite green, not hazel, not brown, but they glowed in a combination of all three that evoked images of a spring meadow filled with goldenrod. I shook off the instant thrill of attraction that rippled through me. He was a patient, not a Chippendale stripper, despite the low slung jeans on his narrow hips and the black t-shirt that perfectly framed his sculpted broad shoulders. Seriously, if Joshua ever needed extra cash, a few turns on the catwalk to any Barry White tune would garner him a truckload of dollars.

Oh, God, what was I thinking? With one last lingering analysis of his muscular arms, I pulled up the patient chart at his feet. While taking measured breaths, I read the vitals listed on his admission summary until I believed I'd be able to look at him without a fluttery sensation erupting in my stomach.

"Don't tell me," I said after an additional minute or two. "Let me guess. You wound up on the wrong end of a nail gun."

Only slightly less dazzling than his eyes was his smile, with even, white teeth inside full, dark red lips. "Nope. Screwdriver."

I'd been joking about the nail gun. Josh, however, wasn't. I arched a brow at him. "Excuse me?"

He struggled to prop himself up on his elbows. "Not a big deal. Jimmy DeMarco was goofing around and managed to slam a screwdriver into my skull." While that knee-melting smile never hardened, he pointed at the hole in his head. "Lucky for me, I've got a lot of bone up here."

Duet in September   286

I puckered my lips into a moue as I gazed at his forehead. "Not much of anything else, though. Where was your hardhat?"

"On the sawhorse. It was lunchtime."

I opened a foil-lined packet and dabbed at the wound with an antiseptic wipe. When he winced at the sting, I had to bite back a chuckle. "Well, clearly, you're not safe at lunchtime, either." I pointed to the hardhat perched on his abdomen. "You might want to consider wearing that thing from the minute you get up in the morning 'til you go to bed at night. What is this? Your second visit to the E.R. this month?"

"My first," he corrected with a hint of umbrage in his tone. "Technically, last Tuesday was still September. So this is my first time here in October."

"Oh, my mistake. Well, welcome back." I turned to the nurse hovering near the triage area. "Helena, would you get me a suture tray, please, and surgical glue?"

Joshua sat up higher. "Surgical glue? Whatzat?"

"It's like Krazy Glue for lacerations," I said and dabbed him again, simultaneously pushing him back into a supine position. "Relax. If the wound isn't too deep and I can stop the bleeding, we can glue your head back together, rather than stitch. Then you won't have a scar marring that beautiful face."

"You think my face is beautiful?" He batted his lush eyelashes like a cartoon heroine, and I dove back into the chart to review his blood pressure and pulse rates until mine returned to normal.

"Easy, Romeo. Save the charm for ladies your own age," I scolded, replacing the chart on the bed.

"You *are* my own age."

"Uh-huh," I said flatly. "Give or take a decade."

"Six years is not a decade."

Once again, I looked up into his face, this time in surprise. "How do you know how old I am?"

For the first time since I walked into the exam area, his expression was solemn. "I may be a wood jockey, but I can do basic math. You were my babysitter for years before you went to college. When I was ten, I remember you telling my mom about your sweet sixteen party." He shrugged. "I figure the age gap between us has stayed the same over the years. Unless you found some kind of break in the time-space continuum that you haven't shared with the rest of the world."

"My sweet sixteen party…" I brushed another antiseptic wipe across his brow as I thought back to those cringe-worthy days.

"Yeah. You wanted a Spice Girls theme. I thought it was a totally lame idea and tried to convince you to go with the Power Rangers instead."

A cloudy memory sharpened into focus. Me, in my god-awful "Rachel" haircut that was so popular back then but made my plank-thick hair look like a bad Cleopatra wig. I sat on the faux leather couch in the Candolero den, regaling Mrs. C. with details of what I'd planned for my big day, from a cardboard version of the double-decker Spice Girls bus to lollipops shaped like microphones. Little Joshua, cute but totally annoying in those days, chimed in every five seconds with the advice that I could be the pink Power Ranger, and he would be the red one. Or blue. I was kinda fuzzy on the details.

"I had the hugest crush on you." Josh's confession blasted away the memory.

With a start, I realized how close I leaned toward him while dabbing at his wound with the gauze. For God's sake, my boobs practically brushed his chin. Then he smiled at me again, as if he knew exactly what I was thinking.

Other Books by Gina Ardito

The Bonds of Matri-money
A Little Slice of Heaven
A Run for the Money
Nobody's Darling (Book I of the Nobody Series)
Nobody's Business (Book II of the Nobody Series)
Nobody's Perfect (Book III of the Nobody Series)
Eternally Yours (Book I of the Afterlife Series)
In Your Dreams (Book II of the Afterlife Series)
Chasing Adonis
Duping Cupid (a Valentine's Day Short Story)
Charming for Mother's Day (A Calendar Girls Series novella)
Reunion in October (Book II of the Calendar Girls Series)
Homecoming in November (Book III of the Calendar Girls Series)

Books by Gina Ardito writing as Katherine Brandon

Kismet's Angel (Book I of the Kismet Series)
Kismet's Revenge (Book II of the Kismet Series)
Kismet's Salvation (Book III of the Kismet Series)
Echoes of Love

About the Author

Gina Ardito is the award-winning international author of more than twenty romances, a legendary singer in confined spaces (her car, the shower, her office cubicle), and a killer of houseplants. She hosts fun, informative workshops for writers around the country. In 2012, Gina was named a Woman of Outstanding Leadership by the International Women's Leadership Association, but to her friends, she's still just a shenanigator.

A native of Long Island, New York, she lives with her husband, two children, a bionic dog, and their two cat overlords. For more info on Gina and her books, you can visit her website at ginaardito.com, follow Gina on Facebook at https://www.facebook.com/GinaArditoAuthor, on Twitter @GinaArdito, or sign up for the monthly newsletter she shares with her ScribBLING Diva pals by filling out the easy form at scribblingdivas.com.

CPSIA information can be obtained
at www.ICGtesting.com
Printed in the USA
LVOW13s1208130317
527020LV00004B/909/P